"Now's the time to change your mind," Matt said. **"If we don't suit, you need to speak up. Once we're married, we're together for life. Until then, I could send you back on the train."**

"The thing is—we can't go back to Chicago."

"We're at an impasse, then," Matt said, his words sounding more clipped than he likely intended.

Eleanor decided she should say something to smooth over the conflict, but no words came. Then she heard a slight sniffle at her side.

She saw that her sister had returned. Tears were streaming down Lily's face.

"It's all my fault," Lily wailed. "I only wanted you to have a True Love, like Mama had with our father. You need to marry someone who is your True Love, too. We're going to marry him, right?"

"That's what we promised to do," Eleanor said. The choice had to be the sheriff's at this point. She did not know where else they would go, but they could not stay here unless they were welcome. Even if she could tolerate it, she would not let Lily's heart be broken that way...

Janet Tronstad was raised on a small ranch in the middle of Montana. Even though she has spent much of her life in cities, she still calls Montana home and has set most of her forty books there. Her books have been printed in various countries and their sales have put her on the *New York Times*, *USA TODAY* and *Publishers Weekly* bestseller lists. Janet currently lives in central California.

Books by Janet Tronstad

Love Inspired Historical

Calico Christmas at Dry Creek
Mistletoe Courtship
"Christmas Bells for Dry Creek"
Mail-Order Christmas Brides
"Christmas Stars for Dry Creek"
Mail-Order Holiday Brides
"Snowflakes for Dry Creek"
Mail-Order Mistletoe Brides
"Mistletoe Kiss in Dry Creek"
Montana Mail-Order Bride

Visit the Author Profile page
at LoveInspired.com for more titles.

Montana
Mail-Order Bride

JANET TRONSTAD

LOVE INSPIRED
INSPIRATIONAL ROMANCE

LOVE INSPIRED®
INSPIRATIONAL ROMANCE

Recycling programs
for this product may
not exist in your area.

ISBN-13: 978-1-335-41891-3

Montana Mail-Order Bride

Copyright © 2022 by Janet Tronstad

For questions and comments about the quality of this book, please contact us at CustomerService@Harlequin.com.

Love Inspired
22 Adelaide St. West, 41st Floor
Toronto, Ontario M5H 4E3, Canada
www.LoveInspired.com

Printed in U.S.A.

And we know that all things work together for good to them that love God, to them who are the called according to his purpose.

—*Romans* 8:28

I dedicate this book to my maternal grandparents, Elizabeth and Harold Norris, who were Montana ranchers. They enjoyed the life and led me to love Old West stories. My grandfather had a shelf of Zane Grey books that made up much of my reading in my younger years and my grandmother enjoyed taking care of their cattle. I'm grateful that they shared their love of all things Western with me.

Chapter One

The snowy winter of 1884

The Union Pacific train rumbled softly as it sped along the tracks in the darkness, but the noise wasn't what was keeping Eleanor Fitzpatrick awake. Every time she snuggled down into her cloak and closed her eyes, she was filled with a sense of foreboding. This impulsive journey—taking herself and her younger sister from their wretched tenement building west of the Chicago River to some remote town in the hills of the Montana Territory—could be the single biggest mistake of her twenty-two years. After all, what kind of a man advertised for a bride he didn't know, even if he was in dire circumstances? Worse yet, what kind of a woman answered his ad?

"A desperate woman—that's who," she muttered softly to herself as she glanced down at the top of the curly blond head sleeping against her shoulder and smiled. Her seven-year-old sister, Lily, was the only family she had left and she would do anything to keep the girl safe.

For the second time that night, Eleanor pulled out the wrinkled newspaper ad from her pocket. The porter's lantern, hanging from a hook at the front of the passenger car, barely gave off enough light for her to see the words, but she read them again anyway.

BRIDE WANTED: Dying sheriff, leaving two young children behind, seeks mail-order bride to be their mother. Applicant must promise to raise the children when he's gone. Will have a small bakery to operate for income. Marriage in name only. Must be honest and a good Christian woman. Reply immediately to Sheriff Matt P. Baynes in Dillon, Montana Territory. Train ticket will be provided.

She had too much pride to answer a mail-order bride ad like that, but her friend, Mrs. Gunni, had done so in Eleanor's name and without her knowledge. It all became clear this past Monday.

As usual, Eleanor had been out looking for work in the huge, noisy factories near where she lived in the heart of Chicago. Everyone knew that those kinds of places always had openings, especially for people like her who were willing to take the most menial and low paying of jobs. But no one would even talk to her. In fact, the hiring foreman hurried past her as though she had the plague, calling out everyone for an interview except her. She didn't know what was wrong.

Finally, cold and defeated, Eleanor headed home and was wearily climbing the very long stairway to the tiny attic room she shared with Lily when—suddenly—she glanced up and saw the huge dour man who delivered their coal, Otis Finch, rushing down the steps, his black coat flapping as he shoved her aside so he could pass. He had something dark gripped in one hand, but he was at the bottom of the stairs before she realized it was Lily's custom-made shoe.

Alarmed at that, Eleanor bolted up the few remaining stairs, threw open the door and found her trembling sister sitting on the only piece of furniture in the room, a cot with an unbleached wool blanket spread neatly over the thin mattress.

"I don't want to be brave anymore," the girl whispered, tears pooling in her eyes. She was wearing her favorite blue dress, and her long skirt was spread out, as it always was, to hide the deformity in her right foot. "I want to go home to Grandmother's house. Please."

Eleanor knelt down and embraced her sister. She, too, often longed for the safety of the home they'd shared with their grandmother until her death three months ago. "You know the bank owns that place now."

"And Grandmother is in Heaven," Lily said, finishing the thought with a sigh.

Eleanor didn't answer. Instead, she tentatively leaned back to see Lily's face better. "Did the coal man put his hands on you?"

Lily wrinkled up her nose before shaking her head slowly. "But he growled at me like this." She made a ferocious face and then demonstrated the sound deep in her throat. "And he said he would be back and fix me for good." She shuddered and continued in a flood of words. "I didn't like that. He didn't say when. What does he mean? He's not a nice man."

"He scared you," Eleanor said softly and Lily nodded. There was no reason for Otis to take her sister's shoe. He had no possible use for it. Eleanor did not understand his power in the neighborhood, but he was a bully. She had heard he could be bribed to do certain things, but he certainly could hope for no money from her. He must know she was penniless.

They were silent for some time, just sitting together wrapped in their hug.

"Let's go outside," Eleanor finally suggested. "That always makes you feel better."

Lily nodded and Eleanor twisted around so that Lily could climb onto her back. It was the only way Eleanor could carry her sister, and she wrapped her cloak around them both before standing upright.

Despite the smoke in the air from the factory chimneys, they each took deep breaths when Eleanor finished the flight of stairs down ten levels to the building's worn entryway. Then she stepped outside with Lily still on her back. The nearby structures blocked most of the view of the sky, but what could be seen was the usual heavy gray. Everything felt damp and cold. The soles on Eleanor's black high-button shoes had been worn so thin that she could feel the icy pebbles on the street beneath her feet. She looked around, but there was no one in sight except for their friend, Mrs. Gunni, who operated the vegetable stall in front of their tenement.

"Was that Otis Finch I just saw running past here?" the woman asked in her slight Danish accent as Eleanor carefully walked over and turned so that Lily could be seated on the stool the woman kept next to her business.

Eleanor nodded. "I hope you don't mind us sitting here a minute."

Although Eleanor had carried Lily down here today, her sister occasionally made the trip on her own. It was a struggle for her and took a long time, but she managed.

"Of course I don't mind," Mrs. Gunni said gruffly as she pulled a blanket off a low shelf in the stall and wrapped it around the girl. "I keep that seat for my favorite visitor, and well she knows it." She gave a quick kiss to the top of Lily's head and studied them both for a moment. "Now, tell me what is wrong that makes such worried faces."

"It was my fault." Lily spoke first, her tears dry by now. The color had come back into her cheeks as she turned to Eleanor. "I didn't open the door. You told me not to and I didn't. But that stinky coal man had a key to our room and he just—poof." The girl made an explosion gesture with her tiny hands. "He came inside. Like in a fairy tale. Just poof—poof." Lily finished her hand movements and crossed her arms, scowling. "He's a wicked troll."

Mrs. Gunni looked over at Eleanor in alarm. "He has a key?"

"Apparently," Eleanor said as she stepped over to hug Lily. "You're not to feel bad. You did everything right. We'll change the lock so he can't get in next time. I'll protect you."

"If I see that coal man again, I'm going to turn him into a toad," Lily declared with determination in her voice. Her shiny yellow curls shook in fury. "An ugly toad, too, with a big lump on his foot so he can't walk and has to crawl everywhere. Let's see if he likes that! He deserves it, too."

"He's certainly no prince," Eleanor agreed, forcing a smile. Her sister never forgot the anguish of her limp, not even when she was dreaming up the most wonderful or horrible of fairy tales. Being a toad might be the worst possible fate in Lily's stories, but being lame in her actual life was never far from her mind.

Eleanor turned to Mrs. Gunni and lowered her voice. "You were right about Otis. I cancelled our coal order, thinking that would do it, but—"

The two women took a few steps away so Lily couldn't hear them talk.

"He's more dangerous than I knew," Mrs. Gunni said softly. "A locked door won't stop him. His older brother came by my stall this morning. He said Otis has something wrong in the head, and the brother thinks he will hurt Lily or you—badly. The two brothers were raised by a wicked aunt, and Otis got it in his head that you're Lily's aunt. He was all upset after that. Aunts are bad people in his mind. He thinks you are a danger to everyone." Mrs. Gunni paused to look at Eleanor intently and her voice softened. "Otis has been telling everyone that you are a mean person and that's why no one will hire you. Plus, even though he's afraid of you, his brother says Otis is determined to get his revenge for what he thinks you did to him."

"But I've done nothing to him," Eleanor protested.

Mrs. Gunni nodded. "I know. He's just not right in the head. One minute it's like he thinks he has to protect Lily from you, and the next, he's breaking in and running off with her custom shoe. His brother is not sure what Otis will do, but he wanted me to tell you Otis has a knife and he might use it."

Both women were silent for a minute. "It's not safe for Lily to stay around here," Eleanor said in despair. "We'll have to move. I can't afford to go far, but—"

"His brother says Otis will come looking for you," Mrs. Gunni answered. "Once he gets a notion in his head…" She threw up her hands. "He thinks of nothing but Lily and the aunt who is with her. He thinks of nothing else."

Eleanor stood there. "What can we do, then?"

Mrs. Gunni walked back to her stall, reached down to the bottom shelf and picked up an envelope. "Maybe you and Lily have a place to go—far away. This came in the mail today."

"What is it?" Eleanor asked, following Mrs. Gunni back to where Lily sat.

The other woman pulled a folded piece of newsprint out of her pocket and handed it to Eleanor. "Read. It will tell you everything."

That piece of newsprint was the ad she now held in her hand on the rumbling train away from Chicago.

When Eleanor had lifted her eyes from the ad, the other woman spoke in a rush. "I thought there would be more letters before the tickets were sent. Lily and I talked—we both thought we would have plenty of time to speak with you. We did not know he would send railroad tickets so soon. He is a trusting man."

"Lily helped you with this?" Eleanor turned to look at her little sister, who beamed proudly as though to confirm it. Eleanor was aghast as more pieces fell into place in her mind. "He thinks I'm going to marry him, doesn't he?"

"Maybe, yes," Mrs. Gunni admitted, ducking her head. Then, like she could hold it in no longer, she burst forth with her final thought. "But this one—he must be a wonderful man! He sent a ticket for our Lily, too. We did not even need to ask. A kind man, he is. But he needs a wife in a hurry. He is sick. He may die soon. And you? You need to leave Chicago."

Mrs. Gunni stopped in seeming exhaustion.

"And the sheriff might be your True Love," Lily chimed in then, her sweet voice barely penetrating the headache Eleanor felt growing.

"But marriage is forever," she protested. She'd set aside thoughts of romance years ago when she realized that if she had a husband, he would have legal rights over Lily. She didn't trust any man that much.

"Well, who can say marriage is forever? This man— he must be very ill," Mrs. Gunni had gathered up her breath again and replied matter-of-factly. "Me—I had many good years with my husband before he died, but you and this man? It won't be long."

"All the more reason why I can't do this," Eleanor

said. "It would be taking advantage of him. Why, he doesn't even want a real wife."

"And you don't want a real husband," Mrs. Gunni said with a grin. "That's why Lily and I—we thought maybe it would work. Anyway, the man needs a nurse, and you have done much caring for your bedridden grandmother—and her being so difficult."

Eleanor was surprised. She'd never said anything negative to anyone about the way their grandmother had treated her and Lily. Not even when the woman had been most scornful of them.

Mrs. Gunni waved her hand as though she understood the relationship was not to be discussed. Clearly, though, Lily had told her, even if inadvertently. Then Mrs. Gunni held out the envelope. "The tickets are here."

"Surely, there's something else we can do," Eleanor protested.

Then Lily twisted around and spoke.

"That Otis man stole my shoe," she declared with disgust on her rosy face. "He said he wanted to see how it was made and I untied it to show him. Then he took it and laughed as he ran out the door. With my shoe!"

"He had it in his hand when I saw him," Eleanor confirmed. They all knew how important that shoe was. Lily had been three years old when she had finally started to walk. They had been living with their grandmother then, since their parents had been killed in a carriage accident two years before that. The doctor said Lily needed a custom-made brace and shoe to walk normally, though, and their grandmother surprised Eleanor by paying a cobbler to make the leather contraption. Without it, Lily tilted to one side and lurched so much that other children teased her.

Mrs. Gunni was silent for a minute. Snow was falling and the wind was beginning to blow. Then she leaned close.

"You see what Otis has done, don't you?" she whispered to Eleanor. "He has made it impossible for Lily to escape if he comes back to your room. She cannot run without that shoe."

Eleanor closed her eyes. The woman was right. *God, help us.*

When Eleanor opened her eyes, all she saw was Lily sitting on that stool with a look of complete trust on her face. Eleanor knew she had no choice. She took the envelope. "You're right."

She stood there feeling her heart turn to ice.

"I believe the good Lord sent those tickets for you," Mrs. Gunni said with an upward glance to what was becoming an increasingly stormy sky.

Eleanor wasn't willing to go that far. She believed God answered orderly prayers said in church, but the wild cries of her heart never seemed to move Him. At least, they hadn't when she'd prayed for her father to stay home and not turn away from baby Lily in disgust over her misshapen foot.

Eleanor kept praying, of course. It was a habit from childhood, and in truth, she knew God was high up there somewhere. She even believed He answered some prayers, but she had begun to wonder lately if He listened to only important people like ministers and bankers and not poor young women like her.

Eleanor faced her friend. Mrs. Gunni was right about one thing. "I don't really have a choice, do I?"

The other woman put her hand on Eleanor's arm. "I hope that this new life will bring more joy than you expect. I'll send a telegram to the sheriff after you leave so he'll know when you and Lily are to arrive. Give the man a chance."

Eleanor nodded. "I'll do my best."

Now, days later, she leaned back in her train seat and looked out the window, wondering how many women had started their married lives with those same, lifeless words. Duty didn't make any woman's heart beat faster. She'd given up thoughts of romance years ago, but she suddenly realized she'd always expected to live a happy life anyway, with herself and Lily and, maybe someday, a friendly cat.

Yes, she thought, a sweet kitten is what they needed. Eleanor wished that she knew if this sheriff was a good man, the type of man who would welcome a nice, quiet pet. It would make all of the difference if he cared enough about weaker beings to see that they were fed and had a home. Then he might be trusted with her Lily.

The next day, in the snowy foothills of Southwestern Montana Territory

Sheriff Matt P. Baynes scowled at the old tomcat that was huddled behind a wooden box on the platform of the Utah and Northern Railroad in the small town of Dillon. That beast of a cat had been stalking him for days and was wise to try to hide from him, even if the feline wasn't careful enough to notice that the box was made of slats and a man could see right through it. Then again, the gray-striped animal might just be taunting him.

"Scat," Matt ordered. The cat stared back, without moving. Matt shook his head. No doubt the beast had looked good in its younger years, but now with its torn ears and patchy fur, it barely seemed fit for polite company. "I expect they'll have something for you to eat over at the saloon."

The tom would just have to make peace with the haughty white Persian cat that had seemingly replaced him when the saloon owner recently hired a piano player who came with her own well-groomed pet. Matt had seen the two animals arch their backs and spit at each other on more than one occasion, but for some reason, the old tom avoided an out-and-out fight—which was odd now that Matt thought about it. The creature had the battle scars to prove he'd win any contest with that Persian beauty, but for some reason, the tom kept slinking away, even choosing to spend the nights on the jail's side of the street. Matt knew that, because when he lay on his cot at night, he couldn't sleep for all the shuffling and snarling cat noise coming from the other side of his thin wall.

Turning back to the railroad track, Matt squinted despairingly into the distance. He had more to worry about than that animal. He was still of two minds over whether he hoped his bride and her sister were on this scheduled train or not. He might need a wife, but he wasn't happy about it. All he knew was that any self-respecting man would meet the train when his future wife came in on it.

His mother had instilled that much sense into him before she abandoned them all when he was twelve years old. Matt shook his head, wondering why the thought of that mail-order bride should call to mind his traitorous mother. It did not bode well—that much he knew.

Being miserably cold didn't help his spirits any either. He had his sheepskin coat pulled tight around his chin and he was still shivering. A March blizzard had been hitting the small town with everything it had for the past week, and he couldn't see the railroad tracks for more than twenty yards in either direction. The train was already an hour late. It might not even make it in today.

Matt shook his head, growing more convinced that no one was coming. He should be relieved. It was fate. He was thirty years old and, so far, not much had worked out with him when it came to women. There was no reason to think it was going to change now, no matter what kind of charming letter he'd received in response to that ad.

"Meeting the bride, Sheriff?" a voice asked, startling Matt out of his ruminations. The snow was heavy enough that he hadn't noticed the intruder. He knew the man worked for the railroad, but he didn't remember his name. Was it Adam? No, that didn't sound right.

"Only polite to meet her train," Matt mumbled in response.

The gossip about his ad had spread all over Dillon like wildfire. He should have known. Nothing much else was going on with the weather being like this and Matt supposed everyone liked a love story as long as it was happening to someone else. He could tell the whole town a thing or two about the pitfalls of love, though, having watched his parents' marriage turn sour.

"Heard, too, that you're planning to go out and round up the Blackwood brothers," the man continued. By now, he was leaning on the handle of the shovel he'd used to scrape the snow off the platform. "You think they're the ones who shot and killed your brother and his wife?"

Matt waited, hoping that the man would grow uncomfortable and leave. The man didn't move and Matt started feeling awkward himself, so he answered, "I figure so. Angus, isn't it? Angus Wells?" The man nodded and Matt continued, "I won't know for sure who did it until I get one of them to confess. The undertaker thought my sister-in-law, Adeline, was shot by mistake, even if she was holding a gun."

"Can't be the Blackwood boys, then," Angus said. "They don't miss much with their shooting."

Angus took the opportunity to spit toward the back corner of the platform. Matt watched in fascination as the liquid froze and crackled when it hit the ground.

"I know the Blackwood boys are good with their firearms," Matt answered. "I'm the one who taught them."

It had been eighteen years ago, he calculated.

"Why would you do a fool thing like that?" Angus asked, his mouth hanging open in astonishment.

"Well, the oldest one was eight years old at the time," Matt replied. "And their father had been gone awhile." Matt left out that the reason their father was absent was that the man had run off with Matt's mother. Both families had suffered. "The fact was that someone needed to teach them boys how to shoot or they'd never see meat on their table again. Besides, they weren't outlaws back then. They were ranch boys, like me and my brother."

The two families had been neighborly before the runaway incident, even though the Bayneses grew cattle and the Blackwoods raised sheep.

"You reckon they'll think back to your kindness and not kill you, then?" Angus asked as he stood there.

Matt snorted. "Not likely. No, they'll do their best to lay me out dead." He didn't add that it hadn't taken long for the Blackwood boys to blame the Baynes family all those years ago. They claimed that what happened to their father could be laid square at the feet of Rose Prinz Baynes, Matt's mother. She'd always been flirtatious, but the boys figured she must have gone to some extra effort to seduce their father or he would have never left his wife and six sons, two of whom were twins and mere babies at the time.

"Well, who's going to take care of your brother's kids if you up and get yourself killed by those Blackwood boys?" Angus demanded to know, like he was their keeper instead of Matt. "No one around here is going to take them in."

Matt nodded wearily. The man spoke the truth. Apparently, there had been rumored threats and bad talk from the Blackwood brothers ever since Dillon started calling itself a town three years ago. Matt had been down in the Idaho Territory longer than that, but it was clear that those boys had been scarred for life by their father leaving them the way he had. None of them had settled down and married. Although, in fairness, Matt had to admit the same could be said for him, and he was older than those boys by a good four years. The truth was that both families had been damaged by those two adulterers who should have known better. To Matt's knowledge, no one had heard from either one of them since, and after all this time, it was unlikely they would—which suited him just fine.

"It's a shame about those children of your brother's though," Angus continued after making a few more futile swipes at the still-falling snow. "That's got to be tough."

Matt nodded again. His brother had never seemed as angry with their mother as Matt had been, but then, Luke hadn't been the one who caused that argument no one talked about. And, maybe his brother had been too sick to notice the grief that twisted their father into knots whenever anyone mentioned their mother. As a boy, Luke had trouble breathing. Matt nursed him as much as he was able, but he never knew what to do for sure. Their father would only dismiss Luke as weak, and so he was not much help.

Luke's lungs seemed to get better as he got older and he had even gone up to Canada close to a decade ago and came back with a French bride, just like their father had done when he wanted to get married. Luke's two children, a boy and a girl, had been huddled together in a jail cell ever since Matt had first stepped into the sheriff's office a couple of weeks ago. He hadn't even seen them at first, given that they were quiet and he was upset after hearing about the killing of his brother. Matt had ridden hard to get here from the Green River, and he hadn't known about Adeline being shot and dying, too, until he got to Dillon.

"Heard you're having a time with them," Angus offered his insight, or maybe it was meant to be sympathy. "Could be you should just arrest them for not cooperating with the law."

The man chuckled like he'd said something witty.

Matt sighed and didn't respond. But Angus kept looking at him, intent on getting an answer, even if it was none of his business.

"I've done everything I can think of," Matt finally admitted, hoping that would stop the questions. Angus nodded sympathetically, though, and Matt found himself relaxing. Finally, he confessed, "Nothing seems to make them feel any better. I might as well have arrested them."

Angus nodded. "The poor young'uns must be missing their folks."

And they didn't like their uncle much either, Matt thought glumly. They had sat in that jail cell like prisoners of war for over a week. Henry—or, as he insisted on being called, Henri—was a boy of seven with a fierce scowl on his face. His sister, Sylvie, was three years old with a trembling lip. Neither of them had said a word other than to mumble to each other in French.

Matt had tried smiling and singing to the children. He'd made shadow puppets on the wall and showed them how to polish their shoes. He'd even gone over to the general store and bought them each a handful of lemon drops. Nothing worked. They continued to look at him like he was a rattler, ready to strike them down the minute they relaxed their guard.

It took a few minutes for Matt to hear the distant sound of the train engine.

The other man heard it, too.

"Here she comes!" Angus looked over and grinned. "I reckon you're some excited."

"Well, they might not be on it," Matt said, by now hoping it was true.

"Oh, they'll be on it all right," Angus said with a chuckle. "I already got a telegraph from some friend of theirs in Chicago asking me to let him know when Eleanor Fitzpatrick and her sister arrive."

"A friend? Who would that be?"

"Some man named Otis Finch," Angus said. "He wanted me to let him know the minute they arrived. Maybe he's a suitor who regrets letting one of them get away." Angus gave a heavy sigh. "Ain't that nice? Him missing her already?"

Matt wondered if the whole town of Dillon had gone too far in wondering about the love life of his mail-order bride.

"I'm sure he's not a suitor." Matt figured he should stop that rumor right now. If either one of the sisters had matrimonial possibilities, they wouldn't have answered his ad.

Of course, it could be a bill collector. Or even be a bounty hunter, if it came to that. Matt was suddenly aware of how little he knew about the woman he was going to marry. And that didn't even count what mischief the sister might be bringing along with her.

Matt turned to Angus. "Don't reply to that telegram until I tell you. We don't know what we're dealing with here yet."

Angus looked surprised, but nodded. "I suppose that's best. Let everyone settle down first."

"Thanks," Matt said to the other man.

He should have never agreed to do this, Matt thought as he watched one of the passenger cars come to a halt right beside the platform. A black ashy smoke, caught by the wind, swept down from the billowing stacks that stood on top of the engine. The lengthy snow-covered train, which had come up from Ogden, was overflowing with travelers and they spilled out onto the icy platform like chickens let loose from their coop.

Matt panicked. He didn't even know what the woman looked like who was going to be his wife. Then he saw a sturdy, gray-haired woman, trailed by a younger woman, both plainly dressed and sober. The younger one moved slowly, like she might have that foot problem mentioned in the letter. That had to be them, he thought with a sigh. They looked nice enough, albeit a little dull and self-righteous. Then he saw a man come up to them and greet them both with hugs. He had to admit to some relief. The letter he'd received in answer to his ad hadn't mentioned age, so he figured Eleanor Fitzpatrick would be on the older side of forty, maybe even of fifty. He didn't care. The more years she had on her, the more likely she'd be to stay and do her duty to the children after he was killed.

Suddenly, it seemed people were rushing to leave the platform, going this way or that. Of course, it was too cold to stand around and talk.

Finally, the only passengers who were left looked like a young mother and her daughter. It was hard to tell their exact ages. The younger one leaned on the older one, and they were both standing straight in the wind, dressed like exotic birds in gray, a muted mauve and bright blue. They were surveying the deserted area in dismay. He knew Eleanor had a sister, but he thought she was full-grown. The younger one here was a child. She had a long dress, so he could barely see the scuffed boot on one of her feet. A small battered trunk sat at the side of the eldest, along with two carpetbags.

He decided his bride had not come, and he was going to turn around.

But the woman, a gray cloak gathered around her, settled the girl on top of the trunk and stepped over to him.

"Are you Sheriff Matt P. Baynes?" she asked with a voice colder than the air swirling around him. Matt was stunned. Her hair, what he could see of it under the brim of her lady hat, was raven black. Her eyes gray as an evening sleet storm. Her skin so fine that it reminded him of the translucent inside of one of the china cups his mother used to line up on the mantel out at their family ranch. He'd never seen someone so delicate and beautiful. She didn't even come up to his shoulders, but she held herself with pride. Despite its chilly tone, the woman's voice had a sweet lilt to it that was vaguely familiar.

"You can't be Eleanor Fitzpatrick." The words burst out of him before he considered how they would sound. "I mean, you wouldn't need to answer an ad to get a husband. Surely, men all over would line up to marry you."

He might be dismayed at her beauty, but she was clearly taken aback at his comment.

"I beg your pardon." He certainly had not expected a woman like this. "I'm just— That is, most women would have mentioned their good looks in the letter."

Jacob Goetts, the man who had convinced Matt it was his duty to marry for the sake of his nephew and niece before he went after the Blackwood brothers, had told him that women teetered on the edge of lying in those matrimonial letters, most saying they were attractive or pleasant-faced, no matter how they looked. Not that Matt cared much about the outside of the woman he was set to marry, but he was suspicious that she hadn't mentioned it. Made him wonder what else she hadn't said.

But he didn't have time to ask. The woman's cheeks flamed at his words and she said, "About that letter, it—"

"We'll have time to talk later," Matt said, suddenly seeing Angus walking toward them. He didn't want the man to come and start quizzing his bride about any suitors she'd left behind in Chicago. He might have his questions about her, but he nonetheless felt very protective of his prize and he didn't want her to turn back before he could convince her to stay. "Let me start over. It is a pleasure to meet you, Eleanor Fitzpatrick."

He had shaved his beard off this morning, but the snow that sat on his hat probably still made him look like an old grizzled trapper in his sheepskin coat. And then, he had that scratch on his cheek from a few days ago when he tried to pick up that wildcat so he could haul it back to where it belonged. His mother's disappointment with his general looks and manner had made him shy away from ladies like the one in front of him.

"Eleanor Marie Fitzpatrick," she corrected him, emphasizing her middle name and then smiling slightly. "Eleanor because that was the name of my father's Irish mother. Marie is from my French mother's side of the family. And the Fitzpatrick is my father's surname."

Her name was like a whole bouquet of dainty flowers, Matt thought and then noticed she was waiting for a response.

"And what do you prefer?" Matt asked while waving Angus away behind his back. He wanted to learn all he could about this woman.

"I was Marie Fitzpatrick when I was a girl." She smiled, showing off a little dimple on her left cheek. That name was sweet, too, Matt thought.

"I'm sure you were as delightful as a young girl as you are now," he said before thinking. Fortunately, he stopped himself short before he sounded as lovesick as

Angus. He figured most of the gladness he felt was relief that Eleanor was here and the wait was over. Only then did he realize the storm was still blowing freezing air on them all.

Eleanor gamely continued the conversation. "But when I was fifteen years old, I decided Eleanor Fitzpatrick was more fitting for a grown woman. Our family situation had changed and it sounded responsible."

"And is that what you are now?" he asked. "Responsible?"

"Yes," she said, sounding resolute but not happy about it.

"You're too pretty to worry about things like responsibility," Matt said softly.

"Someone has to," she answered, looking at him like he should know that.

"Then, let me," Matt said. He was stunned at his own words and, when he realized what he'd said, he winced. *Lord, help me*, he scrambled to pray. He needed to stop this. He was openly flirting with this woman—in a blizzard on a deserted train platform, no less. He planned to marry her, but he wasn't prepared to be smitten with her, no matter how attractive she was. He must have grimaced again then because, all of a sudden it seemed, she was scrutinizing his face.

"Where's the pain?" she asked briskly as she assessed him. "I know the Lord can help us endure most anything. Prayer works. But if you feel bad, I have supplies in the trunk to make you a special tea that will help."

"Tea?" Matt said, realizing he must have mouthed

his short prayer asking for help. Maybe she had read his lips. Or he was so off-balance he might have actually said the words aloud?

"Tea is good for sick people," Eleanor informed him. "I know ones that cut the pain. Most nurses know how to use herbs to make different broths that are useful. And poultices, too."

"I don't need a nurse."

"Of course you do," she said. "Your ad said you were dying."

"Oh, that." Matt felt a headache coming on. He'd rather be facing the whole Blackwood gang than standing here. It was enough to make him feel the cold temperature more deeply. "We really need to get inside out of this storm."

Matt looked down and focused on the young girl for the first time. He took a step closer to her. She had climbed down from the trunk and was leaning on it as she waited patiently. She already looked frozen, her body quite a bit off-center because of that scruffy boot. It was too big for her. But it didn't take away any of her charm. Her skin was pale and her hair so fair it was like spun white gold around her face. Even though her footwear didn't match, she did have two pairs of gloves on her hands. He noted that Eleanor had none—which meant the older one had given hers to her sister. Neither one was dressed for this kind of weather.

"This is my younger sister, Lily." Eleanor had followed him over and now introduced him.

Matt smiled as he nodded to the girl. "You're probably freezing. Jacob Goetts, my—uh, I suppose he's my deputy—put a new pot of coffee on the stove in the office."

He suddenly realized the girl looked too young for that. "He can warm up some milk for you, if you'd rather. I think we might have some chocolate to put in it, too."

He'd gotten the dark sweet for the children a few days ago and he kept a jug of milk for them in the coldest cell in the jail, which happened to belong to Jacob. Lily smiled and Matt picked up their trunk, using a hand to balance it on his shoulder. It was remarkably light. He gripped the two valises on the other side and lifted them, as well. Then he looked down at the little girl. Her smile had faded and she was looking worried as she gazed out into the storm.

Suddenly, Matt understood and he called to Angus. "Give me a hand, will you?"

The man walked over and smiled. "What can I do?"

"You can carry the trunk and these bags to the jailhouse," Matt said. "And tell Jacob we're on the way. See if he can warm up some milk."

Then Matt set the trunk and bags down on the platform and opened his arms to Lily. "Want a ride?"

The anxiety left her face and she glanced up to her sister. "Can I?"

"There's no need," Eleanor said to Matt primly. "I can manage Lily. She's not too steady on icy ground, but we'll make it to where we're going. We always do. I don't want you to have to do anything extra."

The woman stood there looking stern, like a school-teacher who expected to be obeyed. But Matt thought she didn't look strong enough to get her own self to the jailhouse, let alone help someone else.

"Nonsense," Matt said as he opened his huge sheepskin coat and swept down to pick up the girl. She wrapped her arms around his neck and snuggled close.

"Make sure your hands are tucked in," he instructed her.

Then he turned to Eleanor. "Close me up and your sister will be warm as a bear in hibernating season."

As Eleanor worked the buttons on his coat, he noticed her hands were shivering. They were so white they almost seemed gray.

He looked down at the girl whose soft breath warmed his neck. "Can you pull off a pair of those gloves to give to your sister? Your hands will be fine if you keep them under my collar."

Lily wiggled around and, before long, her tiny hand emerged from the opening in his coat with two leather gloves dangling from her fingers.

"Thanks," Eleanor said as she accepted Lily's offering and started to slip them on her hands.

"You'll be glad to know the town put in a boardwalk that goes all the way down the main street," Matt said as he waited for Eleanor to get her fingers inside the gloves. "The jail is, of course, off the street."

Matt noted she didn't look especially impressed as she glanced at the wooden walkway, even though he'd heard it had taken the town months to make the improvement. Maybe the woman was distracted though. Her frown certainly indicated something was wrong.

"Lily will be able to step right along on it when

there's no snow," he added so she would understand more fully.

"Oh, yes," Eleanor said, her head bowed down as she struggled to get the last of the gloves on her hands. "I see now. That's very nice."

Matt figured *nice* was polite, but not enthused.

He realized then that a boardwalk probably did not make this town stand out as better than Chicago. Dillon, even with its new brick bank and all of the false storefronts it had added recently, was still a frontier town. It even occasionally had shoot-outs on Saturday nights. As sheriff, he carried his guns everywhere except into the church. No, he thought, an elegant lady like this was not likely to approve of a place like Dillon.

"I heard they have cobbled streets in Chicago." He wasn't sure that was true, but he remembered some traveling salesman saying it. "I expect that's what fine ladies are used to in a town. Keeps their shoes clean when they do their shopping."

"Not everyone is able to worry about their footwear," Eleanor said. "Chicago has dirt streets west of the river, but it is the smoky factories that keep everyone and their shoes filthy. The city's not all fancy hotels. My grandmother had a fine Victorian house there, but she was blessed. As we were also, when we came to live with her over five years ago after our parents died in a carriage accident. Lily and I loved sitting on her porch in the springtime. It was a shame when the bank took that place."

The woman stopped abruptly as though she didn't usually talk that much.

"Oh," Matt replied, not knowing if he was supposed to offer up some similar details in response. For years, he'd been a ranch hand down by the Green River in Idaho Territory, until he got the word about the death of his brother. He didn't have a porch, but he liked riding night duty with a herd of cattle when the stars were out. Not that it would impress this woman, so he settled for saying "Follow me."

"Of course, we don't expect to be sitting on the porch here," Eleanor added in a low voice, making him think he was right that she was anxious.

Well, he was, too, he thought, wishing he could ask her right out what she had expected. But it was cold and he wasn't sure it mattered at this point anyway. The woman and girl were here. The time for refusing this marriage was over—at least on his side of things. Technically, he was the one who had invited them, even if it had been Jacob's idea and letter that had gotten them here.

Never in all his conversations with Jacob had either of them expected society ladies to come, though, and that's what these two were. Jacob had told him it was mostly widows and poor women who answered these ads. Matt's heart sank. Ladies would expect a gentleman. He remembered his mother wanting him to wear a tie, like the men did in New York City, instead of a bandana like everyone in the Territories wore. He didn't care for poetry. He preferred a banjo to a violin. The list of his failings as a gentleman was long.

He almost sighed. He would have been better off with the older woman who'd stepped down from the train first. She looked like she'd accept a man as he was and not fuss at him. Besides, she wouldn't tangle up his tongue like Eleanor did.

Not that the society sisters were guaranteed to stay long. They'd have difficulty adapting to Western ways if they did. He thought he was only trying to keep an open mind, but he suddenly realized that the thought of them leaving made him feel like a stone had been dropped down his gullet and left to settle in his stomach.

He might not be a gentleman, but he was in trouble. He consoled himself with the fact that he'd probably not have long to suffer their disapproval. Not with the Blackwood brothers to face. All six of them were reputed to be deadly shots. He should be planning his funeral and not worrying about whether some woman was going to find him as lacking as his mother had in the gentlemanly graces.

He looked down at Eleanor. She surely was a fine-looking bride. It would almost be worth wearing a tie to win her regard. And then she frowned, almost like she had something withering to say. He waited, but she remained silent—at least, for now.

Chapter Two

"Just a bit farther," Eleanor heard the man say as she trudged along behind him. He didn't even turn around to see if she was still there. What little optimism she'd had when she stepped off the train was being slowly frozen out of her. She could see snow collecting on Matt's broad back, so she figured it was covering her, too. Her body was shaking so much that she wondered if she'd ever thaw.

This blizzard was strong enough that she had to stop a moment to take a thin wool scarf from her velvet purse and wrap it around her gray hat. She tied it securely under her chin, even though this was the only nice hat she still owned and it meant slightly crushing the jaunty mauve feathers on the brim. While she occupied her fingers with all that, she noticed the man hadn't stopped or even said anything more. He was getting farther ahead.

In fairness, he probably couldn't see her very well, given the swirling snow, even if he turned around. He likely didn't know she had needed to stand still for a moment. Pins were falling out of her hair in the back, but she could not stop that now either. Wind whipped her long skirt until it clung to her legs, making it difficult to move, but she had to hurry to catch up. If she lost that man in the swirl of snow, she wouldn't know where to go. She'd hate looking like a washerwoman when she talked to him about what he expected of a wife, but she had to keep putting one foot in front of the other as she followed him down the icy walkway.

When Eleanor caught up, she tried to see the top of Lily's head. The girl was snuggled down close to Matt, and Eleanor saw only a few stray blond curls. She managed to keep her pace and, at the same time, make note of the town. It obviously prided itself on being neat. There were no broken windows or abandoned buildings, although a couple of the stores did appear to be empty. They passed several clapboard houses with wood slats so new they hadn't turned gray, a general store with a high false front painted green, a two-story saloon with a balcony going around the second level and an outside stairway leading up to that from the street. Across from the saloon, there was an old run-down building that had iron bars on its windows. A large bare tree stood to one side of the place, and snow had been cleared in front of the door.

Matt opened the door and confirmed her fears that it had to be the jail. The inside air smelled of coffee, though, and a battered enamel pot sat on top of the round stove. She noticed her trunk and the bags standing to the side, so the other man must have brought them and left. Matt gestured for her to unhook his coat, and Eleanor stepped over to work on the buttons again. They were made from pieces of what she guessed was some kind of animal bone, and they were slick in the damp cold. She undid the buttons and glanced up to see Matt gazing down at her. His eyes seemed to be unnaturally warm and she felt a blush crawl up her neck. He couldn't have any affection for her, she told herself as she stepped back and he opened his coat. And he shouldn't have any other thoughts, she told herself primly as she studied the floor. Eleanor looked up and realized he hadn't been thinking about her at all.

Instead, he was carefully standing Lily upright on the floor, keeping his hand on her shoulder, waiting for her to be steady. Of course, Lily never would be. Eleanor always made her sister's dresses long to hide her trouble with walking. She hoped the man would not realize Lily's difficulty until he had time to see for himself how sweet she was.

"It's the cold," Eleanor whispered to Matt. "Lily has a hard time when it's like that outside."

The man nodded like it was to be expected and picked up Lily again to carry her over to a chair. The girl sat down, her feet dangling slightly. Eleanor watched as Lily smoothed down her blue skirt like a princess and looked up at Matt as if he was her knight in shining armor.

"Thank you," Eleanor said to him softly. She wasn't sure she wanted Lily to think this man was her hero, but he had been kind. The problem was that they didn't know him and he could turn on them when he learned the truth of Lily's foot. Eleanor suspected Lily was already spinning stories about the sheriff, and she didn't want her to be hurt when he failed to live up to her hopes.

"You're welcome," Matt said as he stepped farther into the jailhouse. He didn't seem to recognize that Lily was mesmerized by him.

Eleanor glanced around. Maybe she was needlessly worried about Lily's admiration of him. By tomorrow, he might do something else and Lily would decide the man was a toad. Right now, the smell of coffee made the building seem pleasant enough, even though there was no hiding the cracks in the plank walls that were stuffed with bits of old newspapers. A kerosene lamp on the desk lit up a circle around it, but the rest of the place was almost dark—probably because it looked like shutters had been closed over the windows.

Still, Eleanor told herself, it was much warmer here than outside. And there were no sounds of angry men fighting like she expected in a jail. The four prisoner cells all had their doors open, so no unfortunate outlaws appeared to be here at the moment. Half of the building was given over to the potbellied stove, some cupboards, that huge desk and a scattering of chairs—one of which Lily was currently using. A nice carpet would make the place look better, but it was not something Eleanor would suggest. She merely pulled the gloves off her hands and stepped closer to the stove. Her fingers were white from the cold, and the air coming from it made them tingle. She stuffed the gloves into the pocket of her skirt.

"Where's your house?" Eleanor asked, now that Matt had moved around enough to ensure he was comfortable. "Is it close?"

He looked at her in surprise and was silent.

"There are a couple of hotels in town," he finally said as he moved a chair closer to Eleanor and indicated she should sit down. "I don't have a house. My niece and nephew have the ranch, of course, but that's some ways away, and I have to be here to do my job, so we have been bunking here. I'm not sure this is a good enough place for ladies though. Maybe it's best if I take you to one of the hotels."

Eleanor froze, and it was not the temperature this time. She hadn't realized how dependent she would be on this stranger. Hotels were expensive and she did not want to give him any excuse to send her and Lily back to Chicago.

"We've been sleeping in our seats on the train for days now, so just being able to lie flat will be an improvement," Eleanor said, careful to make it clear she was truly grateful for any bed. She had used a few of her coins to buy food on the train after they'd finished the bag of apples that Mrs. Gunni had sent with them. Eleanor didn't have enough money left to do more than purchase a few ribbons so Lily could pull her hair back in the wind. Even if Matt offered to pay for a room, Eleanor couldn't accept. He might want the funds back if he decided to call off their agreement.

"I assure you cots here will be fine," Eleanor said to make sure there was no misunderstanding. "We appreciate any hospitality for the night."

Matt carefully picked up their trunk and carpetbags. Then he carried them into one of the cells. "This is the biggest cell. It has two cots and a washstand."

"Thank you," she said.

She could already tell that she was not what Matt had expected. He eyed her like she was fragile and wouldn't be able to do much work. Her mother had been that way, too, and Eleanor knew she resembled her. But she also had her father's Irish strength and she intended to show Matt that she was a worker.

"I could have managed the trunk and bags," she said as Matt stepped back to the center of the room. "Of course, I'm grateful, but from now on, I can do what is necessary."

The sheriff looked over at her in astonishment.

Then she heard another cell open.

"Welcome to Dillon," a lanky man said as he stepped out of the far cell. The shadows in that corner made it especially dark and Eleanor had missed him in her glance around earlier. His short rusty hair was swept back and his face deeply tanned. A white shirt was carefully buttoned around his neck. He appeared to be a decade or so older than Matt and was whipcord thin. He moved gracefully, giving her and Lily a stately bow. "I'm Jacob Goetts. I help the sheriff with things. At your service."

"Thank you," Eleanor murmured. She prompted her sister, and Lily whispered a response, as well.

Eleanor had not known manners like this for some time, not even in Chicago.

"My pleasure." Jacob's lips turned up in a friendly

smile. "If there's anything I can do to make you more comfortable, just ask."

Matt stepped forward and scowled. "I'll see to everything."

"I—" Eleanor began and then decided it was churlish to refuse the help of both men. She smiled stiffly and added, "Thank you."

She could not help but notice that Matt wasn't nearly as easygoing as his friend. But, she told herself, that was probably because he was the man she'd come here to marry. He was probably anxious. Well, the truth was she was feeling unnerved, too. She wondered how long she could hide Lily's difficulty in walking.

"Dillon is a lovely town," she offered. "The jail here is warm." Maybe, if she kept shoveling compliments his way, Matt wouldn't say whatever sour thought it was that seemed to be growing in his mind as his frown deepened. She wished she'd had more time to talk to Mrs. Gunni before they left so she could have asked what happened in these cases if the parties didn't suit. But she and Lily had barely had time to hug the widow farewell, take the bag of apples she handed to them, and confirm that they were taking the early morning train west. Mrs. Gunni had repeated that she was happy for them and waved them on their way.

Just then, Eleanor heard a slight rustle and turned sharply to see the mound of bedding move on the cot in one of the remaining cells. She had thought the blankets had been left in disarray by a past occupant—prisoners being the sort to do things like that, she supposed—

but she saw now those blankets covered two little figures who were staring out at her, their eyes wide open.

"Ohh, my *magnifiques bebes*," Eleanor cooed, her fears and the cold forgotten. What precious little children—or *magnificent babies*, as her mother would have said with her French accent. Eleanor remembered her whispering those words to every baby she met until Lily was born. After that, she didn't seem to think any baby was worth noticing. Eleanor tried to shake off the past. She needed to forget those days.

When she looked again, the boy and girl were both staring at her, and they shifted their feet around this way and that until they were free of the coverings, and then they came racing toward her like they'd been awakened from their crumpled sleep with the promise of their favorite treat.

"Mama," the tiny girl called out as she swung her rag doll in one hand and stepped close enough to clutch Eleanor around the leg with the other.

Eleanor could feel the torrent of emotion coming from the girl, so she bent down and gathered her and her doll up into her arms. Gradually, she lowered the child until she could cradle her on her hip.

"What's your name?" Eleanor asked softly.

"I'm Sylvie," the girl said shyly and held up one hand. "This is Dolly."

"I'm very pleased to meet you both," Eleanor said, nodding courteously to them. Then she turned to the boy. He was older than she'd first thought. "And your name is?"

"Henri," the boy said and added in disgust, "And she takes that doll everywhere with her. Even to bed."

"You like Dolly, too," Sylvie protested. "I see you hug her when you think I'm asleep."

The boy flushed a deep red. "I'm only making sure it's okay. I know I'd have to go find her if you lost her someplace."

"I wouldn't lose Dolly," the girl said, horrified. "I love my Dolly."

"Of course you do," Eleanor said soothingly. She looked to Matt for guidance, and he shrugged, so she added, "And I'm sure Henri was just—ah—protecting your Dolly because he's a good brother and loves you."

Eleanor finished with relief. Lily was the only child in her family and she had never had to keep quarreling siblings happy with each other.

"Yeah." The boy seemed to relax at her words.

Eleanor was pleased with the children's responses, so she thought she'd make the family circle wider. She looked over at Matt. "And, of course, your uncle is protecting both of you and—"

"He's not our uncle," Henri interrupted abruptly.

Eleanor saw the shock on Matt's face before his eyes grew hooded and his face impassive.

"Don't be silly," Matt said. "Of course I'm your uncle."

Henri shook his head adamantly. "You're not tall enough."

"What?" Matt asked, clearly bewildered. "I'm your father's brother. That makes me your uncle."

Eleanor was confused, too, but she could see that Henri was stubbornly convinced he was right.

The boy shook his head again, even more firmly. "Our father's brother was this much taller than he was." To demonstrate, Henri put his hands out about two feet apart. "I know because of the marks on the side of the kitchen door in our house."

"Out at the ranch?" Matt asked, his brow furrowed.

The boy nodded. "My mother measured me against them. She hadn't started marking Sylvie yet. But she made my marks on the doorpost, too, and I saw my father's and his brother's from when they were kids. My father told me that his brother was always that much taller than him and he didn't like it."

"He did gripe about that a lot," Matt said with a smile. "Every time we got measured, he'd be mad. He was always smaller and not as strong. Still, he liked it when our mother got out the measuring stick, even if he could see I was still ahead."

Henri's face crumpled slightly. "My mama's not here. I don't have nobody to measure me now. Does that mean I won't be growing no more?"

The boy's grief was obvious, Eleanor thought, and she almost reached out, but Matt took a step closer to the child.

"I'll be happy to notch the post for you when we go out to the ranch," Matt said, looking uncomfortable but determined. "I can do what needs doing."

Henri shook his head mournfully. "You can't do it. It has to be a boy's *mother* who does that. My father said his mother marked it for him. And he said my mother would do it for me. That's the way it's done. Fathers watch, but they don't mark."

Eleanor saw the two of them stare at each other— the man and the boy—neither one seeming to know how to compromise and yet both of them needing the other's approval.

"I could do it," Eleanor said, hesitantly glancing up at Matt before turning to Henri. "I'm not your mother, but I would be honored if you'd let me stand in for her and do the marking."

"That'd be all right." The boy nodded shyly and Eleanor felt her heart warm toward him.

Then Henri jerked his head toward Matt. "Will he be there?"

"Of course I'll be there," Matt said. "I'll be watching like your father would. And there's no reason to think I'm not your uncle."

"You're not the sheriff either," Henri said, his lip showing defiance. "I've met the sheriff lots of times, and he—" the boy pointed toward Matt "—he isn't him."

"Oh," Eleanor murmured. For all she knew, Matt wasn't the sheriff. She hadn't even seen a badge. Matt had certainly said he was a sheriff in that ad, though, and she saw no reason for him to lie, unless he thought it would make him sound more attractive to women. She eyed him carefully. No, she decided, any man as handsome as him would know women liked him. They probably fluttered all around him wherever he lived.

By now, Matt had knelt down until his face was level with Henri's.

"It's true that I'm not the sheriff you're used to," Matt said. "The sheriff you remember quit after your parents were killed. We should have told you. I didn't think. When I got here, there was no lawman. Jacob was sort of keeping up the jail, but he needed help. I said I would do the job, so the judge made me the sheriff. I have a badge in this desk here."

Matt stood up then and walked over to the desk, opened a drawer and lifted out a badge.

"But you're still not tall enough," the boy persisted.

"I was twelve years old when those marks were last made," Matt said softly. "Your father was two years younger. At that age, I was just naturally a lot taller than he was. And he was sick a lot. He didn't like that one bit when we made those marks, but that changed when we both grew up. He grew a little bit stronger each year. Finally, we were about the same height."

"Why didn't anyone move those marks, then?" the boy said, unwilling to give up the point.

"Like you said, our mother was the one who made the marks," Matt answered. "After that last time, she wasn't there any longer." Matt spread his hands. "She was gone."

"To Heaven?" the girl whispered, wiggling around on Eleanor's hip to look at Matt in fascination. "Like our mama?"

"No, not to Heaven," Matt said softly.

"I miss my mama," Sylvie said to Matt. "Do you miss your mama, too?"

Eleanor watched the shock of the question freeze

Matt. It took him some time, but eventually he said, "Yes, I think I do."

Sylvie wiggled to signal that she wanted to be put down on the floor, and Eleanor obliged her. With her doll held close, the little girl toddled over to Matt and stood right in front of him and lifted one arm. "Up."

Matt pulled the girl up and she hugged him around the neck. "I'm sorry your mama is gone."

Matt patted Sylvie on the back, and Eleanor noticed he made no move to loosen the girl's tight grip on his neck.

"You can sleep with my dolly if you want," Sylvie finally offered as she snuggled the doll close to him. "She makes me feel better when I go to bed."

Eleanor thought she saw a tear form in Matt's eyes, but he only kissed his niece on her cheek and said, "I think your dolly would miss you if I take her."

Sylvie sighed and then nodded. Eleanor thought she looked relieved.

Eleanor smiled at each of the children. The excitement of their first greeting had faded, and they were both gazing at her seriously now.

Finally, Matt cleared his throat and spoke to Henri. "Do you believe I'm your uncle now?"

Henri shrugged. "I guess so. You do look a lot like our father."

Eleanor took a closer look at Matt then. Now that his hat no longer covered most of his face, he seemed very Irish. Dark black hair clung to his skull as the snow finished melting on it. His chin was strong, his cheekbones high. Icy blue eyes challenged her. He was unquestionably handsome. Eleanor's spirits continued to sink as she put all of the pieces of him together. Matt Baynes clearly resembled the portrait of her father that was nestled in the golden locket she and Lily cherished.

Eleanor glanced down at Lily and guessed her sister might be coming to the same conclusion. Instead of being appalled, though, she was staring at Matt in awe.

"You kind of look like my papa, too," Lily said, her voice almost a whisper. That was the only time Eleanor had heard her sister refer to their father by that affectionate term. Lily had been too young to remember him and so she was relying on the photo.

Eleanor hoped Matt hadn't heard Lily, but she saw the shock go through his body and she knew it was too late. *Please, Lord, don't let him reject Lily like our father did*, Eleanor prayed. He had said the burden of Lily's foot would be too much for any man, and maybe he'd been right. *Please, Lord.*

"I'll take care of Lily," Eleanor whispered. "You don't need to worry about her."

Matt seemed to pay no attention to her words as he walked over to the chair where Lily sat, and squatted down. "I guess that'll be the way of it when I marry your sister," he said. "I'll be your father, if that's all right with you."

Lily studied him for a moment. And then she reached out and touched his smooth cheek and nodded. "You're much better than the toads who wanted to marry my sister before."

Eleanor was shocked that Lily remembered her suitors.

"Well, that's good—I think," Matt said as he rose

back to his feet. "I will always try to be better than a toad."

Lily giggled. Matt seemed glad he'd caused some merriment.

But Eleanor was breathing hard. She was having a hard time adjusting to the fact that Lily had remembered her two beaus. Both of the men had been horrified when she told them she wanted Lily to live with them. They both said Lily would never be self-sufficient or married. That she'd be a millstone around their necks for the rest of their lives. One wanted to send her to an orphanage. The other man decided that he would send Lily directly to a workhouse. When Eleanor challenged them, one of them had informed her that she would not make that decision—it would be his if she married him. That was when Eleanor stopped accepting the courtship of any man.

Eleanor glanced up, noticing that Matt was looking at her with a puzzled expression on his face. "We don't need to rush to marry if you need a little time to adjust. A day or two extra won't matter."

After her last disastrous courtship, Eleanor had educated herself on her rights as a married woman and found out she had pitifully few. Her one suitor had been right. She could not protect Lily if her husband wanted to send her sister away.

"I thought we'd talk to the pastor on Sunday," Matt continued. "The man has several churches and he isn't here every week. But, when he's around, he usually stays until Tuesday or Wednesday to get some rest."

"I'll need to get a dress ready to wear," Eleanor said,

stalling. It was a good excuse, but it would soon be clear she owned only three dresses. The frayed mauve one she'd worn on the train here, a bright yellow one that used to belong to her mother and was given to her this past Christmas by her grandmother after Eleanor had found it in the attic earlier, and an unbleached linen one she wore with a long apron for chores like baking and washing the floors. "You know a woman likes to look her best."

Matt nodded.

Before he could say anything more, she added, "And I'd like to talk to an attorney before we go to the preacher."

She didn't have more than a few coins to offer, but she hoped the lawyer would agree to give her some time to pay the rest of his bill.

Matt lifted his eyebrow in apparent surprise. "Questions about our marriage? I can tell you right now that it will be legal, even if it's in name only."

Eleanor blushed and shook her head. "That's not it."

He looked at her curiously. "Well, there's Wayne Lunden down the street. He's a pretty good attorney, I understand. Seems like a nice enough man, too, even if he's a bit impractical. Asked me if I wanted to draw up a will. I said there was no need since I was marrying a good woman and she'll see to the children."

Matt was still studying her and she could feel it. "Wayne's quite the gentleman, but he's almost engaged, if that makes a difference in your need to see him."

"Of course it doesn't," Eleanor protested indignantly. Surely, he didn't think she was seeking a different husband. "You and I might not know each other, but I don't welch on my agreements."

Eleanor no longer needed the heat of the stove to make her warm. And then she remembered the sheriff hadn't even offered them any of the coffee he'd brought them here to drink.

"It's some woman he met down in Denver," Matt added then. "Betty something. She's running a dress shop and is accustomed to the West. She knows how it will be when she moves to Dillon."

"I'm sure they'll be very happy together," Eleanor said stiffly. "I noticed there was an empty dress shop down the street. Will that be hers?"

Matt shook his head. "Wayne doesn't hold with his wife working."

"Oh," Eleanor said, surprised. She thought most men would appreciate the extra income.

They were both silent for a moment. They knew so little about each other, Eleanor thought. She didn't know where to begin.

"I will be working, though, won't I?" she asked.

"Ladies generally don't." Matt looked wary. "I suppose we could hire someone to operate the bakery."

"That's not what I meant," Eleanor hastened to say. "I want to work. I don't know what I'd do with a life of leisure."

Eleanor realized she didn't want the children to hear all of this conversation. She caught Lily's eye and nodded in the direction of the children's cell. Her sister understood and led the two young children back to their cot.

Matt looked at Eleanor but didn't say anything until the children were settled on their bed.

"Most ladies dream of that kind of a life," he finally said quietly. "Parties. Opera. I would think a lady like you would want to marry a gentleman who would give her that. Maybe a banker."

Eleanor tried to force herself to meet his gaze, but she couldn't. Was he saying they didn't suit? A kind man would make the parting seem like it was her idea. She wasn't backing out, but he might be. What if he changed his mind about marrying her? It was night and they had no other place to go.

She was relieved when he continued.

"I grew up on a ranch north of here," he said. "There was no town around back then. Anyway, my brother, Luke, and I were working the home place, and when he got married, I stayed on awhile. As I said, though, he'd always been frail. I ended up doing most of the heavy work and was glad to do it. But, finally, we both realized his wife was turning to me for help when she should have been asking him. It diminished Luke in her eyes. I decided it would work best for all of us if I left. So I went down to Idaho and spent the last seven years, give or take, riding trail on cattle for the Green River Ranch."

Matt was quiet for a minute.

"You were kind to your brother," Eleanor finally said.

Matt shrugged. "Maybe too kind. My father was a hard-nosed man all his life. He was rough on Luke, and I had a tendency to step in to try and stop it. It didn't help Luke though. He grew up expecting others to do for him what he should be able to do for himself. And my father gave him a hard time because of it. My mother, on the other hand, pampered Luke. She was a lady, fancy parasols and all. She used to wave her perfumed handkerchiefs around like they were butterflies ready to fly free. Maybe that's how she did think, because she sure took off like one of those butterflies. I don't know where she is these days. She had always wanted to make me and Luke into educated gentlemen, but I was a big disappointment to her. I can read fine and do sums, but my manners never satisfied her. I thought my letter explained how it was."

"Of course," Eleanor said and then swallowed nervously. "But we don't need to worry about that."

She had read his brief letter on the train. She should have stayed long enough, though, for Mrs. Gunni to tell her all that had been in the one she supposedly had written to him. Lily hadn't been able to remember it when Eleanor had asked on the way here.

"Now's the time to change your mind," Matt said, a muscle in his cheek twitching in what Eleanor suspected must be anger. He continued, "If we don't suit, you need to speak up. You won't need a lawyer to tell you that. Once we're married, that's it. We're together for life. Until then, I could send you back on the train— if the tracks are open, that is."

"I've heard there's an avalanche blocking the rails," Jacob inserted then. "This train got through right ahead of it. No trains can go either there or back right now. So, no point in making any rash decisions tonight."

"Well, we'll have to—" Eleanor started, hoping a solution would come to her. "The thing is—we can't go back to Chicago."

"We're at an impasse, then," Matt said, his words sounding more clipped than he likely intended.

Eleanor decided she should say something to smooth over the conflict, but no words came. Then she heard a slight sniffle at her side.

She turned and saw that her sister had returned. Tears were streaming down her face. Lily had managed to limp back and stand beside them, even though one shoulder drooped lower than the other and she steadied herself by holding on to Eleanor's skirt.

"It's all my fault," Lily wailed, her voice choking and her pale cheeks pinking up.

Eleanor looked up and saw Matt staring at them, bewilderment on his face.

"I didn't mean anything," he said.

"It's all right," Eleanor told him quietly as she squatted down to Lily's level and opened her arms. Lily came right into them as Eleanor continued cooing, "Don't cry, sweetheart."

Lily pulled herself away a little so she could look at Eleanor. "I only wanted you to have a True Love, like Mama had with our father."

"Well," Eleanor said and then ran out of words to respond to the incredible sentence, so she just kept patting Lily on the back. Maybe she had been wrong to keep the truth of her parents' troubles from Lily. "Their marriage wasn't perfect."

Lily's foot had been most of what broke their parents

apart, but Eleanor couldn't tell her sister that. Besides, even when the two had loved each other earlier, their mother had been too weak to stand alone and their father had been too proud to accept life as it was.

"But they had True Love," Lily insisted in a whisper. "You need to marry someone who is your True Love, too. Your prince."

Eleanor looked up to see if Matt was listening. He appeared to be.

"You realize we don't know each other very well," Eleanor whispered to Lily. "And he says he might not be with us for long."

That was as diplomatic as Eleanor could state it. Of course, Matt was the one who had said he was dying, so her comment should be no surprise to him.

Lily nodded with barely suppressed excitement. "But when you give him a kiss of True Love, like the ones Mama used to give Papa, it will cure him. I just know it will."

"Ah," Eleanor murmured. She hardly knew what to say. Lily could never have seen their parents kiss each other; she'd been too young. It was all fantasy. She looked up at Matt in apology. "It's my fault. I'm afraid I've let Lily's imagination go wild and—"

"Nothing wrong with that," Matt said gruffly. "She's a good girl."

Eleanor nodded, but she didn't explain further. She was going to need to find a way to tell Lily about their parents' marriage without bringing up their father's reaction when he had first seen her foot after she'd been born.

"The sheriff might live forever," Lily announced merrily then. "After your kiss, he'll be a prince."

"I don't expect to live that long," Matt said with a smile. "Or with that degree of—ah—royalty."

Lily, looking more pious than she ought, in Eleanor's opinion, replied, "We have to have faith. That's what my sister always says."

"I mean faith in God," Eleanor protested softly. "Not in True Love."

"But they are the same, aren't they?" Lily said. "God wants us to love each other. It says so in Mama's Bible."

"Sounds like she has a point," Matt said with a twinkle in his eyes.

"You're right," Eleanor said to her sister as she ignored Matt and leaned over to kiss the top of Lily's head. Someday, she'd have to talk to Lily about the different kinds of love in the world. But right now, she supposed it didn't hurt for her to dream about True Love as long as she knew there were toads walking around, as well.

"We're going to marry him, then?" Lily said, her voice filled with hope.

"That's what we promised to do," Eleanor said. The choice had to be the sheriff's at this point. She did not know where else they would go, but they could not stay here unless they were welcome. Even if she could tolerate it, she would not let Lily's heart be broken that way.

Matt cleared his throat. If he needed proof that he didn't know how to relate to women, he had it. He'd known Eleanor and her sister for only half an hour and already one had been in tears and the other seemed to be planning to leave him. And Eleanor would follow through, too. He could see it in her eyes; she was upset. In fact, she had the same look an untamed cow had just before she was going to bolt into the bush to try to hide from some cowboy. Of course, he couldn't go after Eleanor with a horse and lasso her, pulling her out into the open and forcing her to trust him enough to lead her home.

"I'm sorry," he said as he squatted down so he would be level with the two sisters. He had nothing left but his desperate need. "I surely hope there is some way we can start over. I'm afraid I'm not very good at this."

Lily had calmed down, but he reached out to pat her on the back anyway. He was shocked when she turned and wobbled toward him. She ran her hand over his smooth-shaven cheek and then leaned close to his ear.

"Eleanor can do anything," she whispered. "She knows how to take care of sick people and she bakes really good French bread. Croissants, too. That's what you wanted, isn't it?"

Matt nodded. He stood up and offered his hand to help Eleanor stand, as well.

"I'm sure your sister would make a wonderful wife," he assured Lily. "But maybe she's sorry she came. I heard a gentleman, Otis Finch, had telegraphed already, wondering if the two of you arrived all right. Isn't that kind? He misses you."

Lily still had her hand on his arm, and Matt felt her stiffen even before he heard her gasp.

"The coal man?" Lily asked, her voice trembling even more. "You can't let him get us."

"I don't know what—" Matt started to say, until he saw clearly how frightened the girl was. He looked up at Eleanor and saw her face had tightened in tension, too.

"I'd prefer if no one answered that telegram," Eleanor said. "The less he knows, the better for us."

"I thought he was a friend," Matt said carefully.

Lily shook her head vigorously. "He's a mean old man and he wants to hurt my foot."

"I certainly wouldn't have permitted that," Eleanor went on, looking down at her sister. "Besides, we shouldn't talk about our troubles with strangers."

"I'm hardly a stranger!" Matt protested. He could see the skepticism on Eleanor's face, but he continued, "I know we've gotten off to a bad start, but I am not going to let anyone frighten you. I'm the sheriff, after all. And I'll be sure no telegram goes to the man. Angus—he's the one who received it—won't answer it without my approval."

"How did he know to send a telegram here though?" Eleanor took a step closer and whispered so only Matt could hear.

"Is there more to this than I know?" Matt asked as he turned to face Eleanor. None of the children could hear their words. He could feel her distress. Something was very wrong.

"If Otis knew where to send a telegram, then Mrs. Gunni, our friend, is in danger. She's the only one who knew where we went." Eleanor's eyes were worried.

"He must have forced her to tell. I need to be sure she's all right."

"I can send her a telegram," Matt offered.

"I don't know her address," Eleanor admitted slowly. "She has a produce stall and sleeps inside it sometimes. I invited her to share the room with Lily and me, but she always said she had a place."

"I know someone who works with the Chicago police," Matt assured her. "We can send a telegram to him first thing in the morning, and he can look for your friend's stall—you know those streets?"

Eleanor nodded. "Thank you."

She then stepped away from him and Matt turned to the children. They had all patiently waited for the end of the conversation.

Then Lily stepped closer to him and leaned forward. Matt bent down. She looked like she wanted to tell him something.

"You'll know Otis Finch is here, because he growls. All the time," she whispered and then hesitated. "And Mrs. Gunni is my friend, too."

"Thanks for letting me know," Matt said as he straightened. He looked toward the desk and noticed that his nephew and niece were both staring at him, looking sober and a bit reproachful. Sylvie had even put her thumb in her mouth.

"Our mama always said big boys shouldn't make girls cry," Henri informed him, his shoulders stiff with self-righteous disapproval.

Matt nodded to him. "She's right. It was wrong for

me to make Lily cry. I didn't mean to though. Some-times, I make mistakes."

The boy nodded and seemed satisfied. "We forgive mistakes. My father said we all make them."

Jacob, who had been watching, cleared his throat. "Maybe we should have some coffee and get warmed up." He moved a wooden chair closer to the far side of the desk and motioned to Eleanor. "You just come sit over here."

Eleanor helped her sister over to a chair at the table and then sat down in the one Jacob had pulled out for her.

The deputy stepped over and told Lily, "I have hot milk for you and the other children."

Lily dazzled him with a smile.

"I've got a plate of shortbread to go with the cof-fee," Jacob announced proudly as he straightened up and walked over to a shelf. "Baked goods are rare here, but Mabel Wells made these for us yesterday. They're Irish shortbread."

The deputy brought down a plate covered with a white cloth and set it on the table. Then he removed the fabric with a flourish, revealing small squares of the treat. Each one had the imprint of fork tines on its top and was sprinkled lightly with sugar.

"The kind our father liked," Lily said as her eyes brightened even more. "Eleanor told me they were his favorite."

Jacob nodded. "Mabel said that when she heard your last name, she knew you'd like some old-fashioned shortbread. A taste of home, she said."

Matt watched everyone drink either hot chocolate or coffee and take bites of shortbread. Even Sylvie and Henri unwound enough to make a comment here and there. Then Jacob told a story of his own mishaps growing up in New York City and everyone laughed.

The good feelings continued as everyone got ready for bed. He and Jacob hung a couple of army blankets over the bars so Lily and Eleanor had some privacy in their cell. He noticed that the children, Sylvie and Henri, didn't sleep with the blankets over their heads like they had been doing. Matt decided it was a good thing Dillon wasn't having a crime wave. They didn't have an empty cell left for anyone. Even the drunks usually found better accommodations on the floor of the saloon across the street than they did in this jail.

It wasn't until Matt was lying on his cot in the dark, though, that he smelled the lotion he'd seen Eleanor applying to her hands. It smelled of lemon. He decided Lily was right. Eleanor could do anything if she could bring the smell of spring into a Western jail in the middle of winter. He only hoped she'd be able to cope with the problems that were sure to come.

Once again, he wondered why Eleanor wanted to talk to an attorney. He frowned. A trusting woman wouldn't do that, would she? Even his mother had never resorted to using a lawyer against his father. Matt told himself he needed to ask her outright. Maybe tomorrow, he told himself as he yawned and tried to settle into sleep. Then he heard it. That old tomcat was shuffling around on the other side of the wall again, likely looking for a comfortable place for his aching bones to lie down.

Matt tapped the wall and got a menacing growl in response.

"Good night to you, too," Matt answered back. "You old reprobate."

It was silent for a few minutes, and then in the darkness he heard Sylvie's tiny voice ask, "What's a reti—retibate?"

Matt chuckled. "An old sinner. No one for you to worry about."

It was silent for a few more minutes, and then Lily's worried voice could be heard from the other cell. "How old do you have to be to be one of those? Am I one yet? Or—" The child's voice grew louder in her excitement. "Is Henri one?"

"No, sweetheart," Eleanor answered that, humor in her voice.

Matt decided he'd never get to sleep. "No one under this roof is a reprobate sinner."

He must have spoken more loudly than necessary for nobody made any sound after that—not even the cantankerous old cat himself.

Chapter Three

Eleanor slept fitfully and then awakened, wondering if the growls she'd heard in the night had been real or part of her nightmare. Surely, no animal would be out in this cold. Finally, she heard someone walking around, likely to put more wood in the stove. It was still dark, though, so she only snuggled farther down into the blankets on her cot.

The worst part of her nightmare had been seeing flashes of Otis Finch's face. She was clearly worried about him. She opened her eyes. A rim of dim light was showing around the edge of the blanket draped over the bars of her cell, so she supposed the sun was rising.

She had no desire to hasten the start of this day. Things had been a whirlwind since they arrived, and she knew it could get worse. When she first read the ad, Eleanor had had a moment's skepticism about why a dying man would advertise for a wife. Then she considered the children involved and thought a decent man might do that, marrying to give the children someone to hold on to when he was gone.

But Matt Baynes was no more dying than she was. He wasn't pale. He didn't wheeze. He certainly wasn't bedridden. In fact, he positively glowed with energy. He would have had no trouble finding a wife unless all of the local women already knew that he was prone to some failing he hadn't mentioned. Something like excessive drink or gambling. As far as she could see, though, Matt didn't have any problems that he hadn't created for himself. The truth was he was so handsome that he could get an offer to marry even with all of his running around. He had no need to put an ad in a newspaper for a stranger to answer.

So she had to wonder if his ad had been a hoax. What benefit he got from bringing her and Lily out here, she could not see, but there had to be something. He had sent the train tickets, which only meant there must be money in his scheme, whatever it was.

Granted, he did have the children like he said, so that part of his story was solid. She smiled just thinking of them. Two more engaging little ones she'd never seen. Of course, if last night was any indication, they didn't know him well enough to be a character reference.

Right about then, she heard quiet whispers and knew it was the two children. They seemed to be standing on the other side of the blanket draped along the bars of her cell.

"Is she our new mama?" the girl's voice asked, her voice filled with a longing that touched Eleanor's heart. "I want her for a mama."

"A mama needs a papa," the boy answered, sounding worried. "She might not want to be our new mama if there's no papa."

"But isn't our uncle—" the girl's slight voice started and then stopped abruptly.

A man cleared his throat.

"Don't be bothering the lady now," he said. She recognized Matt's voice.

The scurrying sound of little bare feet assured her that the children had scampered back to the cot they shared. Then she heard the heavy boots walk away from the blanket.

By that time, Lily was halfway sitting, leaning on her elbow, on the other side of the cell.

"I guess it's time to get up." Eleanor was already seated on her bed with her blankets wrapped around her. It was too cold to take much time waking, so she stood up, the soles of her feet landing square on the plank floor.

"Oh, oh, oh," she sputtered softly. The cold on her bare feet made her shiver. She quickly tiptoed over to their trunk. She grabbed one of the only two other dresses she owned and rushed back to her cot to sit down. A new life demanded her bright yellow dress. It was somewhat old-fashioned, since it had belonged to her mother, but it cheered her up to wear it. Eleanor hadn't worn the garment around the tenement because she feared it would call too much attention to herself.

"Who wants fried eggs and ham?" Jacob's voice rang out cheerfully. Eleanor had noticed last night that the only stove in the jail was the potbellied one in the front.

There was a cast-iron skillet hanging on a peg near it, and the deputy was clearly using that to cook. "Thems that gets here first gets the best pick."

Eleanor slipped into her clean dress and finished twisting her hair into a knot on her neck before turning to help Lily do the buttons on the back of her dress.

"Things will look better this morning," Eleanor promised her sister with a smile as they both smoothed down their skirts. "I'll see if we can get some warm water so we can wash our faces before breakfast."

"I don't want to miss out on the eggs and ham," Lily whispered.

Eleanor nodded. Ham was a rare treat for them these days. So were eggs, for that matter.

The blanket came down easily from the sides of their cell and Jacob pointed them toward where a basin of hot water stood, waiting for them. On the same stand, there was a pail of water for drinking.

"One egg or two?" Jacob asked as they walked by him to the basin.

"Two, please," Lily said before Eleanor thought to stop her. The girl was walking close to Eleanor so she could lean on her and keep upright.

"One will be sufficient for each of us," Eleanor said, changing the order. "There's quite a number of people to feed."

"We got plenty of eggs," Jacob said with the wave of a spatula that showed a basket filled with them, sitting on the desk. There had to be over a dozen still left in the container. "Another courtesy of Mrs. Wells—part of her 'welcome to Dillon' gift." He nodded a second time and pointed to the partially sliced ham. "That's from the Turners. They raise a few hogs. Again, a welcome."

"Well, my goodness," Eleanor said. She was touched. That didn't even count the Irish shortbread Mrs. Wells had given them for last night. "I've never seen such gracious hospitality."

Eleanor helped Lily over to a chair at the large desk but remained standing beside it.

When she and Lily had been evicted from their grandmother's house after her death, none of the neighbors had even expressed their concern for them. In fact, they avoided them like their distress was contagious. That was probably due to the formidable men from the bank who came and carted everything out of the house though. They claimed it was to cover her grandmother's debts, but Eleanor knew nothing about such obligations and she had done the accounts for her grandmother in the last four years of the woman's life. Something crooked had been going on in Eleanor's estimation, but she hadn't been able to hire an attorney to look into the bank's actions. She intended to do so when she earned enough money to pay someone. Maybe she could ask Mr. Lunden after she asked about her rights regarding Lily.

Eleanor heard the doorknob to the jailhouse rattle from the outside. She had already seen that Matt was not around and, when Jacob didn't seem concerned, decided it must be him coming back.

"Folks here are grateful that the children will have someone to see to them," Jacob finally responded to

Eleanor's comments. "They're especially glad you've come."

"But the children already have—" Eleanor stopped because the door opened. Matt stepped inside and closed it. She could hardly continue her sentence, since he was who the youngsters had. He looked at her like he knew what she had been saying though.

Self-consciously, Eleanor glanced up at Matt and continued. "I was just saying how wonderful it is that the children have you to look after them."

"They best not get used to it," Matt said as he stomped his boots on an old towel by the door. He had a fresh scratch on his cheek. "I'll be leaving soon."

"When?" she asked with a gasp. Was his illness closing in?

"Likely by the middle of next week," Matt said, seeming more concerned about the snow melting on the wood floor than anything else.

"You're sure?" Eleanor asked. That was so sudden. He must not be as healthy as he looked. But surely, death took longer than this.

Matt nodded. "Can't say I'm looking forward to it."

"No, I suppose not," Eleanor said, her voice catching. She almost felt like crying and she knew she had no business doing that, so she added as matter-of-factly as she could, "I'm sure the children will miss you."

Eleanor winced. Her throat tightened then. "I don't want you to worry about them. I'll be honored to care for both Henri and Sylvie."

"I expect I'll be back from time to time, for a while,

at least," Matt said in a calm voice. "This first trip will be mostly scouting around."

"Oh." Eleanor pressed her lips together. She wouldn't say another word. But her worst fears were coming true. She knew Matt was sick and that he might die. But the leaving he was talking about sounded much more voluntary than that. It reminded her of her father.

Eleanor had been fifteen years old when her father started taking his absences. Lily was about a week old and he claimed he couldn't stay in the same house with a crippled child, not when she looked like she was doomed to be that way forever. He had tortured Lily's foot trying to make it normal, and when nothing he did worked, he declared the baby a disgrace to the Fitzpatrick name. No Fitzpatrick had ever been born less than perfect, he declared. That meant, he said, that the baby was not his. Eleanor was so relieved that Lily had stopped crying since their father had halted his experiments that she hadn't realized that what he said would change everything. Her father left for the first time, and her mother took to her bed, sobbing so much that she seemed unaware of anything but her own distress.

Eleanor wasn't prepared to suffer like her mother had though. She didn't care if the neighbors knew what Matt was doing. She wasn't going to be a wife waiting at home while her husband was off making merry with who knows who and doing who knows what.

"These places you're scouting," Eleanor asked, her voice sounding cold even to her own ear. "Do you know where they are?"

"I have some thoughts," Matt said, sounding puzzled.

"I see." Eleanor didn't, of course, but really, what could she say? "I would think you'd want to be with your family at a time like this."

Then she sniffed. She was going to cry after all, and she told herself it had nothing to do with him dying. She was just disappointed in herself that she had fallen into this situation. Then she was horrified. She probably sounded like she cared if he was there—which wasn't true.

"I mean, with the children," she managed to say, nodding at Matt's nephew and niece. "They are the ones who you should want to be with—and who want to be with you."

"Henri doesn't care if I'm gone," Matt said as he nodded to the boy. "And Sylvie wouldn't even notice."

"That's true, ma'am," Henri said earnestly as he looked up at Eleanor. "He has bad men he needs to…" The boy's sentence trailed off. "I'm not supposed to say."

This was even worse, Eleanor thought. "You're making the children keep your trips secret?"

"It's for the best," Matt replied. "I'm sure people guess where I'm headed. There's enough gossip floating around Dillon to sail a ship in it. But I'm sure not giving out any specific details."

"I suppose I should be grateful you have the decency to keep it quiet," Eleanor agreed stiffly. Her mother had suffered greatly from the rumors about her father's behavior when he was away.

"People know I have to be going," Matt said, looking puzzled. "They know it's needed."

"But what could be more important than the children?" Eleanor asked, more impatiently than she intended.

"Bringing the killers of their parents to justice is what I have to do," Matt snapped back. "That's what's necessary."

"Oh." Eleanor looked at him. He was serious. Slowly, things started to click in her mind. She looked at the badge he now wore on his chest. She finally understood. She was so appalled she whispered, "You think they'll kill you, don't you? When you go after them to arrest them. You think they'll shoot you down. But you're still planning to do it."

"I have to," Matt said simply. "It was my brother and his wife."

Eleanor studied him. He wasn't posturing. His blue eyes were not defiant. He wore no scowl. This wasn't a moment's anger with him. It was calm, solid intent.

"My goodness," Eleanor said. The tension made her stomach clench. "That's why no one here will marry you. That's what your ad meant. You're not sick at all. You think you'll be shot and killed."

Something flickered through his eyes, but it disappeared too quickly for her to interpret.

"You and the children will be safe," he said softly.

"But you— That's horrible." She couldn't keep it back; she suddenly knew. "And you're going alone, aren't you?"

For a moment, all she could see was the memory

of the night when her father had been gone and her mother sick in her room. Fifteen-year-old Eleanor had to face down an intruder with nothing in her hands but a fireplace poker. She had never felt more isolated. Of course, maybe she was assuming too much. Matt might not be alone.

"Is he a tough man?" she asked. "Will he have a gun?"

Matt grunted. "He's six rough-and-ready men and they'll all have guns."

"You have to get help," Eleanor said. What he described was an impossible task. "You can't do it alone."

He would die, she thought bleakly.

Matt looked at her, searching her eyes. "I'm not likely to find a man in the town of Dillon willing to go up against the Blackwoods. Most folks here haven't seen one of the brothers face-to-face, but they have all heard the stories. A holdup of some miners in Virginia City. A shoot-out in Helena. The family still has their sheep ranch north of here, but the brothers have not been around for some time. Although that's where I'll start, since I believe their mother is still living there."

"Oh," Eleanor said, feeling the air seep out of her lungs. This was worse than she had thought.

"Besides, most of the men here have families," Matt said. "I can't ask them to take a risk like this. It's not easy on a family when a parent is—ah—absent."

A moment passed.

"Well, no need to talk about all of that before breakfast," Matt said, his voice even and his face bland again. "It might not come to pass."

He gave a slight nod toward where his nephew and niece were standing.

Eleanor nodded. Her knees were ready to give out and she stepped closer to a chair and sat down. "Of course. That can wait. We'll talk later."

Matt nodded. "And that's a lovely sunshine dress you're wearing this morning. You look pretty as a picture in it. And, yellow makes the day better, even before we step outside."

Eleanor smiled her thanks. He was trying to comfort the children with the small talk, and she approved.

She spent a few minutes looking at the floor. When she glanced up, she saw that Matt was juggling three tin plates with two eggs and a slice of ham on each. He carefully set each one along the back side of the desk and drew up a high bench. Then Matt lifted up his niece and nephew, setting them on it—Henri on one end, Sylvie in the middle and Lily in her chair on the other end.

"I sent that telegram off to the policeman I know," Matt said with a nod to Eleanor as he started to get Henri and Sylvie ready to eat. "He'll get it to your friend."

"Thank you," Eleanor said. She had never seen a man tuck a handkerchief into a child's collar so they could eat without worry. Most men she'd known wouldn't think to do that.

She tore her eyes off that scene, though, now that Matt had mentioned the telegram. Last night, she had given Matt the street names that formed the corner where Mrs. Gunni had her produce stall. The Danish woman was sturdy and always kept a walnut cane to chase off troublemakers, but Eleanor didn't want to take any chances.

"Mrs. Gunni might not even need to worry about anything," Eleanor said with a glance at Lily. She didn't want her sister to worry. "Other people could see we were leaving, and maybe one of them told the—ah—" Eleanor spun to a stop. She didn't know what to say without mentioning Otis.

"Better to be prepared," Matt agreed smoothly.

Eleanor moved herself to the chair Jacob had indicated last night.

Then she saw that Matt had a third clean handkerchief in his hands.

"Would you like a lady's bib?" Matt asked Lily.

Eleanor watched as her sister beamed up and vigorously nodded her head.

Matt tied the napkin around Lily's neck and then sat down at what would have been the head of the table if it had been anything but a big desk.

"Now, wait for the blessing," Matt cautioned them as he made himself comfortable. "We always thank God for what He's given us and we have to especially thank Him this morning for the ham and eggs."

"And biscuits," Henri whispered as he looked over his shoulder at Jacob.

"That's right," Jacob said as there was a knock at the door. "I expect that's Mabel Wells right now. She told me yesterday to expect—" by this time, Jacob had walked over to the door and he opened it with a flourish "—buttermilk biscuits."

A flushed gray-haired woman with a wide grin stood

there with a basket filled with biscuits. She stepped into the office and withdrew a small jar of jam out of some pocket in her voluminous skirt. She set it on the desk and then reached into the basket and pulled out a small crock of butter.

"I hope you liked the shortbread," the woman said shyly. "My husband, Angus, was going to come with me, but he had to be at the telegraph office."

"Thank both of you so much," Eleanor murmured. Her voice was thick with emotion. "The shortbread last night was the nicest thing you could have done to make us feel at home. And now this morning— It's so generous."

"Well, it's a pleasure to welcome you properly," Mabel said, looking straight at Eleanor. "Angus and I do hope you'll like our small town. I know it's not what you're used to, but we want you to feel like it's a friendly place. I figure food is the best way to say all of that."

"I'll never forget your kindness," Eleanor managed.

Mabel beamed at them all for a moment. "Angus and I will have all of you over for supper some night soon."

Before Eleanor could even answer the woman, she left them with a wave.

Eleanor wondered if all the residents in this small town were so friendly. She looked over at Matt and asked, "Is everyone this way here? I've never seen such a welcoming town."

Matt didn't answer right away and she could see him thinking. She almost thought she had been wrong about the town, when he nodded.

* * *

Matt realized he had never seen the benefit of gossip until now. Whether it was thanks to Jacob or Angus or someone else, the whole town had taken an interest in his mail-order bride and the two children who'd lost their parents.

"I used to think they were just busybodies," Matt admitted. "But it seems they really care."

He could tell Eleanor had been deeply touched by the food and friendship various women had offered. He needed to thank Angus when he saw him next, because he figured Angus had been the one spreading the word.

Matt had never had such a sense of community in his childhood as he did now. Maybe it was because his father was so distrustful of people after Matt's mother ran away that they didn't have much to do with any of the folks around here then, or maybe it was just the stubborn Irish in the man that didn't think anyone should be too close, but Matt had followed his father's ways and kept himself apart, even after he moved down to Idaho. Now he was starting to believe that the people here were some of the finest people he would find anywhere. His father had been wrong.

This past Sunday, Matt had taken the children to the small church down the street and had been blessed by the sermon. Given that his father thought they should stay by themselves, they'd never gone to church after their mother left. From there, Matt had just drifted away from God, figuring the good Lord didn't care much about the Baynes family and maybe He had good reasons. Matt had learned a few things since then. For one thing, he knew bitterness didn't help anyone. He had no call to be angry at God or the Blackwood brothers for grievances in his childhood.

Of course, if those six brothers were the ones who had killed Luke and Adeline a couple of weeks ago, Matt would have no mercy and would arrest them. He'd always protected Luke and he regretted he hadn't been there when his brother needed him most. All he could do now was arrest the murderers, even knowing he'd likely die trying.

Matt stopped his ruminations to realize that everyone was staring at him. And then he remembered. He'd mentioned needing a blessing for the food. The faces around were all looking at him with something akin to hope. It made him feel good and he wanted to make them feel that emotion, too.

"Let's hold hands while we pray," he said. No one he knew had ever suggested doing this, but he knew it would mean something to the people here. They were his family now. He watched them clasp hands before he reached out himself, one hand to Henri and one to Jacob. Then he bowed his head and began. "Our Father, bless us this day and the provisions that our friends have brought to us. We thank You for Your love and care for us each day. Make us a family who love You and each other. Amen."

Matt noticed that no one reached for their fork when the prayer ended. They just stared at him.

"We need some kind of togetherness," he finally muttered. "I want us to be a family that goes to church."

"Like we did on Sunday?" Henri asked, a frown on his face.

Matt nodded.

"Sylvie cried all the time," Henri pointed out dubiously. "She missed our mother most that day."

"We'll have to hold her close, then," Matt answered. He hadn't known how to stop Sylvie's tears on Sunday. She already seemed happier now, though, as she leaned close to Eleanor. "We'll be sure that she brings her doll along."

"She had her doll last Sunday," Henri said in disgust. "I ended up having to carry it because she was crying so much. Maybe we could bring one of these biscuits for her to eat," Henri pointed at the overflowing basket. "She'd like that."

Matt had a feeling Henri would like that, too.

"Let's all have a biscuit now," Matt said as he reached for the basket and handed it to Henri. "You're in charge of making sure everyone gets one. Just pass it to the person next to you."

Henri took his and gave one to his sister, too. "These biscuits will be gone by tomorrow."

"I can bake some kind of a treat for you both," Eleanor offered as she passed the butter and then the jam. "Today's Saturday. I can make some pan biscuits tomorrow on the stove here." She looked at Matt directly then. "If you have some flour and baking soda."

"If we don't have it, we can get it," Matt assured her.

Everyone spent some time eating.

"You really do cook?" Matt finally asked. Eleanor was so beautiful he couldn't imagine her kneading bread dough. She was the kind of woman who should be sitting in a parlor making sure her petticoats were covered and her skirts furled sufficiently to make her waist appear smaller than it was.

"Do you really have a bakery?" Eleanor responded eagerly.

"My father bought it for my mama," Henri announced and looked at Eleanor hopefully. "Can you do French bread?"

Eleanor nodded. "And French croissants. And beignets—those are what you might call French donuts. Tarts or pies. Sourdough bread. Date cakes. Cream puffs. Oh, and Irish shortbread—that's one of my specialties. And anything else a person could want."

Matt noticed Henri was dazzled. And Eleanor looked happy reciting her talents. He responded, "The bakery has been closed up, but she's there all right. Technically, she belongs to the children, but it does them no good at their ages. It's got two big double ovens and everything. It needs some cleaning and the walls probably could use a coat of paint."

"I'm not afraid of hard work," Eleanor announced. "And we'll put some of the profits away for the children's futures—whatever sounds fair."

Matt figured he would have to be a blind man not to see that Eleanor really wanted to operate this business. She knew Lily didn't like that Otis Finch, but there were other men in Chicago Eleanor could have married. She did not have to come out here. But he wagered those men didn't have a bakery to offer. And that fact settled all of his nerves down. It was good thinking on her part. She would probably marry anyone to get an opportunity like this.

He was pleased for a moment, and then the feeling evaporated. Somehow, that thought didn't sit as well with him as he had thought it would. A woman shouldn't marry anyone just for what she could get. There should be some emotion there, even if they didn't know each other well. Then he shook his head. He was being unreasonable and he knew it. He had put out an ad and she had answered it. Feelings hadn't entered into it.

"Wahoo," Jacob yelled loud enough that it made the lantern jiggle a little. "Wait until I tell the boys down at the livery stable. The people who had the bakery before Luke bought it hadn't really gotten it started much. And Luke and his wife didn't have time for anything. We're finally going to have a real proper bakery in Dillon."

"A French one," Eleanor added, her face blissful.

Matt's gut clenched. "Ah, I don't think we should say a French bakery."

"Why ever not?" Eleanor asked in clear astonishment. "Everybody knows that French breads are some of the finest in the world."

"And French women are the prettiest," Jacob added, a little too eagerly, Matt thought.

Eleanor beamed at the other man. "Why, thank you."

Matt was so mad he didn't trust himself to speak. He wouldn't be surprised if Eleanor would have married Jacob to get herself a sweet deal like this.

"This is a Western town. Calling the place French

might seem too fancy," Matt finally said. "Make the customers uncomfortable."

And his father would have objected, Matt finally added silently to himself. Although the man had married a woman who enjoyed the finer touches in life, his father wanted nothing to do with anything that even bordered on what he considered city ways. And he expected the same attitude from his sons. Luke had ignored their father and pleased their mother in this, but then, because of his various illnesses, he'd spent more time with her. Matt, on the other hand, had naturally settled into his father's attitudes when he saw how disappointed he made his mother.

Finally, Matt looked up from his thoughts. He had finished his eggs and ham. And he'd eaten two biscuits. He stood up. "Speaking of the bakery, I better get over and make sure the key works in the door lock. I'll light a fire and warm the place up some before we all go over."

"You can call it the Baynes Bakery," Jacob suggested from where he was still sitting. "Assuming you get down to the church and ask the pastor to hook you two up right and proper."

"We decided to wait a bit," Matt said, hoping Eleanor would contradict him on that. After all, it only made sense to get married soon.

"We should look at the business before we make any decisions," Eleanor said to his disappointment as she turned to him. "And I should be with you if you're going to light any fires. With a stove, the flame has to be just right to get the kind of crusty French bread I'm known to bake." She looked at him then with a bit of indignation in her eyes. "That is, if I can even call it French bread. Maybe I should say it's Baynes bread."

Matt chuckled as he put on his sheepskin coat. He was getting himself a businesswoman for a bride. And a feisty one at that. Suddenly, he wasn't so sure he wanted to follow in his father's footsteps. "I expect French bread would sell better. Maybe we could compromise with the Baynes French Bakery. People know we Bayneses aren't high society, so they won't be put off with the French part."

"You'd compromise?" Eleanor asked, looking astonished.

I would for you, Matt thought, but he didn't dare say that. He wasn't even sure what it meant to him.

"Why not?" Matt said instead as he finished buttoning up his coat. He remembered all the grumbling his father had done every time his mother wanted something his father thought was too fancy. Like those teacups. Or a floral rug for the floor. It was a constant tug-of-war. Neither one of them had been happy. Matt sure didn't want a marriage like they'd had. "It's colder than blazes outside. Dress warm."

Eleanor looked down at herself. "This and my cloak are all I have."

"Bring a couple of blankets, then," Matt said and watched as she walked to her jail cell and brought back two of the old wool coverings. She twisted them around herself, tucking in a corner here and turning another one out there. He couldn't believe it, but she gradually had those blankets looking like a garment of fashion.

He shook his head. French women were wasted in

the Montana Territory. She'd make a stir in Denver. Or San Francisco. Or— Before he could stop himself, he thought about his mother and wondered where she was now. She loved the people and parties, so it would be a big city of some kind. He didn't have a clue though. And it was too bad. He had a feeling his mother would open her arms to her new daughter-in-law if she knew about her. He had a sudden longing to have his mother come to his wedding. Which was nonsense since it would be a simple ceremony with only the kids and Jacob for guests. Maybe Angus and his wife would come, too. Anyway, it would just be saying a few words and then recording the wedding date in the Baynes family Bible, which was likely still out at the ranch house. He'd have to see to that himself.

He remembered suddenly how proud he'd been when his brother recorded his wedding a decade ago. It had felt like the Baynes family was putting down deeper roots and branching out. He had to admit he'd get satisfaction from seeing his own name on one of those marriage lines.

And then he remembered Eleanor wanted to see an attorney. Given her enthusiasm for a bakery, he wondered if she was going to look for a way to get the business without having to marry him. He looked over at her more closely. She looked so innocent in that cheerful yellow dress. Well, he wasn't going to be fooled by a woman like that.

"That's a pretty dress to wear just to go see a lawyer," Matt said, trying not to sound jealous.

"I'm not sure I'll see him today," Eleanor said stiffly. "I want to visit the bakery first, if that's all right."

"I see." Matt wished she would say why she wanted an attorney.

"The bakery belongs to the children, you know," Matt said, trying to sound casual. "It's their inheritance. No lawyer can change that."

Eleanor looked up at him in surprise. "Of course not."

She sounded innocent, but if not, he figured she got the message.

"We best be going, then," Matt said as he walked over to the door and picked his hat off a peg. "No telling what is wrong with those ovens."

For all he knew, there were worse problems than nonworking ovens in this marriage agreement he had with Eleanor. He knew what he and the children were getting from the arrangement—the children needed a mother, and they seemed to like Eleanor quite well. He felt comfortable giving them to her to raise. But he wasn't sure what she was getting from the agreement. She clearly was looking for safety, but she'd left Chicago. That danger had likely passed. She'd do better to marry a man who expected to live longer than a few weeks. A woman needed a husband out here.

He wondered suddenly if that thought had occurred to her yet. He sure didn't want to tell her if it hadn't. He didn't care to think of her looking around Dillon to pick out her second husband before she'd even said her vows to the first one. He glanced down at her. She sure looked sweet, but he'd known her for only a day. He'd have to watch her for signs of a wandering eye. Any woman worth her salt would be planning her future.

Chapter Four

Eleanor stepped out of the jailhouse behind Matt. She had been puzzled at his comments that she might want to change the children's inheritance, but he had nothing further to say although his expression had grown gradually more disgruntled until he looked like he'd bitten into a lemon and was still chewing the rind. She didn't want to ask if he was changing his mind about their marriage, though—not on a pleasant day like today—so she decided she would just pay attention to the small town and hope his dissatisfaction faded. The longer she could postpone any clear rejection, the more likely the sheriff would grow accustomed to her and Lily.

"Dillon is a lovely town," she muttered finally.

He looked over and grunted in what seemed to be agreement.

The snow that covered the roofs was melting. The wind had stopped blowing. Anything in the shadows was frozen still, but everything else was thawing in the sunlight.

Eleanor had barely taken three steps when she noticed a battered-looking gray tabby cat make an awkward leap out from beside the jailhouse and, when it suddenly saw Matt, freeze in place. Matt had his back to the feline, but the beast's eyes blazed with defiance. Eleanor was sure it was a male; it looked ready to fight, even though it was obviously no longer up to a real battle. Its charcoal-and-white fur was matted in places and gone altogether around an ugly scar on one of its back legs. The poor thing. That must be why the animal moved so slowly. His leg probably hurt. As she studied him, he glared at her and slowly laid his ears back until he gave a low hiss deep in his throat. She didn't know why, but she knew in her heart that the animal's hostility was all a show meant to protect itself.

"Uncle doesn't like him," Henri whispered as he stepped out of the jail behind her. "He won't let him stay inside the jail. Sylvie doesn't like him either. He scares her. I think that's why she and Lily decided to stay back with Jacob."

"That doesn't mean we can't be nice to the cat," Eleanor said to Henri as she leaned over and held out an open hand to the feline. "We can be friends, can't we, kitty?"

Matt swung around sharply. "Don't touch that beast. It scratches."

"Ah," Eleanor said, but she reluctantly withdrew her hand and stood upright. The cat's hazel eyes were even fiercer, now that Matt had spoken.

"That old bag of bones belongs in the saloon," Matt said firmly as he motioned for her and Henri to follow.

"That's where the animal sleeps—and has for the past year. He's just got his nose out of joint because of the new white Persian who rules the place now."

"Well, a saloon doesn't seem like a proper environment anyway," Eleanor murmured. It sounded like the poor cat had no real home—at least not one where he was welcome—and, after almost being homeless herself, she knew what that felt like.

"He's a wild tomcat," Matt said, not even turning around. "He needs to take care of himself. If you do for him, it'll make him weak and he won't survive."

She wondered if he dismissed homeless people as easily. No wonder the animal was aggressive. It sounded like he didn't have a friend. Matt certainly wasn't one, and that Persian cat didn't seem to like him.

"Does he have a name?" Eleanor asked as she took Henri's hand and they hurried to keep up with Matt's longer footsteps.

"They call him Whiskey," Matt answered. "Every now and then, the men in the saloon like to fill a saucer for him with red-eye and see if he'll go for it and get drunk. It passes the time, I suppose."

"Why, that's horrible," Eleanor exclaimed as she stopped in the middle of the walkway and looked back to the jailhouse. The animal had slipped away and was probably in hiding by now.

"The cat doesn't seem to mind," Matt said mildly as he started to cross the street. "He can take care of himself."

"And if he can't?" Eleanor whispered. She wondered if he would someday say the same things about Lily.

Matt shrugged. "Then he dies. That's the way it is here." Matt stopped and turned to look at her. "The only other cat he's shown interest in is that Persian beauty, and she doesn't think much of him. No one will miss him."

"Why, I—" Eleanor started to protest, but he walked away before she said that even cats could feel the need for love.

She stared at him as he kept going across the muddy street. She wanted to keep the soles of her black high-button shoes clean, but she had to follow the sheriff. Eleanor let go of Henri's hand and lifted her skirts slightly so the hem of her dress wouldn't get too dirty. She would check with Jacob about the homeless cat later. For now, Eleanor knew she had other things to worry about.

Earlier this morning, Matt had shown her the telegram Otis sent before she got here and, although she had agreed when Matt said the man would give up on his threat after he discovered how difficult it would be to travel the distance to where she was, she had not been truly convinced Otis would stop. Her nightmare proved that to her.

She knew Otis wasn't her only challenge though. Her conversations with Matt confirmed that she and Lily were going to have to adjust to a rougher life than they had known in Chicago. She'd already seen a couple of fights in the street. If she operated the bakery alone, she knew she'd have to plan for attempted thefts. She and Lily would have a broader life here and it would be satisfying, but it was risky. Right now, though, she was going to examine the bakery that she'd be operating. Before long, she would have an income and a home. No one could stop her from taking care of Lily then. So far, Matt hadn't seemed to realize how lame she was.

Give him time to know her, Lord, she prayed silently. If Matt could only learn to care about her Lily, then everything would be all right. Eleanor frowned, remembering how he dismissed that old crippled cat, seeming not to care if the animal lived or died. That certainly didn't encourage her to trust him with Lily.

Eleanor looked up and saw that Matt had stopped at the two-story clapboard building they'd passed yesterday. It stood a few yards to the right of the saloon. She watched as he pulled a large key out of his coat pocket and slipped it into the lock. Eleanor studied the front of the bakery. Two large windows faced the street. Someone had taped newspaper over the windows on the inside of the room, so she couldn't see what was there. In the blizzard yesterday, she'd thought the place was empty.

Now, she looked up and saw a wooden board attached to iron hooks, that hung crookedly alongside the door. It was painted to simply say Bread for Sale. The wind had broken one of the hooks holding up that sign, and rain had warped the wood. She would need to replace it. But the location for the bakery was excellent.

Eleanor could see a woman and man heading down the street, and there were dozens of footprints in the snow showing people had walked by the shop this morning already. It wouldn't be long before she'd have them stopping in for a breakfast bun or an afternoon sweet. And there was a sturdy railing out front where customers could tie their horses. She'd have to be sure that word got around to the ranches that she baked French donuts. She'd heard cowboys loved donuts, although they called them "bear signs." Maybe she'd even talk to the owner of the saloon and offer to provide several trays of the treat so they could pass them around to their patrons. It'd be good advertising.

She suddenly realized with a start that she'd been staring off into space dreaming. When she looked over, she noticed Matt had opened the door and was waiting patiently for her. She hadn't heard any creaks, so the frame on the door must be sound.

Henri raced over to the counter the minute Eleanor stepped into the long, empty shop. He looked through the glass, likely thinking there would be bakery items there, like he was used to seeing. Of course there were none.

"I'm surprised your parents would buy this," Eleanor said to the boy as she followed him closer to the counter. "I don't imagine your ranch is very close. It would be hard to come and go every day."

"Mama said me and Sylvie would stay here with her. Father would stay at the ranch," Henri outlined the plan, not showing any sign of discomfort, which meant he likely didn't understand what he'd revealed.

"I see," Eleanor said. She glanced over at Matt and he shrugged.

"I thought they were doing fine," he said softly so only she could hear. "But then I was working down in Idaho. I'd write every couple of months, but I hadn't been back for a few years. The Montana Territory is hard on women though. Most of the ranches are isolated and it's lonely."

"My father bought the bakery so I could go to school," Henri said proudly, obviously unaware of Matt's comments. "Mama said I had to have book learning since I told her I want to be a doctor someday." He lifted his head and squared his shoulders. "Sylvie's too young to go to school."

"I know some miner donated a building for a school," Matt admitted. "But I heard that no teachers wanted to live this far west—especially when the town can't pay very much."

"But a teacher is coming," Henri said emphatically. "Mama told me. Then the school will open. She said it would be a surprise for us because the lady teacher would stay with us in the bakery."

"I'm glad they finally found someone who would come," Matt said. "I'm a little surprised my brother would feel obliged to provide room and board for the woman, but maybe that was part of the compensation offered."

Henri shrugged. "I don't know. My parents stopped talking about it when I was around." He frowned. "Do you think they thought I shouldn't go?"

"Of course not," Matt assured the boy. "Every child needs to go to school. And getting the bakery is the best way to do it—for the winter, at least. I'd guess you would all live on the ranch in the summer."

"And every weekend," Henri announced, no longer looking worried. "Mama promised. Father was going to come in on Friday morning and I'd leave school early to go home. Then he'd bring us back on Sunday."

"They could probably make the trip from the ranch to town every day during the late spring and early fall, too," Matt said. "With a horse and buggy, it takes about an hour. It's the brutal winter weather that is half of the problem. Adeline and the children wouldn't have fared too well if they were hit by a storm on their way to the ranch. It'd be too dangerous to try from November to mid-April."

"When I am twelve years old, my father said I can ride a horse to school from the ranch." Henri's voice cracked then, as he remembered what had happened. "I could have done it, too."

Eleanor walked over to the boy and put her hand on his shoulder. "I believe you could have. Your father must have known you were a very responsible child— I mean, young man."

She stood where she was for a minute and then looked around. A glass-fronted counter ran along the back side of the shop. A faded picture of a waterfall hung on that wall. A closed door set in the wall likely led to a kitchen. A large multipaned window on the left lit up that side of the room. The pink wall color had turned a little yellowish. "We'll want to brighten the place with paint."

"White would do," Matt said. "Although I did hear a peddler came through Dillon last summer and sold some paint powder—Venetian red, Prussian blue, Turner's Patent yellow. Mix any of them with the white they stock in the general store and you'd have lots of colors."

"We have choices, then," Eleanor murmured in satisfaction. There was a small shelf on the right wall where she could display her family's three rose-china cups and matching saucers that she had packed in the trunk to bring with them. "If we added some trim in Prussian blue, white might work well for the main walls."

The bright blue would draw attention to the china pieces. She had grown up loving those cups, with their cream insides and delicate pink outsides that had oval pictures of rosebuds on the fronts. Her parents had bought two of the sets for their wedding and ordered another a year later when Eleanor had been born. When her mother was pregnant with Lily, she had talked of sending away for one more to celebrate that birth, but it never happened. Her mother hadn't even mentioned the cups after Lily came. One of Eleanor's hopes was to add that fourth cup and saucer and give them all to Lily when she turned twenty-one years old. Somehow it would make their family story feel complete.

Not that she needed to worry about something so distant, Eleanor thought, as she kept looking around. The ceiling was taller than usual, here in the store, and if she wasn't mistaken, the swirl design was made from a molded layer of tin that had been painted white. She'd seen those kinds of ceilings in Chicago and always thought they were elegant. A cluster of carved oak chairs and square tables were stacked together along the right side of the room. An opening beside the counter led to a stairway.

"What's up there?" Eleanor asked. If it was anything like the downstairs, she'd be well pleased.

"I understand that it's the owner's home," Matt said as he started toward the steps. "I haven't been up yet. I didn't bring the children here because they were more comfortable with Jacob around. He was the one to take care of them before I got to Dillon. I only came here a few times to check that everything was fine downstairs. Windows closed, that kind of thing. I did hear there's not a cooking stove upstairs and that food is sent up from the kitchen with this contraption."

Matt took a step to the left and opened a large square door beside the stair. Eleanor could see the ropes that formed a pulley to raise the platform at the bottom. It must go all the way straight up, she figured.

"It's called a lift," Matt said. "It opens outside the main door upstairs. I understand it's heavy enough to carry fifty pounds."

"We could send Sylvie up," Henri said in excitement.

"It's not a toy," Matt said sternly. "It would be dark in there and your sister would be frightened."

Henri nodded. "I wouldn't be scared though." The boy had walked over and was studying the platform. He looked up. "I wonder if I could go."

"No," Matt said quickly. "No one is supposed to ride in them."

"It's for pots and pans," Eleanor explained. "And it is much easier than carrying everything up and down those stairs." Eleanor looked around. "A lot of thought has gone into this place."

"Lily could take the lift and not have to use the stairs," Henri pointed out.

"Oh," Eleanor said. She hadn't thought about that.

Matt shook his head. "We don't know if it is safe for anyone to ride in it. Besides, Lily doesn't need something like that."

Eleanor stifled the urge to correct him. Instead, she prayed, *Lord, help him to see Lily as You do—her weakness and her strength. Then maybe he and I can talk and she'll be safe.*

Matt began to climb the steps and Eleanor motioned for Henri to follow the man. She didn't want the boy to feel left out of anything so she followed behind.

The stairs going up were narrow and there was a locked door at the top, so Matt had to bring out the key again. Henri opened the door to the lift and it squeaked. Then he looked inside the tunnel downward while Matt turned the key to the living area.

"I'll fix that," Matt said as Henri closed the lift door. "You go ahead."

Henri nodded as he stepped into the living area. Matt motioned for Eleanor to follow the boy, and he waited for her to do so before he went in right behind her.

"Ah," Eleanor murmured as she stood a few steps inside the entryway.

She turned her head slightly and could see the sun shining through the row of windows on the left side of the building. It made the large room look cozy, albeit very dusty.

"It's a sitting room," she added in delight. She had missed that part of a regular house the most when she and Lily lived in their tiny room in the Chicago tenement building. There, they had to sit together on the cot to visit and they had no place for company. But this was such a nice place for a family and friends to gather in the evenings.

Eleanor was pleased as she looked around. A polished walnut mantel stood above a dark brick fireplace. She remembered the fireplace directly below this one. It had been made of a lighter brick and boasted a white mantel. Up here, a fire poker stood beside a large wooden box that still had kindling in it. Out of habit, she walked over and lifted the poker to be sure it was sturdy. She remembered well that night she'd had nothing but a tool like this one to use in her defense when she was a girl and faced with an intruder. She reminded herself to be sure there was a heavy fireplace poker downstairs, too.

Looking further, she saw two emerald green stuffed chairs, one on each side of the divan, all clustered together in front of the fireplace. She was impressed that the fabric was velvet. A large floral rug, deep gray with huge pink roses, was spread out beneath the chairs and sofa to give the area a warm feeling. Henri ran over and sat down hard on one of the chairs and a light puff of dust filled the air.

"Father got us all new furniture," Henri announced proudly. "Like this. It's out at the ranch. 'What's the point of having money,' he'd said, 'if you don't spend it?' But—just when he was going to order chairs from a catalog—some furniture came free. He wasn't too happy about it, but he said he'd have to take it."

"That last part sounds like Luke," Matt muttered quietly. "The first part sure doesn't though." He looked at Eleanor and explained. "He and I grew up stretching a penny until it hurt to spend it."

His brother had been even more afraid of hard times than he was, Matt thought. He supposed it came from Luke being frail as a child. And maybe from having others do too much for him as a result. A man had to know he could depend on himself or he was always insecure.

Eleanor nodded. "How old was your brother when you left here?"

Matt thought. "Probably twenty-one years old. I was twenty-three. Adeline was pregnant with Henri then."

"People can change in that amount of time," Eleanor suggested.

Matt shrugged. "Not Luke. He knew the land we had was never going to be able to feed a huge herd of cattle. He would watch his pennies. My dad kept talking about there being gold in the back field, but that was foolishness. Although that mine he had us dig gave the young'uns someplace to go when their parents told them to hide, so I guess it was worth something, after all."

Eleanor nodded. She preferred to believe Henri that his father had changed. She figured Matt simply wasn't ready to give up his memories of how things had been. His family had started seeing things differently, even if Matt hadn't. It was the only explanation. She turned to glance over at Henri. "All that chair needs is a good cleaning. And you're doing an excellent job of getting the dust out."

Henri grinned back at her.

A graceful walnut table, obviously meant for dining, stood against the far wall with its eight matching chairs all in their place. A dark ruby cloth ran down the middle of the table. The oak planks on the floor were smooth and shone in the sunlight from the windows.

"Whoever owned the bakery before lived up here," Eleanor finally said in deep satisfaction. "They didn't rent it out." For the first time since they'd had to leave their grandmother's house, Eleanor believed she and Lily would have a comfortable home again. Something deep within her relaxed at the realization. She would be able to provide for her little sister.

"Looks that way," Matt agreed as he opened one of the three doors leading off the main area. "In here, we have a bedroom with two black wrought iron twin beds. Wallpaper with blue, gold and tan stripes. Some old belts on one of the beds, so I'm guessing it's the boy's bedroom."

Henri jumped out of the chair and went into the room to see. Once he was inside, she and Matt heard a loud whoop.

Smiling, Eleanor stepped through the door behind her. "Here's a bedroom with two white wrought iron twin beds. Wallpaper with pink roses here. An empty glass vase is standing on the dresser, so it must be the girl's place."

No one opened the third door, and Eleanor wasn't about to. It was likely the room the man and wife had shared. She noticed Matt glance at it, but he didn't seem any more eager than she was to explore the space.

Eleanor had noticed some rose bushes by the front

door. They were dormant twigs now, of course, but in the spring, she might be able to convince them to bloom. That vase in the bedroom made her believe they had brought forth flowers in the past.

"It's all in good shape," Matt said as he opened some drawers in the buffet standing against the wall to the left of the dining table. "Dishes and silver. Even some nice glassware."

"I'm surprised anyone would sell this place," Eleanor said, turning to Matt. "It looks like it was their home for years."

"It wasn't for that long," Matt said. "Jacob told me it was an older couple who built it, thinking their son's family would move here and run the bakery. Turns out the son had other ideas, so the couple moved down to Denver, where their son bought a general store. The bakery never did have much business. A few loaves of bread each day and that was it."

Eleanor nodded. "Do the rooms up here go with the bakery job?" She realized she was forming dreams, not knowing the facts. Matt could always rent out the upstairs. "If I operate the bakery, I mean."

"Absolutely," Matt said. "There's plenty of space for you and the kids." His face pinked up. "And, after the marriage, there's a place for me, too."

Eleanor felt her mouth dry up at the sudden mention, until she couldn't speak. She knew what the man had said in his ad—that he wanted a marriage-in-name-only—but they needed to talk before they stood in front of a minister and wed each other. After all, he'd also said he was dying, and he'd really meant he expected to be killed. In all her time on the train, picturing what life would be like in Dillon, she'd never imagined what life would be like if she was married to a man who wasn't dying and looked to be very capable of changing the marriage-in-name-only request.

Of course, the big problem was her concern about his control when it came to Lily. Unless there was some legal loophole, Eleanor wouldn't be the only one putting her future in this man's hands; he'd be able to make the decisions in Lily's life, too. On the way back, she'd look down the street and see if there was a sign for Mr. Lunden's office.

"Oh." She finally realized Matt was studying her, no doubt waiting for a response to his remark. "Yes, after the wedding." She felt her face heat up, even though she saw no reason for it. Of course they would live in the same house when they were married. That didn't mean they would share a room or a bed.

There was so much to think about. She looked around searching for something to say. "We best clean the kitchen downstairs first. I'll want to be able to open the bakery as soon as possible. Maybe Tuesday. I think we can do that—if there's supplies in the kitchen."

"I don't know what's left," Matt said as he turned toward the stairs. She thought he looked a little disappointed, but that was silly. She listened as he continued. "Some things might be ruined, but not much. It sounds like Luke bought the place a week before he was killed. Anything like flour and sugar stored here should still be good. And the spices, of course. I doubt they kept any milk or eggs after the sale. We can check, but you'll want to make a list of what else you need."

Eleanor was already doing that in her mind. "Yeast. I doubt they'd leave that, even if they used it in their baking. I'll need to order some."

She turned to join Matt and Henri who were standing inside the doorway that led to the stairs.

"Would any of the stores here have dried cakes of yeast?" Eleanor asked.

"I like cake," Henri offered, his face lighting up.

"Not that kind of cake," Eleanor said as she used her hands to make a circle. "It's a round hard piece of compressed yeast about this size. Called Fleischmann's Yeast. Comes in a red-and-white tin." When she got no glimmer of recognition, she continued, "It became famous after the centennial exposition in Philadelphia in 1876. I need it to make fluffy French bread."

"Never heard of it," Matt said. "Most folks around here have barely heard of Philadelphia, let alone their baking practices. Everyone makes sourdough bread here. Or soda biscuits. So, we don't need that kind of yeast."

"That's why they'll pay good money for French bread," Eleanor said with enthusiasm. "It's something they don't know how to make themselves—at least not if they don't have any yeast."

"I think my mama had those round things," Henri said, looking like he was trying hard to remember. "She had a big box of them and she used them when she made bread."

"Do you think I could use them?" Eleanor asked the boy. "I'll pay you for them when I've sold the loaves."

Henri nodded eagerly. "We had to pick them up at the store, and it was heavy. She put a full box in the kitchen cupboards next to that old blue teacup."

Eleanor heard Matt draw in a breath.

"Blue like a robin's egg outside and ivory inside?" he asked the boy in surprise and, at his nod, continued, "That was one of my mother's cups. She loved those things." Matt paused like he was remembering something pleasant. "She'd saved money for years from the few coins she got at the store for selling eggs. Over time, she bought one cup and saucer for each of us in the family. She was proud of them and had them displayed in a row on the mantel. She always said she was going to teach her sons to drink tea properly someday so they would not be ashamed to dine with royalty." His face went from light to darkness quickly, and then in what seemed like desperation to Eleanor, he turned to Henri. "Maybe that cup isn't one of hers? Could your mother have brought it with her when she came here from Quebec?"

Henri shook his head. "My mother always said she had nothing when she came to this wild country to marry my father, except for her mother's old receipts and a carved rolling pin. Oh, and a pearl beaded purse she was saving for Sylvie." The boy looked at Matt. "My father said my mother was a jewel and he didn't need anything else if he had her. Was he wrong?"

"Of course not," Matt said with a nod, and then he

just stood there. After a few minutes, Henri wandered off toward the window that looked down on the street.

"I guess my father didn't know there were any of those cups left," Matt finally said to Eleanor. He turned so his back was to Henri and then continued, "Luke must have hidden that one in the cupboard until my father died. I thought the old man had broken them all that day, but I guess the fourth one wouldn't have been on the table. My mother had brewed some tea and she was trying to teach me and Luke the proper way to drink it. I would have been twelve and Luke was ten. Luke didn't mind, but I was determined not to do it. I argued back with her something furious, and I must have gotten loud, because my father came in from outside. He took one look at what was happening and threw those cups against a wall. Said he wasn't having his sons drinking tea like they were highfalutin ladies."

"Oh, I'm sorry," Eleanor said as she put her hand on his arm. He was trembling. "Truly."

Matt nodded and looked down at the floor. "Even then, I knew it broke my mother's heart. And her spirit. She'd been disappointed in me and my manners for years. It was a week later that she left us. No note or anything. She was just gone."

"Oh," Eleanor gasped. She knew how it felt to be deserted, but even her father had told them he was leaving. She'd been able to say goodbye. She didn't know how she would have borne it if he'd just disappeared.

Matt didn't say anything, but he blinked hard a few times before he put his palm over the hand Eleanor had laid on his arm.

"I wished after that I'd just drunk the stupid tea," Matt said with his head bowed. "For once, I could have raised my little finger in the air like she said to do. Instead—it was my fault that she left. If I had just forced myself to do what she asked, my father wouldn't have come inside to see what was going on. He wouldn't have smashed that china. My mother wouldn't have left. The Blackwood brothers wouldn't be on the prowl, and my brother would be alive today."

"Oh, no," Eleanor said, her heart squeezing in sympathy. That was an alarming list. "That can't be true. Surely, it isn't all your fault."

Matt shook his head. "No, don't be kind. I have to face it. I set the whole thing going the way it did. I was being rude and clumsy. I might not have intended what happened, but I need to stand up to the fact that my stubborn refusal to drink that tea set everything tumbling down the way it did."

They were silent for a few minutes.

"A gentleman would never have acted that way," Matt said finally.

"But it's not too late," Eleanor said, trying to be encouraging. The burden Matt was carrying was too much. "If you were to forgive yourself and your mother, maybe—"

Matt only grunted, but the worst of the darkness did seem to have passed. "I suppose there's nothing to do about it now anyway. My mother's gone, and after all this time, I doubt she will ever come back."

"Have you ever looked for her?" Eleanor asked. Her parents had both been killed in that carriage accident, but if one of them was still alive she would move heaven and earth to find them.

Matt shook his head, and before he spoke, she knew he was going to change the subject. He'd finished confiding what happened and he wanted to move on.

"We have to go out to the ranch soon anyway," Matt said, proving her right. "We might as well go today. You need that yeast and we might not get another nice weather day for a week."

"That sounds good." Eleanor looked at Matt closely, but that seemed to be the end of it for him.

Matt nodded. "I'll check with the telegraph office to see if they have word back on the telegram I sent. Then I'll talk to the livery about getting a wagon for us. You and Henri can walk back to the jailhouse." He looked over at where Henri had wandered and saw the boy standing by the window on the opposite side of the room.

"Think you can remember the way back to the jailhouse?" he called out to Henri.

"We can both remember the way," Eleanor said firmly. She certainly did not want the sheriff to think she was not capable of even getting herself home. Eleanor looked down and saw that Henri was as affronted as she had been. He walked over and she offered her hand to him. He took it as they went down the stairs.

"Oh, we need to check the ovens before we leave," Eleanor said as she glanced back at Matt when they came to the main level of the bakery.

He stepped around her as they walked behind the

counter, turning to say, "Let me check first. There might be rats."

That stopped Eleanor and she stood still. One of the benefits of being at the highest point of the tenement building had been that even the rats didn't want to climb that far. Of course, they had likely also discovered that there wasn't much food in the tiny attic room at the top of the stairs.

"I'll keep the rats away," Henri said in a nervous voice that told her he was as scared of the rodents as she was.

"There's nothing to fear," she said for both of their sakes, but neither one of them took a step closer to the kitchen door until Matt called, "All clear."

The caution about pests made Eleanor look around carefully when she did step into the room, with Henri hiding himself in the folds of her full yellow skirt.

Tall narrow windows brought an abundance of light into the large room. In contrast to the front of the bakery, the walls in here were freshly painted white. A large, heavy worktable was scrubbed down and sitting square in the open space. She could already smell a mixture of cinnamon and ginger in the air.

"Everything looks clean," she pronounced in relief and patted Henri on the head to reassure him. He took a step forward without her as though to show he hadn't been afraid.

"Never seen a stove like this one," Matt said as he stood on the left side of the room and examined one of the two huge cast-iron stoves, both of which had a double oven. "Looks like it's a German-made one, probably designed for bakeries. Weighs a ton."

One side of the stove Matt was examining consisted of the fire well and had the usual six plate burners—two large and four small ones. The left side held two stacked ovens. Another stove next to it looked identical, until Matt pointed to the burners and said, "Four large and two small ones."

Eleanor noted that each oven had warming bins at the top that would be ideal for rising the bread dough. She could do eight, or maybe ten, loaves of French bread at a time in these stoves, she told herself in satisfaction. Before opening for business in a morning, she'd likely have a dozen large loaves ready to sell along with a batch each of croissants and beignets. She'd be able to bake that amount again by ten o'clock. Of course, she could also do more during the rest of the day if she put a bell on the door to let her know when a customer entered the front.

"Whoever set this bakery up knew what they were doing," Eleanor commented as they all headed back to the door. She was glad they had come here this morning. It would be easy to work in this place. She even saw a corner where she could set up a small table for the children to sit while she was busy.

She noticed a hallway with a door at the end.

Matt must have seen her, for he explained, "There's a living room and bedroom past that door. I suppose it's for the early morning baker. It has a back porch off it, which leads to a small yard."

"Everything sounds so spacious," Eleanor said.

"Oh, and there's bags of sugar and flour stored in some tin bins," Matt said and then pointed. "There's a pantry through the other door. It's got spices. A big container of cinnamon and salt, too. Even a few long white aprons. Lots of cotton towels."

Eleanor nodded. She could spend some time on the drive out to the ranch deciding where she would place the tables in the bakery. The large worktable would, of course, stay in the kitchen, and that smaller one for the children would do fine in the corner. There were several other side tables, though, that could be set along the walls in the outer area of the bakery. With chairs around them, they would be nice places to sit and eat a pastry.

"I think I'll order some large tins of loose tea," Eleanor said as Matt bent down to lock the main door. People would want something hot to drink while they ate pastries at those tables. "We can serve hot tea here, but customers might like to buy some of their favorite kinds to take home and brew later."

"There's more than one kind?" Matt asked in astonishment as he righted himself and put the key in his coat pocket.

"Of course," Eleanor said, equally surprised he wouldn't know that.

"Why would anyone need more than one kind?" he asked with a frown.

They locked eyes for a moment. Eleanor was silent.

"I'm not going to do battle over tea," Matt finally said. "Maybe the ladies above the saloon will want their favorite kinds. But the men here will want coffee. Black and strong. And they won't want to be facing saloon girls when they have their morning coffee—especially not if their wives are with them."

Eleanor gasped. "You can't mean—?"

"All I'm saying is that I'd put a big pot of coffee out before I offered anything else if you want to stay in business for the families," Matt said.

"Tea isn't immoral," Eleanor said stiffly. "Just because some women drink it doesn't mean anything is wrong with their—well—" Eleanor finally paused, realizing she didn't know how to say it. "No one should be judging people when they drink their morning beverage anyway. I'm sure the ladies from the saloon will be properly dressed for their tea."

"All I'm saying is that we're a small town," Matt said quietly. "And it's easy to get off on the wrong foot if you're not careful."

"I'll serve everyone in my bakery," Eleanor said firmly. "I'm not going to ask them where they slept the night before."

"That's probably best," Matt said, sounding wearied.

"And what if someone doesn't like coffee?" Eleanor asked.

"There's always been milk," Matt said. "Or lemonade, if it's available. In the fall, there's fresh apple cider. Me, I'll even take cider over coffee some mornings."

Eleanor eyed the man. "We'll mostly serve Chinese black tea in the bakery, sweetened with brown sugar or lemon if so desired. I'll have to see about ordering tea and lemons from the general store. Maybe some Darjeeling later. Or one with rose leaves added."

"Most folks here drink Arbuckles' roasted coffee," Matt said stubbornly. "You won't go wrong serving that. It's a good, American drink."

"There's nothing American—or moral—about coffee," Eleanor protested. "Arab countries were the first to brew it. It became popular in places like Persia and India. Then, I believe, it came to America, but it certainly did not come from here. Coffee beans don't grow here. All kinds of people drink it. We can't claim it as ours."

"Well, maybe it didn't start here," Matt persisted. "But we drink enough of it to claim it as our own."

With that, he turned and started to walk down the boardwalk, only to stop when a large man came up to him, waving a small paper.

"We'll wait," Eleanor said to Henri as they stood there. Something was up, and she hoped it was that Matt had received a telegram saying that all was well with Mrs. Gunni.

"She's in jail," Matt said after he walked back to where Eleanor stood.

"Jail!" Eleanor gasped. She couldn't believe that. Mrs. Gunni was known for being careful to give the correct change to a blind man and to children too young to know if they were cheated. "She'd never break any laws. I'd trust her with anything."

Eleanor looked down and noticed the distress on Henri's face. She whispered, "Nothing to worry about."

Eleanor hoped that was true, but Matt's face said there was worse information to come.

* * *

Matt stood there, feeling like he didn't know what to say. Eleanor was obviously frightened for her friend, but she stopped to reassure Henri before she addressed her own fears.

Matt figured the best thing he could do was to follow the example Eleanor had set and avoid any panic.

"That's right," he said heartily with a glance down at the boy, too. "It was for Mrs. Gunni's protection, apparently. And at her request. The officer I asked to look into it found her stall smashed and finally located her hiding in a corner somewhere." He hesitated and looked at Eleanor before speaking carefully. "She was scared but didn't think Otis was behind the cart damage. The officer said she asked him to put her in jail where he could keep watch over her. But she insisted that he get word to you that she hadn't told Otis anything. Someone else must have been the one to tell Otis you had gone to the railroad station."

"Anyone around her stall could have known that much," Eleanor said, obviously distraught. "I need to go back and help her."

Eleanor turned as though to hurry back to Dillon's railroad platform.

"But what about—?" Henri's thin voice rose in panic as he looked at her.

Eleanor saw him and hesitated. She looked up at Matt. "I really should return."

"You can't," he said flatly as he reached out as if to stop her. He realized he couldn't do that before his hands even got there, so he left his arms open, hoping she might come close of her own will. His heart clenched at the thought of what she'd find if she went back to Chicago. "Angus is going to contact some of his friends at other train stations. Otis Finch might have written to every stop."

"But he will find Mrs. Gunni. He has friends in the police department," Eleanor said as she stepped closer to Matt. "She needs to be somewhere safer."

Matt watched as Eleanor twisted her hands. Her face looked calm, but the rest of her was very tense. He made himself stand still. After a few moments, she moved close enough that he could feel her trembling. And then she leaned forward as he closed his arms around her.

Matt held her to keep her from falling. Her reaction told him how upset she was. "The only safe place I know for your friend is here. Do you want me to send her a ticket? I know the policeman I've talked to could put her on a train right away. He'll trust me a few days for my funds to get there."

"Oh, could you?" Eleanor whispered. "I'll pay you back for the ticket."

Matt could feel her breathing; she was that close. "Don't worry about that. I'll make arrangements before we go out to the ranch."

"Thank you," Eleanor said, closing her eyes. "That would be good."

Matt stood there for a few minutes, just holding her. The feeling of satisfaction baffled him. He'd held women before, even crying women. But he felt attached to Eleanor in some strange way that was new to him.

It was like he was meant to help her and that somehow aiding her made life better for him. Her concerns had become his. He wondered if it was because they were going to be wed.

No, he told himself, it couldn't be the marriage. That wasn't even going to be real. If he needed any reminder of how ill-equipped he was to be a family man, he only needed to remember that she'd already decided to talk to Wayne Lunden. Matt thought that maybe his sudden tenderness was because he was close enough to facing his death that it made him more sensitive to the distress of others. She was truly afraid. Yes, he thought, that must be it. He still was reluctant to let Eleanor go, though, and he held her until she pulled herself away to fuss with her hair.

"I'm sorry," she murmured. "I'm not usually so overcome like this. I wouldn't want you to think I'm that high-strung. I'm really quite sensible."

"You're worried about your friend," he said, offering them both an excuse for the closeness they'd felt. "It was only natural."

"Yes." Eleanor looked relieved. "Yes, that's it. I'm sure."

Matt stood there, unable to move. The sun was still shining and the air was warm, at least for a winter day, so there seemed no need to take a step in any direction.

Finally, Eleanor smoothed down the front of her dress. "Well, I need to go get the children ready. I'll let Jacob know we're taking the children for a wagon ride out to your family's ranch."

Matt nodded.

"Come," Eleanor said as she took Henri's hand. "We should get back to our girls."

The boy smiled up at her. "Yes, our girls."

Matt felt a little left out watching them. He was relieved that his nephew and niece liked Eleanor as much as they did. He certainly could not guarantee that he'd be there to raise them to adulthood. But—contrary as it was—he suddenly wished he could do just that.

He wondered, with a sudden pang, if his father had ever looked at him and Luke and wanted to do better by them. It seemed unlikely, but Matt supposed he would never know most of what had passed through his father's mind. The man had not talked much about feelings. One thing Matt did know with certainty, though, is that he would want revenge for Luke's death, even if it meant Matt died trying to obtain it.

With that in mind, Matt turned and began to walk in the other direction. Now that the children had Eleanor, he was going to start his investigation at the place where it all happened—the Baynes ranch. First, he needed to ask the livery man to put a dozen pitchfork tosses of hay in the back of the wagon. There was no danger in these first few steps he was taking, so he felt no qualms about the children coming with him. The hay would keep them warm if they nestled down, and he wasn't altogether sure that there wasn't some cow or horse in the old barn that might need feed. Henri had told him that his father had kept no animals anymore except for the horses that had been brought to Dillon, and Jacob had assured him that a neighbor man was going to check and be sure of that. But Matt had a hard time imagining his brother not even having a milk cow on the place.

Maybe he was wrong though. Just because their father had never budged on anything and Matt had played by the same arguments he'd learned as a boy, that didn't mean Luke hadn't changed his mind on things. Matt realized he'd grown older and more responsible, but the things he thought about life hadn't changed. He stayed away from people like his father had taught him. He was honest, but he didn't give a penny away unless there was no other choice. Thanks to his mother, he knew how to act like a big-city gentleman, but he refused to ever do it. His father's scoffing haunted him, even now when he considered tipping his hat at a lady walking down the street.

It could be that his brother, Luke, had overcome their childhood better than he had. He suspected it was his marriage that changed his brother. For instance, Luke had bought that bakery. Matt was surprised at that. Not only because it must have cost a goodly amount but because it gave his wife an independence. Their father never would have given their mother something like that. Maybe Luke had decided drinking canned milk was fine, and he didn't need a cow on the place, especially if his family was in Dillon at the bakery for most of the week.

The more he thought about it, the more uncomfortable he became. It was perplexing that his brother had changed and he hadn't. When Matt looked at the matter straightforwardly, he wasn't sure it was wise for a man to take on the faults of his father just because he hadn't given the matter enough thought to do something different. He didn't even like some of the ways his father had lived his life. And, at the end, the man had died bitter and unhappy. Matt didn't want that, and it certainly wasn't too late to change.

He wondered if a marriage-in-name-only could do for him what a real union had done for his brother. Then he wondered if Eleanor would like it if he made some adjustments in his attitudes. The only way to know, he figured, was to try it and see if she noticed. He hoped very much she would be looking close enough to see any changes he made. That would mean she cared, wouldn't it? All of a sudden, he felt like he was getting ready to ride a wild horse. There was the possibility of a fall. Maybe she wouldn't see any difference, or if she did, she might not care. But, he decided, he was going to try.

He thought he remembered how to kiss a lady's hand well enough to pull off that action without looking like a fool.

Chapter Five

Eleanor was flustered. Matt had asked her to stand and wait while he lifted the children up to the back of the wagon. Then he returned and took her hand. Before he began helping her onto the wagon seat, though, he executed a small bow and bent to kiss her hand.

"Oh," she gasped, staring at him. She could still see the imprint of his lips on her glove. "What did you do that for?"

"I wanted you to know I have some manners," Matt said with a grin. "Of course, it works better if it's not winter. I'll have to do it again in the spring when your fingers are bare and you can feel the kiss."

"Oh," Eleanor whispered. She wasn't sure she was ready to feel his lips on her skin.

Saying no more, Matt stepped closer to the wagon and held out his hand. Eleanor accepted his help, and before she knew it, she was hoisted up to the front of the wagon.

"I never said you didn't have manners," Eleanor finally found her voice so she could protest.

Matt didn't answer. Instead, he walked around and climbed onto the wagon.

"You didn't have to say anything," Matt said softly as he reached under the seat and brought out a wool blanket the color of old nutmeg. He wrapped it around her carefully. "There's no reason you should think I know how to act."

"It's not important," she murmured.

"Yes, it is," he said as he brushed his fingers across her cheek. "A gentleman always takes care of his lady. Makes sure she's warm when it's cold outside."

They stared at each other for a few seconds. It was long enough for Eleanor to feel a blush crawling up her neck, but she still didn't turn her eyes away.

"Well, then." She swallowed and finally managed to say, "Thank you."

No one had ever taken care of her, Eleanor thought. And she didn't know what to make of it.

Matt picked up the reins and signaled the horses to begin. When they finished passing the buildings that made up Dillon, Eleanor turned and looked behind her. Several other blankets, all of them from the jail, covered the whispering children as they huddled together on the floor of the wagon. They seemed content to be surrounded by the hay that Matt had requested from the livery stable.

The blankets might be frayed around the edges, but they were warm. Things would get better, she told herself. She had already informed Lily about the rooms above the bakery, and her sister was excited. Even now, Henri was apparently giving Lily his impression of the house above the bakery. She could hear him talking about that lift that brought the food up.

After some distance, Matt pointed out to Eleanor the first marker for the path to the ranch.

"We always turn left at that tree with the crooked branch," he said with a nod in that direction. "You'll notice you can see a few ruts in these hills ahead. If you need to go to the ranch without me, just follow the path as best you can. You'll get there. Past that tree, there's only the ranch out that way."

Eleanor nodded. She saw the incline ahead where Matt was guiding the wagon. Dead grass showed atop the ground where the snow had either melted or blown away, but here and there, she saw the thin lines made by hundreds of wheels in the past, including one set of tracks that looked recent. Maybe someone had been out to the ranch to tend to animals or something. Matt would know what it was, she thought, as she continued studying the area. This land would never match the green of Ireland that her father bragged of so fondly, but it was a decided improvement over the filthy streets west of the river in Chicago. She was satisfied with her new home. And then she leaned back slightly so she could look up.

"I didn't know it was so beautiful out here." Eleanor let her eyes rove over the endless blue sky. On the train ride here, she hadn't been able to see it because of all the storms. Until now, she hadn't realized how gray everything had been when she had scanned the sky in Chicago.

Matt looked over at her and grinned as she righted herself and faced forward again. The blanket had fallen off when she admired the view overhead, shifting the hood of her cloak until it too fell, and she shivered visibly as a chill crawled down her back.

"Here." Matt pulled the blanket up until it came over her head. "This will keep you warm."

Without the hood, her hair was unruly.

"I'll look like a beggar woman," Eleanor protested as she turned to face him. She had nothing against the women who put their hands out for a coin or two when they had no other way to eat. But she had left her one decent hat back at the jail, and now there was no style to her at all. In dismay, she lifted her hand to push back a few stray hairs. She was certain that her nose was red, as well.

"It doesn't matter," Matt assured her with an easy grin. "The children don't care and you don't need to impress me. I've already proposed."

"No, you haven't," Eleanor protested without thinking and then realized. "I'm sorry, I suppose you have proposed if you meant the ad."

"Of course I meant the ad," Matt said. "I wrote that I needed a wife."

Eleanor nodded. She didn't want to pursue this conversation, but it hadn't been a proper proposal. That much she did know, even if she wasn't going to be difficult about it. "I suppose if the words in the ad were your own words, then maybe it counts."

"Well," Matt sputtered as he glanced sideways, act-ing startled when she met his gaze. He quickly shifted his eyes away. She could tell he felt guilty about some-thing; it was plain on his face. The man wasn't much of a liar, she decided. She tried to stop the slow smile forming on her lips.

"Did you think no one would answer the ad?" she guessed. Surely, the man was not that clueless. Maybe no one had told him he was handsome. The ad certainly hadn't mentioned his appearance.

Matt shook his head, suddenly focusing on the reins in his hands as though the horses couldn't make their way up the hillside without his complete attention. El-eanor didn't say anything although she was sure the team and wagon had made this trip several times be-fore.

"It's not that," Matt finally muttered.

"What is it then?" Eleanor asked. She didn't want to be intrusive, but she felt she had a right—a duty even— to know if the ad had been some kind of a mistake that he now regretted.

"I didn't write the ad—or the letters," Matt said, his voice tight. "Jacob did."

"I came to marry *Jacob*?" Eleanor heard her voice raise in astonishment. The deputy was a nice man, but he was probably forty years old. She hadn't realized age made any difference to her, but Jacob felt more like an uncle than a husband, even if he had put on his best white shirt to welcome her and Lily.

"No, you came to marry *me*," Matt said, his voice

firm. "I just didn't know what to say, and so Jacob did the honors."

"Well—" Eleanor could think of a dozen rules of courteous communication that had been broken, but she didn't mention any of them. It had never occurred to her that Matt hadn't written the ad and the letter himself.

"Jacob said it is done sometimes." Matt sounded defensive.

"Well," Eleanor began again and stopped. Suddenly, she realized her position. She hadn't penned the letter that was supposed to be from her either. In fact, she hadn't even known the letter had been written until it received a response. She cleared her throat. "I'm sure Mrs. Gunni would agree with Jacob that in some circumstances it's fine for someone else to do the writing."

"Your Mrs. Gunni knows about these things?" Matt asked.

Eleanor nodded her head. Her friend did indeed apparently know.

"Good, then," Matt said, his voice sounding satisfied. "We'll not mention that again."

"I surely won't," Eleanor agreed in relief. She did feel a little guilty that she hadn't confessed her lack in the letter writing, but she looked over and noticed Matt was focused once again on the reins in his hands. Maybe the horses did need his attention. She'd have to tell him later, she thought. Certainly before they got married. She wouldn't want to disturb him now as they made their way up another hillside. The snow banks were deeper as they traveled, but the horses stepped high enough to pull them through.

For a few minutes, there was nothing but the sound of hoofs hitting the wet ground and the low murmur of the children's voices behind them. They passed another cluster of trees.

"Are you going to tell your sister about Mrs. Gunni coming?" Matt asked after a while, keeping his voice low enough that the children couldn't hear.

"I don't want Lily to worry," Eleanor whispered back. "We don't know how long it will take Mrs. Gunni to wrap up her business and come. She probably has some produce she needs to sell first. It hasn't been long enough for it all to be rotten. Especially not the apples. Or the onions and carrots."

Eleanor tried to forget that Otis might be harassing Mrs. Gunni right now. Surely, she was safe if she was in the jail or even on the train already. Otis had allies in the police department, but she doubted they would be able to work fast enough to stop Mrs. Gunni's move to the railroad station.

Matt turned to look behind. "My guess is that Henri won't be able to keep it secret for long. They're all still talking. They'll be getting to it eventually."

Eleanor moved slightly so she could glance back and see her sister. Lily wore a blanket over her head, too, but some of her blond curls flew free and shone in the sun. The girl was happy. Eleanor had managed to help Lily into the wagon when Matt went inside the jailhouse to get more blankets, so he didn't know that her sister's foot injury wasn't something that would go away with a night's sleep.

Eleanor kept her face focused on Lily as she cleared her throat. The girl looked up.

"I have a sweet surprise for you," Eleanor said. "Mr. Baynes is sending a train ticket to Mrs. Gunni so she can come visit us for a while."

Lily's expression was blank for a second as she seemed to adjust to the news. Then a grin spread across her face and she screeched, "Mrs. Gunni!"

Eleanor nodded, enjoying the delight in Lily's eyes. Then the girl turned to Henri.

"She's my friend, too," Lily announced proudly. "She knows everything. And she has a stall with apples that she sells. And usually she also has carrots, onions and potatoes. Once, she had a big turnip that would have won a prize if there had been a fair close by to judge it. Everyone said so."

Henri nodded companionably and bragged, "I have a golden apple that my father said was a prize. We can't eat it though. It's too hard. My mother found it. My father never said what kind of apple it was. He just said we were saving it for an emer—" He stumbled over the word and then tried again. "Emergency."

Having pronounced the last word, Henri looked down and adjusted the blanket over his sister, Sylvie, who was dozing with her head against his leg. "I'm saving the apple for my sister. It's still under my bed at home. I'll show it to you when we get there."

Eleanor made sure Henri was engaged once again in his conversation with Lily before she said softly to Matt, "They must have been very poor if an apple was all they had saved for an emergency. Of course, they had just bought the bakery, so maybe that was why they had so little."

Matt shrugged. "I've wondered how they managed to purchase the place, but they clearly did. They must have had other savings, too. Maybe Henri just didn't know about it. And if they needed help, they could have always asked me. I have a fair bit of money put aside and Luke knew that. I'd offered to give him some from time to time. He never took it, but he would have if he needed it for his family."

Eleanor nodded and turned her attention back to the children.

"Mrs. Gunni will know what kind of an apple it is," Lily assured Henri confidently before looking up at Eleanor. "I can't wait until she gets here. Mrs. Gunni can share the room where Sylvie and I will sleep, can't she?"

"Oh," Eleanor said in confusion. "I thought I'd be paired with you."

"Me?" Lily looked shocked.

"Well, yes. We are sisters," Eleanor said, not understanding why Lily would expect anything else. They'd shared that tiny cot for months in Chicago.

"But you'll be *married*," Lily protested, her eyes indignant. "Mrs. Gunni said wives always have to sleep in the same bed as their husbands." The girl seemed incapable of continuing, but she stared at Matt's back with some concern as she whispered, "Don't you want to share a bed with him?"

"Lily!" Eleanor turned around, appalled. "That's not something you mention around strang—"

"I'm not a stranger," Matt interrupted her before she could finish. "I thought we settled that earlier."

"Of course you're not," she assured him, hoping the conversation would end with that. "It sure is a nice day for a ride out to the ranch," she said, her voice sounding strained.

"I thought it might be too chilly," Matt added gamely.

"No, no," Eleanor said. "It's warm enough, I think." Her cheeks were heated, in any event.

"I've always had to share a bed with you," Lily offered, likely thinking she was helpful. "You just have to get used to the other person. Unless they take all of the covers—which sometimes people do."

"She doesn't have to worry about me taking all the bedding," Matt said solemnly.

"And if she takes all the covers just roll toward her," Lily advised. "You'll be warm then."

Eleanor was glad her cheeks were already red from the cold.

"Hush!" she whispered to her sister and then turned to Matt. "Everyone, hush."

"We're only talking about blankets," Matt protested, his voice warm and rich. "Everyone uses them. We have blankets with us now."

"It's not funny," Eleanor reprimanded him. "And a gentleman would never be having this conversation."

Matt took a breath and his laughter escaped, rolling out over the hills in great gasps of merriment. Eleanor had to smile; the sound was infectious.

"The children," Eleanor began, forcing her voice to stay even. She turned to look and found they had moved on in their discussion and were paying no attention to the adults on the wagon seat in front of them.

"Well, I guess we don't have to worry about them," Eleanor admitted. She looked over at Matt and noticed he'd finished his bout of amusement.

"You're sure they're not still watching us?" Matt whispered, with a gleam in his eyes.

Eleanor nodded. And then, before she realized what he was planning to do, he leaned over and lifted her hand, kissing it before she could even think of pulling it away.

"Oh," she gasped, but the sound was lost in the sudden quickness of her breath. She told herself she should move away before the children saw them, but she couldn't seem to summon up the strength to do so.

Then the wagon hit a rock, and Eleanor noticed a jarring action that swung her away from Matt.

"The road," she said to no particular purpose as she settled herself again, only this time a little farther away from Matt.

"It was more like the stars for me," Matt said, his voice warm.

"Well, no one said you had to kiss me," Eleanor told him with more starch than was likely warranted. "Unless Jacob wrote that out for you to do, too."

Eleanor wanted to pull that blanket up over her head again.

"No one could make me kiss anyone," Matt said, his head turning around to look at her. "I thought we weren't going to mention those letters again."

"I didn't mention them," Eleanor said, her voice coming out thin and squeaky. "Not exactly."

"Humph." He shifted so he faced the trail ahead. Then, for some reason, he started to whistle. Eleanor put her hands up to tuck back the stray hairs around her face. She looked back to the children and noticed that they didn't seem aware that anything had happened. And, really, they were right. Nothing had happened, except for the tingling she still felt in her toes.

And then she looked at Matt. What was he doing?

Matt stopped midwhistle and pulled on the reins. He'd noticed the fresh wagon tracks for some time now, but he had expected them to turn off in some new short-cut in the direction of one of the other distant ranches. Driving over this hill, though, he knew there was no other place to go from here except for the Baynes family ranch, the one he had grown up on and that he had eventually left to his brother.

"Something wrong?" Eleanor asked.

"I don't know," Matt said as he reached behind the seat and pulled his rifle forward. He usually drove with it in his lap, but he'd wanted Eleanor to sit closer. It had been a long time since he'd done something so foolish, unless he counted that kiss. He hadn't expected that kiss to twist his insides like it had. But he had his rifle in position now, and he picked up the reins and signaled the horses to keep pulling them forward.

Eleanor must have sensed his unease, because she turned around and ordered Lily and Henri to please put their heads down and pretend that they were napping. She also told them to help Sylvie stay down, too.

"You should move back with them," Matt said. "It'd be safer."

She shook her head and straightened her back. "No, I don't want to frighten them unnecessarily."

Matt looked at her. "If I tell you there's trouble, I want you to scramble back there as fast as you can. If the Blackwood brothers are around, they've already shown they don't mind shooting at women, since they shot Adeline."

"I thought you said they struck her by error," Eleanor said, her face turning pale.

"That's what the undertaker concluded," Matt replied. "But the Blackwood brothers hit what they aim for. I doubt they've made a mistake since they were kids running around barefoot and shooting at rabbits."

Eleanor nodded but seemed to have nothing more to say. He was grateful she didn't, because he needed to concentrate. They were almost at the crest of the hill heading down to the ranch. He pulled the horses to a halt and wrapped the reins around an iron bar that curved around the back of the seat. He'd decided to walk up to the top of the hill and see what it looked like on the other side. Before he did that, though, he needed some information.

"Did your father have any horses in the corral?" Matt asked as he looked back at Henri's face.

"Just Bess and Blackie," Henri said, the back of his head pressed down obediently on the hay. "The ones in the livery stable in town."

Matt nodded. If the livery stable would have rented a wagon without a team, he could have used those two horses for the trip today.

"Be careful," Eleanor said softly.

He turned to give her what he hoped was a reassuring grin and saw that she was twisting a corner of that old blanket like she was worried. That would never do. He wasn't used to having anyone care about him, and it wasn't fair for her to start now. Not with the future he had once he started tracking down his brother's killers.

He had to put Eleanor out of his mind, though, he told himself as he dropped to his knees and crawled forward a few yards to lie flat so he could see the ranch sprawled out in the coulee below. Large patches of snow showed along the far side of the wide dip in the land. Bare ground stretched from the barn to the path leading into the ranch. There were no horses in the corral, and it was unlikely there were any other animals in the barn since it seemed to be closed up tight.

A large cave was dug out of the hillside some yards behind the house, its entrance nothing but a flat, black half oval showing against the snow. That was the mine he and his brother had dug years ago for their father in his gold-lust days and where the children had been sent to hide when the strange men rode up to the house. Henri had told him that their mother had lifted him and his sister out of a back window and told them to run there and they had done so.

The house had been enlarged after Matt left. Raw boards had been used to make an extra bedroom on the right of the log house and those planks had grayed until the addition looked like a poor relation to the sturdy dark logs that stood strong after thirty-some years. Two glass windows shone from the front of the house with the door centered between them. Those windows had been added since Matt had been here, too. Farther back, the chimney was straight.

His brother had kept the ranch in good repair.

Matt's study of the place stopped when he saw the two crosses made out of small branches wired together. They marked the two mounds where Luke and Adeline must be buried. Jacob had mentioned a funeral and graves to Matt, but it had all been finished before he arrived in Dillon and he hadn't wanted to leave the children to make the trip out here. Suddenly, Matt squinted. Something was tied to the middle of both of the crosses—something that wasn't part of the gravesite. He couldn't imagine what it could be, but then he realized that it could be anything. The wind was blowing furiously, and it was likely some stray newsprint or a cluster of weeds.

He studied everything else, and the only other thing to puzzle him was the number of footprints around the house. There were too many. The funeral had been too long ago for those footprints to still be here. It must be a neighbor, Matt thought. Jacob had told him a rancher had come riding down the hillside after Luke and Adeline had been killed. That's what had saved the children's lives, since the outlaws had been heading to the mine when the neighbor showed up. Maybe that man had come back. Some of the footprints were small, so likely the rancher had brought his wife over when he came to check on things recently.

Matt decided nothing was alarming and he stood up and waved to Eleanor. He saw her smile as he walked back to the wagon. Her response made him step a little faster. A man could get used to a welcome like that.

Matt drove the wagon down to the house. The wind was less bothersome at the bottom of the hill and he walked around to help Eleanor climb down from her perch. At his nod his niece and nephew scrambled out of the back. Eleanor had walked to the rear of the wagon to help Lily, but he stepped closer. "Let me."

He could see Eleanor was going to refuse his offer, but she didn't say anything, so he swung Lily down. He noticed the girl's limp wasn't any better than it had been last night.

"We should have the doctor come over later and look at her foot," Matt muttered in an aside to Eleanor. "It's sure slow to heal. Did she fall or something?"

"It'll be fine," Eleanor said quickly as Lily hobbled over and wrapped her arm around Eleanor's waist before they started walking toward the house.

For a woman who wanted to consult an attorney, she seemed reluctant to talk to a doctor. But Matt shrugged. He supposed she knew her sister better than he did. He'd see if she'd let him examine the foot later; he knew enough about sprains to do some good.

"I'll build us a fire inside," Matt said as they neared the house.

"Is it the first time the children have been back

since—?" Eleanor leaned closer and whispered as he put his hand out to open the door.

Matt stopped. Now, this was why his niece and nephew needed a woman to see to them. Of course it must be difficult for them to come back here, and he was just charging ahead like a bit of fire would solve all their problems.

"We could go to the barn," Matt offered as he looked at Henri. The boy's eyes were starting to tear up, but he shook his head.

"I want to see inside," his nephew said. "To be sure everything is still there. It's what my father would do. It's our home. We need to take care of it."

Matt realized then that he couldn't sell the ranch. He'd asked around to see if there would be any offers, and if there had been a good one, he had expected to exchange the place for a bank draft. The two children had more use for money than a ranch that they wouldn't be able to manage. It was a pity though. If he wasn't going after the Blackwood brothers, he could settle down and run the ranch for Henri and Sylvie. He'd always wanted a place like the one where he'd grown up. Maybe he could find someone to rent it.

"Let's hurry, everyone inside," Matt said as he opened the door and stepped back.

Henri and Sylvie rushed past, but Eleanor stood there with Lily, obviously waiting for him.

"I'll take the horses to the barn first," Matt told Eleanor and then turned and walked back to the team. He led the two animals, one a mare and one a stallion, to within a few yards of the barn where, for no good reason, he stopped and rested his hand on the stallion's head—suddenly beset with thoughts on his life. Whoever would have guessed he could send away for a bride and receive one as perfect as Eleanor. If he set himself to working the ranch here— He looked at the two horses in harness and noted they seemed content. If he and Eleanor could find that peace with each other, the two of them could have a real marriage. He'd never wanted to hitch himself to a woman before, but he had a growing feeling for this one.

Of course, that would mean he'd have to give up on bringing his brother's killers to justice, and he wasn't sure that was right. A man had to know he'd done his duty or he wouldn't rest easy. Matt had always planned to offer the Blackwood brothers the option of surrendering and taking them in to stand trial. He had no doubt of their honesty and believed they would confess if they had done the killing.

But those Blackwood brothers had never been fools. Guilty or innocent, they weren't likely to go with him willingly. If the eldest one, Ethan, didn't shoot him, the two youngest—the twins—would. If they failed, he'd have to face the remaining three brothers. There was no way for him to survive all of them.

The truth of it was that he remembered them as friendly, chubby-cheeked kids and he had no drive to shoot any of them, despite what they'd likely done.

"Lord, I leave it in Your hands," he finally mumbled as he started again to lead the horses to the barn. Turning to God with his problems was a new way to live for him, but he was determined to do it. In the meantime, he'd take the harness off the horses and give them a rubdown. Then he'd head back to the house and help Henri find that apple he felt was so important.

Chapter Six

Eleanor stood next to Lily. The girl was prone to slipping on icy ground and they had painstakingly made their way into the house. Eleanor was grateful Matt had taken the horses to the barn and couldn't see them. He would have known something was wrong if he had watched them.

But they were inside now. Henri and Sylvie had obviously raced to a back bedroom and she could hear their excited shouts coming from there.

"Ah," she said, helping Lily loosen the blanket that was wrapped around her head as they walked farther into the house. Sunlight streamed through a large window to their left and they stood in its warmth for a moment, savoring the day.

Lily closed her eyes, lifting her face to the brightness and sighed. "This place feels like a home even when it's empty." She opened her eyes and grinned. "I felt like that room we had in Chicago was a dungeon. The tiny window was so high the sunlight never came inside."

"It's the pictures on the walls and the curtains on the windows, too," Eleanor replied. "That makes it feel like a home, also."

She could tell a woman had lived here.

"I like it," Lily said with a contented sigh.

Eleanor helped Lily limp along in the direction of the noise.

"I can go by myself," Lily announced proudly when they reached the hallway, and Eleanor saw it was true. The walls were close enough that the girl could balance between them. Her sister would do fine at the bakery, too, Eleanor thought. There were handrails on both sides of the narrow stairs and the counter downstairs could be fitted with them, also.

"I'll go back there soon." Eleanor watched until she saw Lily was making progress. It was good for her to feel independent when possible.

Besides, Eleanor realized as she turned back, she wanted a minute or two alone. It was that kiss. She hadn't expected to feel flustered by Matt. He was supposed to be an anemic, dying man who would inspire pity rather than passion in her. The truth was that she hadn't expected to like him. Not like that. She blushed just recalling the feelings, and then she chuckled remembering him kissing her hand—of all things—and looking shy and boyish while doing so. Of course, nothing could come of this whirl of emotions. He had been very clear on that. She figured he would leave Dillon even if he survived the Blackwood brothers. His life, after all, was down on some ranch in the Idaho Territory.

She realized as she stood there that God might actually rescue her from this arranged marriage like she had prayed on the train ride here. If Matt left Dillon, she'd have the bakery to operate and two more children to care for. She and Lily would flourish. Henri and Sylvie might miss their uncle some, but she'd be sure they had good care. She already loved them. There was really no reason to concern herself with anything beyond a brief marriage-in-name-only to Matt. She realized to her dismay that the freedom she'd have would give her no pleasure. She'd miss him.

Of course, it would be for the best if he left, she told herself as she looked around the house. She noticed the air had the faint smell of dust. A doorway led to a room that must be the parlor. She stepped inside, and the new chairs in the room surprised her; they scarcely looked used. And she would expect to see that kind of burgundy velvet upholstery in some of the wealthier homes she'd visited years ago with her grandmother. It was very unusual for a ranch house in the middle of the Montana Territory though. The room had a sturdy, rock fireplace with a log mantel, which gave the room some frontier style.

Eleanor walked over and picked up the delicate china teacup sitting on the slab of log. This must be the china Henri had mentioned in the bakery. She noticed the dried brown circle inside the cup and frowned. Someone had made tea and not washed up. She couldn't imagine who had left the cup like that, but she'd clean it before they left here today. Dust was one thing, but dirty dishes another.

"Come see my room," Henri shouted from the back part of the house and Eleanor stepped out of the parlor and walked down a small hallway to his open door. Lily and Sylvie were sitting at the end of the bed, and a jubilant Henri was bouncing up and down on the feather mattress, grinning. "This is where I sleep. It's a good bed. Not like the cots at the jailhouse. You can't jump on those—not even Sylvie—they'd fall right to the floor."

"I'm sure they would," Eleanor agreed. However, she did not miss the point of Henri's description. "Maybe your uncle will bring us out here for a few days sometime and you can sleep here again."

She was surprised when all of the joy drained out of Henri's face. "He wants to sell my father's ranch. I heard him talking to some man about it. Why would he do that?"

"Oh," Eleanor said, sorry she'd brought the subject up. "Maybe he's worried those bad men will come back and damage things."

"I won't let them," Henri said sternly, straightening his shoulders. "If I'm here, I'll jump out of my bed and charge them." He made a pretend gun with his fingers. "I won't run away this time."

"No," Eleanor said in horror. "You can't do that. They had real guns. There's no shame in hiding and getting out of their way."

"My father didn't run," Henri said stubbornly. "I should have stayed with him. He had a real gun and it will be mine someday."

Right then, Eleanor heard the main door to the house open, and then Sylvie looked up, her eyes wide open.

"Is that the bad men coming back like you said?" the girl whispered to Eleanor. Fear was clear on the toddler's face as they all heard heavy footsteps. "I don't have a gun. Will you lift me out the window like Mama did?"

"No, I don't think—" Eleanor began but then didn't need to continue, because Matt was standing in the doorway to the bedroom. His coat was damp in places and he had strands of hay on his shoulders. His hat was in his hands.

"There are no bad men around here," Matt said from the doorway. "There's a lot of footprints, but I expect a neighbor came to check on the place and brought his wife along. But it can't be outlaws. They wouldn't bring a woman with them out here, and the prints of some of those footsteps were definitely made with lady shoes."

"That must be who had a cup of tea," Eleanor said and, at Matt's puzzled look, explained, "The cup Henri mentioned, the blue china one, is sitting on the mantel, and it's clear someone had a cup of tea in it not that long ago. And no one washed it after."

"That's odd," Matt said as he turned and started walking back.

Eleanor followed him into the parlor.

Matt walked over to the fireplace and picked up the cup, turning it slightly so he could look inside. Then he held it closer to his face. "Smells like tea, all right."

"The saucer is there, too," Eleanor said as she took a couple of steps to close the distance between them.

Matt set the teacup back on the mantel and scowled as he turned around and studied the parlor. "We certainly didn't have that couch and chairs when I lived here." He walked closer. "They look like the ones my mother always talked about getting though. Tufted velvet in burgundy. She talked about tufted velvet for months. My father said something like that would be ruined in a week here on the ranch. She said it wouldn't hurt us boys to learn some manners so we could be presentable if we ever got to a city of some kind."

"They do seem impractical," Eleanor noted as she watched Matt pace around the room. He appeared agitated and she hoped to distract him.

"She was always teaching us things," Matt continued. "At first it was reading, writing and figuring sums—that was all right, but then she started trying to turn us into gentlemen. Teaching us how to bow if we meet the queen or how to pick out the right fork if we have more than one on the table beside us and how—"

"How to kiss a lady's hand?" Eleanor continued with a smile.

The scowl faded from Matt's face and he grinned. "I didn't do too bad, did I?"

"You couldn't have done it any better," Eleanor assured him. She was proud that her voice was steady and held no hint of the sudden hitch she felt in her breath.

"We'll see when spring comes and you don't need gloves," Matt assured her cockily. "That'll be better."

And then they both froze. Eleanor looked into his eyes and knew the realization had hit him, too. He wouldn't be around when spring came.

"I'm surprised your mother wasn't a teacher." Eleanor rushed in to fill the gaping silence that promised to remain there forever.

Matt nodded gamely. "That was her plan until she met my father. She'd even gone to school so she could teach. She gave it all up when she met my father."

"She must have loved him," Eleanor murmured.

"I don't know," Matt answered. "I never saw any evidence of it—certainly nothing like Lily's True Love. That much is for sure."

They were silent for another minute or two. Finally, Matt walked over to a small desk in the corner.

"I'm afraid we haven't made a fire yet," Eleanor said.

But Matt didn't seem to hear. He was looking at the items on top of that piece of furniture.

"I'm glad Luke kept this." Matt lifted up what had to be a large leather-bound Bible. Once he had the book in his hands, he opened it and a white piece of cloth fell from between the pages.

"Well, I—" Matt looked over at Eleanor as though she might know what it was doing there. She didn't, of course. Then he bent down and held out the fancy lace handkerchief to her. "Is this yours?"

"Of course not," she said. "I've never been here before."

Matt nodded and leaned down to sniff the fabric.

"What does this smell like to you?" he asked.

Eleanor reached out and took the finely made handkerchief. Not only was the piece of linen edged with lace, there was a small rose embroidered in the right corner. The cloth had obviously never been used, and she brought it closer to her so she could smell it. "It must be dabbed with rose water."

Matt's face turned grim. "I had no idea that brother of mine made a shrine to our mother—keeping her handkerchief like this. She left almost eighteen years ago. This handkerchief has no right to be in our recording Bible. Births. Deaths. They're all in here. Marriages, too. But she doesn't belong."

"Oh," Eleanor said, wondering what kind of a response Matt wanted. "I don't think rose water lasts for that long. Maybe the handkerchief is not hers. It could belong to your sister-in-law. Didn't you say they both came from the Quebec area? Maybe it's a coincidence."

Matt looked relieved. "That must be it. I would hate to think Luke would get such an odd idea in his head. Our father certainly wouldn't have tolerated it, but then, he's been gone for years. He didn't hold with us even talking about our mother."

"That must have been hard." Eleanor could understand only too well how, if the father avoided any mention of the mother, it might make a child of theirs want to build a bit of a shrine to his absent parent.

"A boy needs his mother," Eleanor added softly.

Matt frowned. "But a man needs to stand on his own two feet. He can't be missing his mother like this." He waved the handkerchief slightly. "Luke always was a little too soft. We babied him. I did, anyway."

"Maybe it's not what it looks like," Eleanor said.

Matt nodded thoughtfully and called, "Henri, come out here for a minute."

Eleanor could hear the soft footsteps of all of the

children as they came obediently down the small hallway. They hesitated before stepping into the parlor, though, and she could see they were apprehensive.

"Maybe you should lower your voice," Eleanor whispered to Matt. "They seem like they're afraid of you."

"Of me?" Matt's voice was still loud, but it was also astonished.

"Well, you do sound upset," Eleanor said. "No child wants to be disciplined, especially if they haven't done anything wrong. A loud voice often precedes that."

Matt looked at her, but nodded.

"Ah, there you are," Matt said very softly as he turned to the children and smiled.

Eleanor winced. She thought he looked like a wolf watching his prey, but then she saw the laughter in his eyes. "I just have a question—that's all. No one did anything wrong."

"I did," Sylvie confessed in her trembling voice as she looked up at her uncle with tears forming in her eyes. "I'm not supposed to jump on the bed, and I did in Henri's room."

The little girl closed her eyes. "I'm sorry."

Eleanor saw the humor leave Matt's face and a look of tenderness replace it. She noticed Lily and Henri gave the appearance of being guilty, too, but Sylvie did not seem likely to tattle on them.

"Oh, that's okay," Matt said as he squatted down and opened his arms to the girl. She ran into his embrace and he continued, "That old bed in Henri's room has seen its share of jumps over the years. That's the bed your father and I shared when we were growing up.

Why it probably couldn't even tell a little lady like you was jumping on it after the abuse we gave it. I bounced on it every chance I got when I was your age. Your father did, too. It's fun, isn't it?"

Sylvie nodded shyly and lifted her head from where she'd leaned against Matt's shoulder. Then she kissed the man's cheek before stepping away and walking back to her brother.

Everyone was silent for a moment, likely from shock, Eleanor thought.

"What I wanted to know," Matt said after wiping something out of his eye, "is whether or not this handkerchief here belonged to your mother."

Matt held up the scrap of linen with all of its fancy trimmings.

Henri looked at it carefully. "No. She had handkerchiefs like—" He scrunched up his face in thought and then said, "I'll be back."

Henri ran into one of the other bedrooms and came back with a simple hemmed piece of unbleached cotton. "These are my mother's. She said there's no point in having a handkerchief that's too nice to use."

"Maybe she had a special one for church and such?" Matt asked quietly.

Henri shook his head.

Matt frowned. "And did your mother drink her tea from the china cup on the mantel?"

"Oh, no." Henri sounded horrified. "That cup is never to be used. My father was afraid we'd break it. She kept it in the high cupboard next to the—" Henri looked to Eleanor. "It was next to the red tins you wanted."

Eleanor was grateful for the reminder and nodded to Henri. "Thank you. I almost forgot about the yeast."

"I'll show you where it is," Henri offered eagerly. "I can't reach it from the floor, but I can climb up on the counter, and maybe then I'll be tall enough to get it."

"I'll fetch it for you," Matt said as he, too, turned to the doorway leading into the kitchen area. "We don't want anyone falling and breaking a leg."

"I wouldn't fall," Henri protested.

Henri was heading into the kitchen across the hallway, but Matt was still standing in the parlor, appearing bewildered. He obviously hadn't taken a good look around until now.

"When did you get the new couch and chairs?" Matt asked.

Henri stopped at the doorway and turned back to answer.

"After we bought the bakery. My father was supposed to go down to Ogden with a big wagon to pick them up. He wrote that he couldn't do it, but our grandmother sent them to us on the train, and he couldn't let them sit there at the railroad station, so my grandmother hired a man to bring them to us."

"Your mother's mother?" Matt asked, with a puzzled frown. "I didn't think your mother had any other family."

"No, it was my father's mother. Grandma Baynes. She couldn't come, she said, but she sent the furniture so that we'd have—" the boy paused as though recalling something he'd heard "—a 'civilized place' to sit when we had visitors—except the only visitors we had were those bad men and they weren't nice, so they never sat on the furniture."

Henri ended triumphantly, obviously proud that he'd remembered so much. Matt was standing there, looking stunned.

"That's her," Matt said as he turned to Eleanor. "That's my mother. It has to be."

"Well, that must be good news," she said and then realized it was the wrong thing to say. "I mean, it's good to know she's alive."

"If she was, why didn't she tell us?" Matt said, the thunder clear in his voice this time. "Do you know how many nights I couldn't sleep wondering if she was alive or dead?"

Eleanor looked over at the children quickly. Fortunately, they seemed more fascinated than afraid. She wanted to keep them that way.

"She did send the furniture," Eleanor reminded him. "That was notice in its way."

"But no one told me," Matt said, still fuming.

"Ah," Eleanor said.

"Why didn't you let the sheriff know you had a grandmother somewhere out there?" Matt turned to ask Henri. "You wouldn't have had to spend all that time in the jailhouse, waiting for me to get to Dillon."

"I did tell the first sheriff," Henri said stiffly. "But he asked me where she lived and I didn't know. Nobody asked again." Henri took a deep breath. "Until now."

"Well, of all the cockeyed ways to go about things,"

Matt muttered as he walked out of the parlor and crossed the hall into the kitchen. He yelled back, "Where again are those red tins you want?"

If it wasn't that she needed that yeast to make good French bread, Eleanor would have suggested they leave it for another day. But she wanted to get the bakery open as soon as possible so she could start making money. She wasn't sure what her percentage of the profits would be and she needed to start making enough money to pay the sheriff back for the two train tickets he'd sent her. And the other ticket for Mrs. Gunni. And then there was the cost of the attorney, too. She'd try to see that man tomorrow and ask what he'd charge to make sure she wasn't giving away legal rights for Lily if she married. She'd feel much better about everything else if she had a contract stating she was the only one to make decisions on Lily's behalf.

"They're on the top shelf," Henri whispered to her.

Eleanor nodded. Henri might be willing to face the outlaws, she thought, but he wasn't so sure about being around his irate uncle. She patted the boy on his head and nodded to Lily.

"All of you stay in here," Eleanor instructed the children, and they all nodded in eager relief. "You may sit on the furniture, but be careful not to get any dirt on it. I'll talk with your uncle for a minute and we'll be back to build a fire."

The children hurried to obey.

Eleanor turned and walked across the hall. She was standing in the doorway to the kitchen when she realized that she knew just how Matt felt.

"I wasn't sure you were coming," Matt confessed as he turned around to face her. "I'm sorry I was impatient. I was—upset."

Eleanor nodded. "I understand."

Lord, help me, but I do. She wasn't sure she should have the sympathy that she did for the man. She knew she had to tell him about her life, though, even if she had long ago decided to stay silent on the problems.

Matt saw Eleanor in the doorway and the words burst out. "How can you understand? Your mother didn't leave you because you weren't good enough for her." Matt stopped himself. It wasn't Eleanor's fault. "I'm sorry. I'm just surprised Luke knew she was alive and didn't tell me. I thought we parted on good terms, but maybe not. Besides, I always felt like we were agreed on our mother, if nothing else."

"Maybe he was going to tell you," Eleanor suggested mildly. "The furniture is new and the shooting happened fast. There might not have been time."

Matt shook his head. It was all well and good for Eleanor to sugar up life, but he lived in reality. "He had to have known before the furniture and he kept it quiet. But it doesn't matter. I'll handle it."

With that, he reached up and started bringing down the tins of yeast. He set them on the counter, one after another, just like they were small wooden blocks. He knew he should be gentle, but he wasn't. He found himself banging them as he stacked them.

He heard a wisp of a sigh, and then Eleanor began to speak. "I understand how you feel because my father left our family almost like your mother did, although he used a different excuse."

Matt looked down and saw that she was staring straight ahead at the edge of the cupboard. Her voice was flat.

"I'm sorry," he said softly, but she didn't seem to hear him.

"I loved my father and he was good enough to us," Eleanor continued. "That is, until Lily was born. Then he changed overnight. At first, I thought it was because I talked too much—chatting, really. I was fifteen and silly sometimes. He seemed tense and I couldn't seem to be quiet. Anyway, he didn't want to be home anymore and he'd take off and stay away for weeks with people he met somehow. Gamblers. Women. Sailors, sometimes. We never knew where he was, who he was with or if he'd come back. Eventually I understood it wasn't me he hated. It was the baby. Lily had a misshapen foot. He said she was a disgrace to him—that in his family children were born perfect or they weren't born at all. He must have said it many times before I heard it."

Eleanor looked up at him then. "I'm sorry, but I haven't been truthful with you about Lily. She can't walk right."

Matt could see the turmoil in her eyes. "Don't worry. It doesn't matter."

He saw tears forming in her eyes.

"Yes, it does," she whispered and continued. "My mother cried endlessly because my father blamed her for Lily's foot being the way it was." She looked up. "You haven't seen it. It's bad."

"It's okay," Matt said. He felt helpless to comfort her. He wanted to step forward and hold her, but he could see she wanted to say her piece. She wasn't even facing him now; she seemed to be looking back in time.

"She kept saying she was sorry, but my father never answered her. And, then he was gone. She missed him or, at least, missed the way things used to be. I was at a loss, too. I didn't know what to do. There was a lot of gossip about my father being gone. My mother wouldn't even look at Lily, so I took on the caring for her." Eleanor glanced up at him then, her heart in her eyes. "She was just a baby and would have died if I hadn't fed her. The woman next door told me how to give her goat's milk in a bottle." Eleanor smiled and her face softened. "Even as a baby, my sister was sweet. She used to gurgle and try to talk to me. I was so afraid I'd do something wrong and make her sick. Or that my father would come back and hurt her. I don't think he would mean to do it, but he might anyway in a fit of frustration."

"Surely, he wouldn't—" Matt started and saw how she stiffened. She clearly thought her father was capable of it. "You don't need to tell me anything else. I can see how you were put in a bad spot."

He was afraid she was going to cry, but she pulled herself together. "I'm only telling you this so you know I do understand. And I think your brother would have told you, if he could, about your mother, but maybe it was impossible. I know I would have done something to help Lily if I had known what to do. Maybe your brother didn't know what to do either."

Suddenly, Matt didn't care about why his brother had kept silent about their mother. It was more important to comfort Eleanor.

"You did what was needed," Matt whispered as he stepped closer and opened his arms. She walked right into his embrace and he felt complete. "Anyone can see that Lily feels loved, and that's all because of you. You did what you had to do, and it was the right thing."

"I do love her," Eleanor murmured against his shoulder. Her voice was thick with unshed tears. "She's everything to me."

"We have to hold on to our family, don't we?" Matt said softly, inhaling the lemon scent Eleanor wore. "When we can't count on our parents, we need to embrace someone else. A brother. A sister."

Eleanor nodded as she stood back and looked self-conscious. She pulled a handkerchief out of the pocket on her cloak and dabbed at her eyes. "Thank you. I don't usually cry so much."

He didn't think she'd managed to let any of her tears escape, but he wasn't going to argue.

"Anytime you need to cry, I'll be here," Matt said without thinking. He wanted to be the one who helped and nurtured Eleanor, but he couldn't really promise what he had. "If I can be here, I mean."

"Of course," she said while smoothing down the skirt of her yellow dress like the refined lady he knew her to be. "I'll be fine. I know you have your plans."

She swept her hands out to indicate those plans were many and unrelated to her.

Matt stopped himself from saying anything more. Nothing good would come if they started having feelings for each other. He did not want her crying if he was shot and killed. She was the kind of woman who would mourn for a long time. He should have paid more attention to the ad Jacob wrote on his behalf. They really should have asked for someone older, someone who was used to the hazards of frontier life. Men were killed in gunfights here—maybe not every weekend, like it used to be, but enough that most folks didn't shed more than a tear or two when a man was gone. He should have asked for a practical-minded bride like that.

Eleanor cleared her throat. "We need to talk about Lily."

Suddenly, there was a squeal from the back of the house.

Matt looked at Eleanor and he could see the alarm jump up in her eyes.

"It's probably nothing—" Matt started to say, but Eleanor was already out the door.

Matt admired the swaying of Eleanor's dress as she hurried down the hall. The color alone brightened his day. He wondered if he could convince her to wear that dress when they got married.

As the squeal had indicated, the children were in Henri's bedroom. Matt suspected the boy had finally unveiled the apple his father and mother had given him. It was probably completely withered by now, and knowing Lily as he now did, he figured they had probably already decided the apple was poisoned and part of some horrific fairy tale.

Matt stepped through the door and saw the children all sitting quietly on the bed. Eleanor was standing completely still, as well. Everyone was focused on the apple Henri was lifting up, and it was—

Matt squinted and took a step closer. "Why, that's gold!"

Henri nodded happily. "My father said it was worth a lot of money and would help us in that emer—gency." Henri frowned and looked at his uncle. "Is it an emer—gency now?"

"I don't know what it is, except astonishing," Matt said. He felt like he had the air knocked out of him. "Who found it?"

Henri nodded. "First, I found it. Then my mother came looking for me and I gave it to her. It was in the mine."

"The mine out back?" Matt turned to the window and pointed to the place where the children had gone to hide from the outlaws. "That mine?"

Matt would have told anyone that the hole in the hillside back there was worthless, despite his father's grand dreams of finding a vein of gold there.

Henri nodded. "There were more rocks like it there, too, but my father said we shouldn't touch them."

"How did anyone know it was there? Someone needed to handle it to get the gold out of the rock," Matt asked, beginning to wonder what was going on.

"It was behind a real big boulder," Henri explained

as he made a huge circle with his arms. "And it wasn't on the ground. It was inside a saddlebag."

"So, it just appeared there?" Matt wanted to be sure. "No one dug it out or found it in pieces somewhere?"

"No," Henri said decisively. "It was in the saddle-bags. I know because my father was worried about whose bags they were. They were hiding behind the big rock, but I looked there because I wanted to see what kind of bugs would be there. Instead, I found this."

Henri held up the golden apple even higher and turned it around to show off the nugget's shine. Matt knew it wasn't raw gold as he looked at it. Someone had worked that nugget over some.

Matt was beginning to wonder if the reason his brother and sister-in-law were killed was because of that gold. Men would do more than shoot down a woman to get their hands on that kind of an apple. And how had it ended up in that old mine?

"Could you show me where the saddlebags are?" Matt asked Henri. He was suddenly glad that his nephew was too young to be arrested for hiding sto-len property. He wondered about his brother though. Maybe he was so used to Matt helping him that he fig-ured other people should, too.

Henri led the way outside and then turned to the back of the house. The ladies had decided to stay in-side and Matt was grateful for that. He wasn't quite sure what he'd find. He couldn't believe his brother had changed so much that he had the courage to carry out a robbery. Nor was it reasonable to think he would steal from outlaws and not report the theft to the sheriff. Maybe he didn't trust the man who had been the law in Dillon before Matt came. It would not take much to believe that gold was related to the wanted poster from the robbery of those miners over by Butte some months ago.

Most of the snow had melted on this side of the ravine and Henri had no difficulty walking right up to that old mine.

"I saw the saddlebag behind that rock." Henri stood at the mine opening and pointed into the darkness.

Matt walked over to the place. Shadows covered most of the dirt behind the rock, but he could see an indentation where something heavy had sat for some time. Nothing was there now though.

"Did your father take the saddlebag into the house?" Matt asked when he walked back to the opening and looked down at Henri.

The boy shook his head. "My father said we didn't want anything to do with that bag. He took a few more pieces and let me keep the apple though. Said it was our right because they put that bag on our land and just left it there."

Luke knew better than that, but Matt didn't say anything. At least it explained where his brother got the money to buy the bakery. He was probably hoping he could get his wife and children safely tucked away in town before the thieves came back to claim their stolen gold. It was unfortunate the move hadn't gone as fast as he had no doubt hoped.

"Did that bag have any markings on it?" Matt asked Henri as he gave one last look into that mine. Almost anyone who had been in the territory for some years would know about the Bayneses' foolish gold mine.

"My father said there was a letter *B* on it," Henri offered. "But he didn't know what that meant."

Matt figured it probably stood for Blackwood, but he could not prove that. There might be a clue of a different gang, too, when he went back and read his wanted posters again.

Suddenly, Matt realized that the sky was turning dark. He cautiously walked closer to the mine opening to look over the landscape in each direction. There were not many trees or even tall bushes, and he could see if anyone was approaching on horseback. No one was around, but Matt didn't feel easy about it.

"It's time we were getting back to Dillon," Matt said as he nodded for Henri to head back to the house.

"But Eleanor needs to measure me first," Henri said anxiously. "On the post by the door. You said she could."

Matt nodded. "We'll be quick about it."

Together they stopped just outside the mine opening. Matt's gaze swept the opposite side of the ravine to see if anything unusual was there. Even a small lump could be a man lying flat, waiting for them to show themselves. He saw nothing worrisome. He stepped out and studied the side of the ravine above him. Nothing alarming was there either.

"Let me walk a few steps ahead of you," Matt said as he put his hand on Henri's shoulder briefly. "If I say run, you race to the house as fast as you can."

The boy nodded.

Matt had brought his rifle out of the house with him and he let it hang loosely from his hand as he took his first step forward. He wasn't moving so fast that he didn't notice someone was standing beside the back window, watching them, though. It had to be Eleanor. He felt a jolt of satisfaction that she cared enough to watch over them.

They both walked rapidly toward the house and were soon back inside its protection. By then, Eleanor was standing in the hallway.

"Did you find out anything?" she asked as both Matt and Henri stamped their feet by the door to remove the fallen snow they'd collected on the soles of their boots.

"Not much," Matt said as he walked a few steps into the house. He stopped before he got so close to Eleanor that he'd be tempted to embrace her. It was best for both of them if they stayed apart. He had no business thinking about a future together with her until he knew if he had one.

"My uncle said I could get marked on how tall I am," Henri announced as he walked into the house farther. "We do it on that door there."

The boy pointed to the kitchen.

"That's the one, all right," Matt said as he reached along the side of his belt and opened the sheath for the smaller of his two knives. Then he looked down at his nephew. "Call the girls. They'll want to be measured, too."

Henri frowned. "Sylvie doesn't get to be."

"She's older now," Matt said. "And she might want

to. And then there's Lily. She's almost your age. She should be on the doorpost, too."

Reluctantly Henri nodded and shouted, "Lily. Sylvie."

When Matt looked up from watching the boy, he was barely in time to see the splash of yellow as Eleanor rushed into the back bedroom. She'd obviously gone to help her sister come out here. He remembered what she had told him. Maybe he should get the doctor to look at Lily's foot. He frowned at that. He wasn't sure how helpful the doctor in Dillon would be. The man primarily patched up gunshot wounds.

Sure enough, Lily was leaning heavily on Eleanor when the three females came out of the bedroom.

"Is it true?" Lily was excited and asking Henri. "Do I get to be measured just like you? In your house?"

To his credit, the boy smiled graciously as he nodded. "Boys and girls both. I'll be the tallest, of course."

Lily nodded and kept beaming.

Matt handed his small knife to Eleanor. "For the notches."

She turned to Henri. "We'll do you first this time."

The boy walked over to the doorway and stood with his back to the post. "Am I growing bigger?"

Matt could see the freshest mark on the frame. But what caught his breath was the lineup of older notches that were from the days when he and his brother had stood there, usually under protest, and had their heights measured. The years rolled away, seeing those marks. He could almost hear Luke complaining that he still wasn't as tall as Matt. He wondered if his brother had

ever looked at those old cuts and thought about Matt
down on the Green River. Neither one of them had been
much for writing letters, but a few had passed between
them each year.

"There you are," Eleanor announced in triumph as
she finished making Henri's notch. "And I do believe
you are a little taller than before. You'll be grown-up
before you know it."

Matt decided that's why the mothers did the marking
and the fathers watched. He couldn't see any distance
between this mark and the last one. Only a woman's
eyes would see how much a little boy wanted to grow
big.

Lily squirmed with impatience as she clearly tried
to stand as high as she could. She stretched until her
skirt was hiked up enough to give Matt his first look
at her foot. He frowned; it didn't face forward.

Matt glanced up and saw Eleanor staring at him, a
closed look on her face.

"You don't need to worry about Lily," she said. "I'll
always take care of her."

"I'm not—" Matt started, but Eleanor shook her
head.

"We'll discuss it later," she said as she returned to
her task and cheerfully asked Lily to move an inch to
the right so she'd have the best place for her own notch.

Matt settled back to do what fathers were supposed
to do—he watched. What he saw, though, wasn't only
notches being made on a doorjamb. He saw the children
behaving like siblings. Henri protective of Sylvie and

a little competitive with Lily. They were working out the roles that would play out over their lives.

It suddenly struck Matt that when he had put that ad out there to try to get a mother for his niece and nephew, this was what he had wanted. Not just someone to be sure they were fed and clothed but someone who would care about them as they made their way in life.

He could tell by the way Eleanor spoke with each child, like they were important, that she was going to be an excellent mother to all three children. He did not have to worry about Henri and Sylvie if he was killed. Although, the thought suddenly came to him, he had always been of the opinion that a boy needed a father. If he was gone, would Eleanor remarry?

Of course she would, he told himself, ignoring the bitterness in his mouth. He reminded himself of how pathetic those young Blackwood boys had been when their father left. They hadn't even known how to shoot a gun. A man in this part of the country needed to know that. Matt looked at Henri, considering. He knew his brother hadn't started teaching Henri to shoot, but maybe Matt should give him some pointers.

"It's never too early to learn to shoot a gun," Matt said, not really meaning to announce it aloud. He was so used to being alone with the cattle that he often spoke his thoughts instead of keeping them inside, where they belonged.

"A gun?" Eleanor glanced up, expression horrified, from where she knelt, having finished Sylvie's markings. "Who's going to learn to shoot?"

He stood there. Strands of dark hair fell back from

Eleanor's head as she looked up. The slight smile that she'd worn most of the morning was gone. Her eyes challenged him. "I don't believe violence solves anything."

"A gun has many uses," Matt said. The more he considered it, the more right it appeared to him. "We're all going to learn to shoot a gun."

"Me, too?" Lily said, a delighted grin spreading across her face.

"Not Sylvie," Henri said, scowling.

"Well, maybe not Sylvie," Matt admitted. "But the rest of us can at least learn how to discharge a firearm."

Now that his sister was not included, Henri was clearly pleased.

"But the children are so young," Eleanor protested.

Matt looked at the woman, hoping she would understand without him having to say the words in front of the children. Eleanor's face cleared and he believed she knew what he was thinking. Henri and Sylvie weren't so young that those outlaws wouldn't have killed them if they'd had the opportunity. It was only the neighbor coming by that had chased the men away. If Henri had had a pistol, and—

Suddenly, Matt realized what had been nagging at his mind ever since he'd heard about that neighbor. The story didn't make any sense. What gang of six outlaws would back off because a lone rancher came over the edge of the ravine? None that he knew of, especially when they had already gunned down a man and his wife.

"The neighbor that came to help you that day," Matt asked Henri carefully. "Do you know who it was?"

Henri shrugged. "I don't know his name. But he's the one who brought the furniture that Grandmother gave us. He drove the wagon right up to the front of the house. I got to hold the door open so the man and my father could bring the furniture inside. My father offered to pay him for his help, but the man said he did it because Grandmother asked him to. He was glad to help, he said."

"What did the man look like?" Matt asked, trying to remember all of the men who lived close enough to do a favor like that.

"He was tall," Henri said, biting his lips in concentration. "And Father knew him. He called him—" Henri closed his eyes tight and then opened them. "Something with an *E* and a *P*."

Ep? Matt thought. "Maybe Epsalm? Eprahim?"

Henri shook his head at each. "My father said you never should have taught that man how to shoot a gun."

"It was a Blackwood boy?" Matt asked, his mind scrambling. "Was the man's name Ethan?"

Henri nodded in relief. "I think so."

Matt's heart sank. The only explanation that was left was that the men who were shooting at Luke and Adeline were the younger brothers of that family and that they left when Ethan came riding up and made them stop. They wouldn't shoot at their older brother; that much Matt was confident about.

He looked to Eleanor, not sure what he wanted

from her at that moment, but she seemed to know. She walked over and put a hand on his arm.

"We'll pray about it when we get back home," she said softly. "You don't have to do anything right now. Let's ask for guidance."

Matt put his hand over the one she had placed on his arm. It felt good not to be alone in these decisions any longer. For whatever time they had left, they were a family and they prayed about their lives.

"Do we still get to shoot a gun?" Lily asked anxiously.

"We'll see," Eleanor said as she stepped away from Matt but not before whispering to him, "We need to talk."

"Yes, ma'am," Matt said with a grin. They probably did at that. There was a lot to say before he went off looking for the Blackwood brothers.

She walked back into the kitchen and he followed her. He could tell she was uncomfortable, because her face was expressionless, like she didn't want him to know how she felt.

When they stood facing each other, she reached up and unhooked the golden locket from around her neck. He'd noticed that she always seemed to wear it.

"Is the latch broken?" he asked, ready to fix it if that was so. She clearly treasured the necklace.

She shook her head as she held the locket in her hand. "I was hoping you would loan me enough money to see Mr. Lunden, and I thought you would want this as a guarantee."

"I don't need a guarantee," Matt said as he stepped

back. What kind of a man did she think he was? "We're going to be married. I trust you." With money, at least, he added to himself.

Eleanor nodded. "But I'd rather not owe you."

"You tell Wayne to send the bill to me," Matt said. Maybe then the man would have to tell him what this was all about.

"Oh, he couldn't do that," Eleanor protested. "He doesn't even know me."

Matt smiled at that. "Trust me. Everyone in Dillon knows you. And they know you've come to marry me, so Wayne will expect to give me the bill."

"But what if—?" Eleanor said with a frown as she held out the locket again. "Please. I'd feel better if I didn't owe you."

"Well, I guess I can keep it in my pocket for you," Matt finally said. "At least until the wedding. You'll want to wear it then."

Eleanor nodded. "That is acceptable. It holds the only photos Lily and I have of our parents. They bought it on their honeymoon."

He reached to pull it out of his pocket. "You should have it with you."

Eleanor shook her head. "I'm not asking you to trust me with no security that I'll pay."

"I already know you're responsible," he said, but he didn't try to return the locket any longer. Maybe he did need to know she was staying. He could stand to lose the money he'd be paying the attorney. What he couldn't risk was her taking a notion to leave him with no warning. She was still skittish of him.

Matt wondered what kind of questions she had about the marriage that would require an attorney to answer them. He suddenly felt uneasy, thinking about Wayne Lunden. He liked the man, but he was single and had started growing a fancy moustache and shining his boots every day. Even without those things, he was a handsome man and could offer a woman more than widowhood and a bakery to operate.

"Remember Wayne's spoken for," Matt said, and watched Eleanor's spine stiffen. "He's all excited about the woman, Betty, he met in Denver a few months ago."

Matt knew he should be more trusting of his future bride, but he had no reason to be. He'd never courted Eleanor. She couldn't have any feelings for him.

"I wish Mr. Lunden and Betty a happy life." Eleanor looked offended and her words were clipped. "Don't worry. I have no interest in attracting a husband."

"You did answer that ad," Matt reminded her, feeling somewhat off-center himself.

"Well, yes." Eleanor paused. "I, of course, did not mean you when I said that about getting a husband."

"Well, what did you think you were getting with that ad?" Matt asked indignantly.

"I—" Eleanor started to answer and then stopped, a flush spreading over her face.

Matt winced. How could he have forgotten? She could not possibly answer that question politely. She'd thought she was getting a dying man. More corpse than husband. It was his own fault for listening to Jacob. But his deputy had been right that he needed someone to care for the children when he was gone.

"Tell Wayne he shouldn't bill you more than fifty cents," Matt said finally. "He claims that's his average charge for legal services. He says he's not in this to get rich."

Not that Matt was in either of his jobs to make a bundle either. Even with humble fees, a lawyer would give her a more comfortable life than a temporary sheriff or regular cowhand could. He almost expected Eleanor to say that she didn't care about money, but she just nodded and walked out of the kitchen.

He shifted his feet and stared at the planks in the floor. Money wasn't his concern. He had few expenses and had saved a fair bit in the last years. No, his problem was the sour feeling he had when he thought about his life these days. He thought he'd made his peace with dying when he decided to go after the Blackwood brothers.

Of course, he hadn't had as much to lose back then. He hadn't yet lain on his cot at night remembering a certain woman's smile as he drifted off to sleep. He hadn't even felt the soft kiss of his little niece or the pride he felt as his nephew tried to stand his tallest. His future was exploding. He was wanting things he thought he'd never desire, like a wife and children of his own.

But his dreams had come too late. He had no future to offer Eleanor or the children. He was good with a gun but not lightning fast. He knew the odds did not favor him for coming out of this conflict with the Blackwood brothers alive. That's why the previous sheriff had lit out without telling anyone. Everyone in Dillon knew the chances in going against them. He didn't even want to think about how slim they were. Most of all, he didn't want to picture Eleanor in tears. He had to stop any closeness between them.

Chapter Seven

Early the next morning, as the sun was barely showing some light, Eleanor climbed out of bed and washed
in the basin of water she'd brought into the cell last
night. They were going to wait to move into the bakery
until they could clean everything. She walked over to
where her mauve dress hung on a peg. She had damp-
ened it and brushed it out last night, hoping the wrinkles would disappear by today. A few of the worst ones
looked like they had, she thought before slipping out of
her nightgown and pulling the garment over her head.
She adjusted the seams as she slid it down. She'd had
to sew new darts in the front and they still didn't hang
quite right.

Unfortunately, she had outgrown most of her dresses
a year ago. She had taken down the hem length in each
of them as much as she could. It was only on this mauve
dress, though, that she had been able to move the upper
seams enough so that the front section wasn't so tight.
Her grandmother had scolded her for looking tawdry

when she wore the other dresses, so she cut those down to make new skirts and shirtwaists for Lily. Her grandmother had not offered to buy new clothing for Eleanor though. Of course, she could understand that if her grandmother had been as deeply in debt as the bank claimed. She was still puzzled about that since she had kept her grandmother's accounts and knew the woman hadn't been making payments on any loans. If there was time enough today, she planned to mention these concerns to the attorney, too.

Eleanor refused to let worry spoil her morning. The dress would be sufficient for her meeting with the attorney and later for going to church. It might be old and threadbare in places, but it was high-collared and respectable. She swept the hanging blanket aside and stepped into the main room of the jail, surprised to see in the faint light that Matt was sitting at the desk drinking a cup of coffee and reading a newspaper.

She had smelled the coffee but believed it was Jacob moving around.

"I thought you'd be out chasing criminals," she said, striving to make her voice lighthearted.

"Not on Sunday," Matt said calmly as he looked up from his reading. "Troublemakers usually do too much drinking Saturday night to be up for much the next morning."

"I suppose so." She could not help but notice that he'd already shaved and slicked down his hair. Even in the shadows, he was handsome.

She suddenly noticed that he'd been eyeing her, too.

"That's a nice dress," he said.

She wasn't used to compliments. "This dress is old and falling apart."

Then she realized what she'd said and winced. "It's still perfectly serviceable, of course. Thank you for the compliment."

"You're welcome," Matt said with a nod and then went back to his reading.

She was glad that he hadn't thought she was hinting for a new dress. But she was surprised he didn't notice the gown was almost worthless. The wool fabric had stretched where she'd redone the seams and it was beginning to pucker.

"I can sew," she added so he'd know she didn't need much in the way of money for clothes. Technically, she wasn't very good yet, but she could do it.

"That's nice," Matt said but didn't look up.

Eleanor stood there a moment and debated whether she should ask if there was another cup of coffee. Finally, she decided she best get on with her errand and walked across the room to pull her cloak down from its peg.

"Wayne Lunden?" Matt lifted his head and asked after she got her cloak put into place.

Eleanor nodded as she reached for her hat. Matt had told her last night that the attorney opened his office for an hour the first thing on Sunday morning, from seven o'clock to eight o'clock.

"I'm surprised he opens at all since it's for such a short time," Eleanor said with her hand on the doorknob.

"Like I mentioned, Saturday night brings its share

of fights to a town like Dillon, and men don't always want to wait for Monday to get things settled," Matt said while she stood there. "And Wayne figures everyone is more civil when they're not quite awake."

"Of course." By now, Eleanor had dropped her hand from the knob, and so she reached up to straighten her hat, all too aware of its bent mauve feathers. Then she closed the tie on her cloak. She was already wearing her only pair of gloves.

Matt seemed to have nothing else to offer in the way of conversation, so she opened the door to the jail, stepping out onto the walkway. The air was frigid, but everything was quiet as she looked around. Shadows still lingered in the doorways of the few shops. A thin layer of frost covered the windows and a light shone from the saloon, although she suspected it was a lamp that had been left burning last night and was not an addition this morning. Shivering slightly, she looked for that old tomcat but did not see him. Hopefully, Whiskey was tucked away somewhere warm. The attorney's office was only a few buildings down and she made her way quickly, especially once she heard the sounds of an argument coming from the saloon across the street.

When she arrived at the attorney's, she gave a firm rap on the door. She expected to hear footsteps, but instead she heard what sounded like a low moan from inside. Then came the jarring sound of breaking glass.

"Goodness," she whispered as she leaned over and tried to look through the window. Maybe the man had fallen. A loose shutter blocked most of her view. All she could see was a bit of the wood floor. She knocked a little louder.

"Come in and be done with it," an irritated male voice called out.

Eleanor wondered if the voice belonged to the attorney or if a disgruntled client was sitting in the room, waiting for him. Either way, she meant to see Mr. Lunden, so she reached for the knob. The door hadn't been latched and opened easily.

Eleanor squinted. She could see the outline of what looked like a perfectly good oil lamp on the desk, but the man, hunched over it with his head in his hands, hadn't lit it. He sat in the half darkness.

"Mr. Lunden?" she whispered.

He grunted. Or maybe it was a groan.

"Your sign outside says you are open for business." She had checked the hours posted to be sure. "It's a quarter past seven on Sunday morning."

"Then, I must be open for business," the man mumbled as he lifted his head and reached for the dented mug sitting in front of him. She looked at that blue enamel cup closely. There was no rust or darkening around the dent; it looked recent. Her grandmother had refused to have any enamelware in her kitchen because it was too costly. Not many men could afford to treat expensive dishes so casually. His clothes looked high priced, too, even if they were wrinkled. His black hair was mussed and his blue eyes half-closed. He steadied his trembling hand and took a drink from the cup before saying, "I'm Wayne Lunden, Attorney-To-Those-In-Need. How can I help you?"

The man wasn't slurring his words and there was no smell of alcohol, but Eleanor decided he must be drunk. His white shirt had a dark spot on the collar, and its top buttons were opened. The black, trimmed moustache looked neat enough, but the rest of him gave her pause. And no one would sit in the dark, brooding like he seemed to be, unless something was wrong. Although maybe—

"Are you ill?" she asked gently as she took a step closer.

"Sick at heart," Mr. Lunden agreed with a sigh as he looked up and studied her a moment. "Do I know you?"

"No," Eleanor said, unsure what his problem was and uncertain if she should probe further. "I just came in on the train Friday. Coming from Chicago to—"

The man gave a dry chuckle. "Of course. You must be Matt's mail-order bride. He's a fellow to be envied from what I've heard. As sweet a lady as a man could find, according to Angus Wells from the train station. I should have followed Matt's example. He put up an ad and—one, two, three. Here you are and ready to marry him. Matt didn't even have to write the ad himself."

Eleanor felt slightly offended. "Matt told me he meant the words that Jacob wrote. That's the way it's often done. He didn't lie."

"Humph," the attorney said as he shook his head. "When a man starts talking marriage to a woman, there's always lies. On one side or the other."

Eleanor wasn't sure she liked the tone in his voice, but he had a point. If it wasn't lies, it was other things. "That's what I wanted to talk to you about."

He looked at her, puzzled. "Lies?"

"No, the marriage," she clarified. "I wanted you to help me draw up a contract to go along with it."

"You don't need a contract." Mr. Lunden waved her concerns away and took another deep drink from whatever was in that cup. "The ceremony says it all—you promise for richer, for poorer. In sickness and health. To honor and obey. That's pretty much it."

"But I don't want to obey," Eleanor protested. "Not in all things. That's why I need a contract."

The man stared at her like he must have heard her wrong. "You don't want to obey?"

"Not in all things," Eleanor repeated.

The whole room went silent for a moment. Even the shutter that had been flapping slightly in the wind seemed to stand still.

"Do all women feel that way?" Mr. Lunden finally demanded to know.

"I'm not sure," Eleanor said, wondering if she should leave. The man was still staring at her like, well, she wasn't sure what it was like, but it made her uncomfortable.

Then suddenly he slammed his hand down on the desk. "That must be why she's called off the engagement."

"I beg your pardon." Eleanor took a step back and turned slightly.

"No, don't leave," Mr. Lunden pleaded as he sat up straighter in his chair. "I'm sorry for being so overwrought, but you see, my fiancée—" He paused and bent his head. "Except she's not anymore."

"The woman from Denver?" Eleanor took a step closer and prompted softly, remembering what Matt had told her. "The one you met on a trip recently. Betty?"

Mr. Lunden nodded and then sighed. "She's the most wonderful woman. But she wrote and told me she has decided not to marry me. Me. Not marry me."

The man seemed to be demanding something from her.

"I'm sure it's not personal," Eleanor murmured.

He looked at her in astonishment. "It doesn't get more personal than that."

"No, I suppose not." Eleanor wanted to leave. "Perhaps I should come back later."

"No, no," Mr. Lunden said as he reached for a pen. "You're a client. It will only take a minute to write out something for you to use."

"It's no trouble to come back," Eleanor said. "I need to return anyway since I have another item to discuss with you."

"No time like the present," Mr. Lunden said as he pulled a sheet of paper toward him. "What rights exactly are those that you want to maintain as a married woman?"

Eleanor told him about her concerns over Lily. "But don't mention that in the contract—about Lily, I mean. I don't want Matt to resent her."

"General terms," the attorney nodded. "But you'll tell Matt?"

"I'll have to eventually," Eleanor replied when Mr. Lunden looked up at her. "I just need a little time. I don't want Lily to know either."

"I'm not sure a contract will be valid if you don't tell him before the marriage," the man murmured as he started writing again. "He should really sign it, too."

Finally, he lifted the pen with a flourish. "It's the best I can do. You'll need to give it to the minister—and again before the ceremony. And Matt, too, of course. You might not need to tell him everything, but he needs to know you're taking the *obey* word out of your vows."

"I'll tell him that much after church." Eleanor tucked the paper away in her purse. "Matt said to send him the bill."

Mr. Lunden grinned. "I doubt he'll appreciate this piece of work. I think it's better if I don't charge anyone."

"I always pay my debts," Eleanor said firmly. "I'll just need to get the bakery open for a few days, and then I'll be in with the money."

"Don't worry about it. We might even be able to come to terms on some baked goods to cover the bill. Can you make a sour cream–raisin pie?"

"I sure can," Eleanor said with a grin.

"Excellent," the attorney said as he rubbed his hands together. "My mother used to make those."

"I'll be happy to make one for you," Eleanor said. "In addition to payment—or more baked goods. But now I have to rush off so I can be sure my sister gets to the church in time for the services."

"I'll see you there," the man said as he smoothed back his hair and adjusted the collar on his shirt.

"You go to church?" She spun around, surprised.

"Not often, but I will today," he said, his grin growing wider. "I'm hoping to see Matt's face when you give him that contract to sign."

"I don't need to do that today," Eleanor said as she started walking toward the door again. "We plan to wait a few days to get married. Matt said the preacher usually stays in Dillon until the middle of the week."

"I wouldn't count on that," Mr. Lunden said cheerfully.

Eleanor turned back. "What do you mean?"

"I understand there will be a special announcement in church today," he said. "I've heard the preacher is leaving—packing up and heading to another church somewhere west of here. I'm not sure when his final day will be."

"Well, he'll certainly stay out the week," Eleanor said as she pushed her hat down more securely on her head and reached out to the doorknob. "Most ministers give a month's notice, so I'd think a week would be the minimum."

"Maybe," Mr. Lunden said. "Things go a little faster around here than in places like Chicago though. But if you're certain—"

"I am," Eleanor said as she opened the door. It wasn't snowing today, but it was cold and somewhat windy.

"Thanks again," she said as she stepped outside.

It took her only five minutes to walk back to the jail. She hesitated outside the door, noticing the frost that covered the small windows. She turned around and surveyed the scene. Dillon, with its assortment of buildings, was a pretty place when it was all white and the sun had risen enough to make the snow glisten in the sunshine.

She shivered slightly. Even if it had frayed collars and cuffs, she was glad she was wearing her mauve wool dress today. It didn't have the fashionable puffed sleeves like the frocks most ladies wore back in Chicago, but it was warm, and she was grateful for it.

Besides, she wanted to save her yellow linen dress for her wedding day since Matt seemed to like it. She smiled, remembering the light in his eyes when he first saw her in that one. Maybe wearing it would make him less likely to argue when she presented the contract she had in her purse. She frowned, suddenly wishing there was no need for a formal agreement that stated so clearly that she didn't trust him.

But then, she reminded herself, she had to be responsible. Men had disappointed her in the past, beginning with her father and including the few men who had courted her. Lily depended on her to make sure no one would turn her out in the future, and Eleanor knew she was the only one who loved Lily enough to guarantee that.

Eleanor looked down and noticed the jailhouse door was open a few inches. She needed only to press lightly against it before it swung open and she stepped inside. In this kind of weather, she thought it was odd that the door hadn't been closed firmly. As she looked around, though, she saw why it hadn't been. That gray-striped cat had obviously nudged it open and was now curled up beside the warm stove. Eleanor turned and saw at a glance that Henri and Sylvie were still sleeping in their cell. She heard a shuffling sound behind the blankets where she slept with Lily, so her sister was getting up. Matt and Jacob were gone. She figured they must be out on some sheriff business.

As she looked at the scruffy cat again, the animal raised his head and eyed her suspiciously.

"You have no reason to worry," she assured the animal softly. "I don't begrudge you a comfortable bed." She was careful not to move close though. Whiskey looked ready to attack and she didn't want him to feel trapped.

Then she glanced over to see Lily looking forlorn and standing between two of the hanging blankets that surrounded their cell. She held on to one of them as she rubbed her eyes, like she was still sleepy. Eleanor noticed a small tear in the sleeve of her nightgown. Like their dresses, it needed to be mended.

It took a moment for Lily's eyes to spy the huge gray-striped cat lying by the stove, but when she did, she squealed softly. "A kitty! I've always wanted a kitty!"

The cat's head jerked up and he looked at Lily in alarm.

"Careful," Eleanor called out. "That's not a kitten."

But Lily had already started to scoot closer to her prize. She held on to the bars of the cell as she pulled herself along. Eleanor noted that the cat then rose to his feet, his hair standing up and a low hiss coming from his open mouth.

"He's not used to company," Eleanor said as she quickly stepped over and put her hand on her sister's shoulder. "Don't go close. He's afraid of you."

"But he doesn't need to worry about me." Lily looked up in confusion. "I just want to pet him. He looks like he needs a friend."

Eleanor thought Lily was probably the one feeling in need of a friend. They were in a new place and didn't really know anyone yet. They both missed Mrs. Gunni.

"But he doesn't know what you're thinking," Eleanor said, keeping her voice soft and her eyes on the cat. Only a young girl, desperate for a pet, could see this wildcat as a kitten.

They were both silent for a moment.

"What's his name?" Lily finally whispered.

Eleanor winced but told her sister the truth. "Whiskey."

"Oh," Lily said, as her eyes widened in shock. "Is that—?"

"Yes," Eleanor confirmed. "That is what Grandmother said we should never let cross our lips."

"Because then the evil one would have our tongues," Lily finished the old saying and thought a moment. "Does that mean he has Whiskey's tongue?"

"Whiskey can't talk," Eleanor replied. "So, we'll never know."

Lily sighed as she moved even closer to the stove. "The poor kitty. Not to be able to talk."

"Don't touch the stove either," Eleanor cautioned her sister. The cat was looking less warlike and more curious by now, but that might not mean much. As they all just stood there, Eleanor had to admit the animal was now watching Lily without fear. Maybe the cat recognized she had trouble walking, too. Whatever the reason, when Lily slid to the floor next to the stove, that cat crawled over and tentatively rubbed against the girl's bare toes.

Lily giggled and looked over at Eleanor. "He likes me."

Eleanor grinned. "It sure looks like it."

By then, the cat was rubbing against Lily's full leg and starting to purr softly.

Just then, Eleanor heard the door open and a gust of frigid air came inside, blowing snow with it. The day had grown colder. She looked up, thinking she might not have latched the door earlier, but then she saw that Matt and Jacob were standing there.

"You're back," Eleanor said, trying to keep her voice bright and cheerful.

"Of course," Matt said as he took a step into the jail. Jacob followed.

"What's that beast doing in here?" Matt demanded to know as he stood beside the door brushing the snow off his coat. He turned to Lily. "Did you let him inside?"

Lily shook her head vigorously. "He came when I was asleep." She reached over and touched the back of the cat before continuing. "He was like the prince in a fairy tale sneaking in during the night to make the princess wake up."

Jacob chuckled kindly.

Matt grunted. "There are no princes around here."

Eleanor thought that was obvious by looking at Matt. He looked more like a rampaging king than something as tame and refined as a storybook prince. Still, she thought he could be more understanding. "Lily has always wanted to have a kitten of her own and to meet a prince, too."

"Humph," Matt said as he removed his hat and brushed the snow off. "She better get dressed if she plans to get to the church in time to hear the preacher."

"Of course," Eleanor said as she walked over to help Lily. "Let's go get you dressed."

Out of the corner of her eyes, Eleanor saw that the cat had slowly crawled along the wall until it was in the corner by the door. With one burst of speed, it slipped through the door, which was still open a few inches. She had tried not to look at the animal directly, thinking that would stop Matt from seeing it. But she knew he had noticed the cat and was still not happy that it had been inside his jail. He went over and shut the door firmly.

"It's too cold outside," Eleanor protested. "It won't be able to get back in."

"I'm not coddling that cat," Matt declared. "It can find a warm corner somewhere else."

"You keep all kinds of prisoners here," she retorted. "I'm guessing some of them aren't very nice. I don't see the harm a stray cat could do."

"I don't nursemaid anyone," Matt said then. "Man or beast."

"I see," Eleanor said stiffly as she helped Lily start walking back to the jail cell. "Does that include Lily, too?"

Matt gave a curt nod. "Now that you mention it, I don't believe children should be given too much help. It makes them weak."

"I see," Eleanor said as she pulled the hanging blanket back and slipped inside their cell with Lily at her side.

"I don't want to be weak," Lily whispered when they were enclosed in their little chamber. "I do my best."

"I know," Eleanor said as she helped Lily sit on the cot. There was nothing she could do about Matt's attitudes now though. "I brushed your blue dress last night so it would be all ready for church today."

Lily nodded, and they were silent while Eleanor took down the dress from its hook on the wall.

"We'll act like ladies in church," Eleanor reminded her sister as she held the dress out so Lily could put her arms through the sleeves. "Smile at everyone who smiles at you, and say good morning to those who speak to you."

Lily's curls bounced as she moved to slip into the rest of the dress. "Will there be other little girls like me in church?"

"Maybe," Eleanor responded as she turned and nodded in approval. "You look nice."

"The girls will want to know if we are going to stay here," Lily said timidly. Her brow was troubled and she bit her lower lip as she continued, "What should I say?"

Eleanor walked over and sat beside Lily on the cot. "Do you want to stay here?"

"I think so," Lily said slowly. "I like the sheriff." She grimaced. "Won't people think we're outlaws, though, since we live in the jail? I've never lived in a jailhouse before."

"Everyone knows Matt is the reason we're staying

where we are," Eleanor assured her. "None of the other children will think you're an outlaw."

Lily looked at the floor and whispered her next question. "Will they tease me because I can't walk right?"

"Oh, sweetie," Eleanor said as she leaned over to hug her sister. "Everybody walks differently."

"Not like me," Lily persisted. "I walked better when I had my shoe."

"I know," Eleanor acknowledged. She wondered if she should have waited a day or two before taking the train out here so that she could have attempted to get that custom-made shoe back from Otis. Mrs. Gunni knew the man's older brother. Maybe he would have helped them retrieve it. Although, Otis might have even thrown it away by now.

"Time for breakfast," Jacob shouted from the other part of the jail.

Eleanor pushed back the blankets and put her arm around Lily to help her step past them.

"I set up the bench at the desk for you," Jacob said as he stood in front of the potbellied stove. He used a small tin fork to lift a piece of bacon from the cast-iron skillet and set it on a plate. "Matt got a complaint about some problems at the saloon. He's checking to see everything is fine there. It's his job, you know."

Eleanor helped Lily walk over to the desk and sit down on the bench.

"Will the sheriff make sure the kitty is safe?" Lily asked Jacob in a small voice.

Jacob gave Eleanor an apologetic glance.

"Well, I don't know about that," Jacob said, looking a

little awkward. "That cat's more like an old cougar than a kitten, though, so you don't need to worry about him. I would be careful around him. He'll fight anyone."

"He's my friend," Lily protested.

"We don't expect the sheriff to take care of the cat," Eleanor clarified as one of the other cell doors opened.

"Why, look who's here," the deputy turned and exclaimed heartily as Henri and Sylvie walked over to the large desk and sat down on the other side of Lily. Both children still looked sleepy and Sylvie had her doll with her.

Eleanor was relieved to have the conversation about the feline cut short. She wouldn't let Lily know, but she, too, was disappointed that Matt hadn't shown any kindness toward the cat. The animal was probably useless in Matt's estimation and that did not bode well for what his feelings about Lily would be when it became more apparent that her foot was never going to improve. She might always be useless in the way Matt measured things. It was clear the cat could no longer hunt for its dinner; its lame foot would prevent that. That's why the poor thing was reduced to entertaining drunks in the saloon. She hoped they at least fed him some milk and not just whiskey. She shuddered to think what might happen to Lily in her old age. She might not ever be independent. She might have to live on the indifferent pity of others, just like that cat did.

Eleanor sighed. She was grateful she had that contract in her purse. She needed to be sure no man she married would ever turn away her sister. Only the law could stop him and that document would make her case.

She wondered again if she had let Lily believe in fantasies for too long. Life certainly didn't mirror any fairy tale that she knew. The happily-ever-after endings were the problem.

As she stood there, a frown slowly grew on her face. What kind of a world would it be if there were no happy endings?

She shook herself then. God would have to help her figure out how to tell Lily about the harsh side of life, from their father to the sheriff. It would help, she thought, if Matt didn't rush about scowling at harmless cats. She didn't want to paint too black of a picture for Lily. The child had to have some hope.

And, so do I, she reluctantly admitted to herself. So do I.

"Hurry up," Matt said as he impatiently gathered everyone together so they could leave the jail and head down the street. He'd slicked down his hair and brushed the snow off his hat. He figured that would have to be good enough for church. He'd missed having his second cup of coffee and he felt it. He should have known better than to go over to the saloon earlier when he got a call for help. How grown men could get so irate and tangled up in a poker game when they all agreed no one had been cheating, he did not know.

"Is the kitty safe at the saloon?" Lily asked quietly from where she stood hanging on to Eleanor.

"Don't worry about that cat," Matt advised. He realized he hadn't seen the beast over there. He had seen the white Persian female cat, but the tomcat had been absent. "Old Whiskey knows when to hide."

By the time Matt had walked across the street and into the thin-walled saloon, fists were flying and he was hard-pressed to know which was worse—the fired-up cursing or the thuds of punches hitting their mark in another man's stomach. The owner of the place was hiding behind the counter, no doubt mourning the loss of the dozen broken bottles on the shelf behind the bar. Several streams of brown liquid were dripping from that ledge onto the floor and the whole place smelled strongly of rotgut whiskey.

Matt had to threaten to lock every one of the men up to get their attention.

"Lock us up in the *jail*?" one of them whispered in the silence that followed Matt's pronouncement. The man held a spindly chair over his head, ready to bring it down on someone else. "With your Chic-ago mail-order bride?"

The man slowly lowered the chair to the floor and sat in it, still looking confused. "I've wanted to see her, but not looking like this."

"And those little kids?" the man who had just escaped being hit asked in astonishment. "That sweet baby girl that doesn't even talk much yet? The one that carries around her doll like it's a real, live infant?"

That man looked around and found himself a chair to sit on, too.

"Well, it is the jail," Matt answered. He noticed those two chairs were the only ones left unbroken. "It's not like there's doilies hanging off the bars."

"But it wouldn't be right," the first man protested self-righteously. "We don't look so good for company."

"You wouldn't *be* company," Matt protested. "You'd be prisoners."

"Still—" the man said.

A few groans told Matt that the others—the ones left awake and standing, anyway—agreed.

"No, it wouldn't be right," a third man said, shaking his head until he burped. The smell of sour whiskey filled the whole saloon.

"We were just loosening up ourselves," a fourth man said from where he lay on the floor, one of his eyes already starting to go purple and close shut. "We wouldn't dream of putting those kids out on the street in the cold."

"Good, because I wouldn't put them out," Matt countered.

"You mean, they'd be in there with us?" the man on the floor asked, horrified as he sat up and tried to comb back his hair with his fingers. "What if we cuss or something? Why, that ain't fitting."

"That's why you'd use the manners your mother taught you or you'd answer to me," Matt said calmly.

"Oh," the man on the floor said, his voice going deep and low, until it almost sounded like he was in pain.

Everyone was silent for a moment. Then all the men who had been standing sat down on the floor like they had been deflated.

"We'll stop fighting," the man who first spoke said humbly.

"We didn't mean anything by it anyway," the second man added.

Both of them smiled to show their sincerity.

Matt wasn't fooled. "I'll stop by after church to see that you're behaving."

A half dozen heads nodded eagerly.

Matt sighed and left as fast as he could. It was Sunday, after all, and he didn't want his family to be late for church, especially when the snow was starting to come down in earnest. It took only a few minutes to get everyone on the way to church. And now the sun was shining bright, although some of the windows in town still had lamps lit inside.

It felt good to have his family with him, Matt thought as he looked around as they all walked. He noticed that the shapes of the buildings didn't line up straight on the horizon. Some structures, like the saloon, were two stories and had false fronts painted in blues and greens. Others were one-story wood buildings with no color to them but that which nature gave. The wind blew slightly and walkways were slick with ice from the night before. The sky above was a dark gray that reminded him of Eleanor's eyes when she was upset.

Matt glanced down at her as she walked so straight beside him. Most women would be leaning away from the storm that was brewing, worried about their hats and the frigid air. But Eleanor seemed to face everything head-on, and that applied to unpleasant weather. Her hat was securely anchored, since she'd tied it to her head with a scarf, but the wind had loosened her upswept hair and a few tendrils trailed along her ivory neck. Her cheeks were red from the temperature and her eyes sparked with determination as she set each foot down on the walkway.

He realized suddenly that he wouldn't have put those brawling men in the same jailhouse as her anyway. What was a sheriff going to do without a jail? He needed to get Eleanor and the children moved into the upstairs of that bakery as soon as possible.

In the meantime, he needed to keep his wits about him. Having a woman like Eleanor by his side would cause a stir, walking into church. He needed to stay close by her this morning. It wasn't just the men in the saloon who would want a look at his bride. Most of the bachelors around would probably want a chance to persuade her to marry them instead of him.

Not many men would say anything directly in front of him; he knew that much. There were some benefits to wearing a badge. He reached down and patted his right hip where his gun usually rested. His hand came up empty. Like usual when he went to church, he had left his gun in the jail with Jacob. Matt glanced back and saw his niece and his nephew trailing him. He looked for Lily, thinking she would be with them. He did not see her at first. Finally, he saw she was clinging to Eleanor's other side and still having a hard time walking.

"That's quite a nice church," Eleanor murmured softly when they came in sight of the newly built structure. Her eyes looked up at him, approval shining in them.

Matt walked a little prouder. He was glad the suggestion to put a false front on the place had failed. A humble whitewash was better. "A town needs a good church if it's going to attract decent families."

As a single man, he'd often done his praying while he was tending the cattle at night. The dark sky often brought out his desire to pray. But he had to admit, he liked the thought of worshipping God with people around instead of cows. And, a family needed to be regular churchgoers if the children were going to avoid growing up with all of the rough edges he had in his life. He wondered how different things would be today if his family and the Blackwoods had gone to church together as they grew up.

Things would be better than they were now. He was sure of that. Matt had already decided to try to be a better example than his father had been, but after this morning, he figured he needed to work on it. He felt guilty for the sharp way he'd talked about that wildcat when all the poor thing wanted was to make his bed by the stove. And the way he'd added that bit about Lily.

Matt glanced down at the woman walking by his side. She'd turned to speak to Lily and mostly he saw the serviceable hat she wore. As he looked at the hat carefully, he noted that the short mauve feathers on the brim had been crushed at some point. She could use a new bonnet, and as he remembered, the trunk they'd brought on the train was mighty light. He doubted she had another dress except for the delightful yellow one she'd worn yesterday. If he was going to do better than his father, he would have to provide for her. He'd start with a couple more dresses. That should please her.

He didn't know much about Eleanor and Lily's life before they came here, but he sensed it hadn't been as easy as he'd first thought, for either of them. Still, he was beginning to worry about Lily. Eleanor seemed to do everything for the child. If that continued, how was Lily going to be able to stand on her own two feet? In the world they lived in now, it was important for everyone to take care of themselves. He'd made a mistake by helping Luke too much as they grew up. In the end, Luke resented it and had a hard time learning how to take care of himself. Matt had come to wonder if Luke and his wife might still be alive today if Matt had taught his brother how to fight a battle instead of doing it for him.

They had almost reached the front door of the church when Angus Wells rushed over to Matt.

"It's—ah," Angus stumbled over the words, but Matt sensed the man's discomfort.

"Excuse me," Matt said to Eleanor. Angus clearly had news he didn't want to share with an audience. "I'll join you in a minute or two." He motioned to the door. "There's a bench right inside where people take off their coats and scrape their boots clean. I'll meet you there."

Angus waited for Eleanor and the children to step into the building before he pulled the white paper out of his coat pocket. "I just got this from the Gunni woman in Chicago. She's on her way here. I got the telegram just before me and my wife started out for church."

"Well, that will please Eleanor," Matt said, feeling relieved. At least he'd done one thing right in her eyes. "There is no need to hide that kind of news."

"The problem is," Angus said, lowering his voice, "she thinks she saw this Otis fellow at the train station in Council Bluff, Iowa. She didn't know if he was coming this way, but she wanted to warn you."

"Oh," Matt said. That was not good news.

"She said she didn't think he saw her and he could have been going in a number of directions," Angus continued and then was silent for a minute. "Are you going to tell Eleanor? She should be warned so she can protect herself."

"I'll protect Eleanor," Matt said, already planning how he would do that. They needed to all move into the rooms above the bakery, whether he and she were married yet or not.

"How are you going to do that if you're out looking for those Blackwood boys?" Angus asked.

"I'll leave Jacob here for her and the children." He'd never planned to take the deputy with him when he went after the other men anyway. There was no point in them both getting shot. He'd have to suggest Jacob share that room with Henri.

Angus nodded. "And I'll keep an eye on who steps off the train. At least, as best as I can. At this time of year, a lot of people are wrapped up in scarves with their hats pulled low, so you can't see their faces." Angus thought a moment. "Don't suppose you have a photo of the man?"

Matt shook his head. "I expect Lily could draw you a pretty good picture of him though. She's gifted that way."

"Have her do that." Angus gave the telegram to Matt.

"It's cold enough today," Angus added as he shifted his feet and looked nervous. "I don't suppose you've heard we have a lady teacher coming to town?"

"Yeah, Henri mentioned it," Matt replied. "Sounds good."

"I—ah—I didn't know who she was until today," Angus stammered. "The missus and I don't have any children, so we didn't go to the meetings."

Matt could tell the man was having a hard time with the conversation, but he couldn't understand why. "I don't suppose it matters much who she is."

"She's a local woman," Angus said. "Sort of anyway. Hasn't lived here for some time, but folks know her—at least about her."

"Well, she can't have lived here all that long ago," Matt said. He supposed a family could have moved in during the years he'd been gone. "But it saves time to have a teacher who knows the area."

"So, you're all right with that?" Angus asked, sounding relieved.

"I don't know why not," Matt said as he looked up from the telegram and frowned at the darkening sky. The storm was going to get worse. He would have to move everyone to the bakery this afternoon. The jail was hard to heat in a bad storm. He'd talked to the town leaders about that, but they figured anyone foolish enough to land in jail shouldn't expect the luxury of a good fire.

Matt turned around and noticed that Angus had left. He shook his head and walked up the steps to the church. At least a blizzard and a new teacher would give folks something to talk about instead of his mail-order bride. He stood in the wide entryway to the church and stomped the snow off his boots. He noticed Eleanor talking to Mrs. Wells beside some of the wall pegs used for coats. On the other side of the room, Lily sat on the bench by herself.

Matt noticed at once that something was wrong. Lily's face was frozen in a defiant look that grew more determined as the seconds passed. He wasn't sure how it had happened, but that wild saloon cat was standing on the floor at her feet, looking ready to use its claws on someone. Two rough-looking boys, both of them older than Lily, were leaning over her, laughing in a mocking fashion. He wasn't sure what the boys had said, but he could tell by their posture that it hadn't been nice. Out of the corner of his eyes, he saw Eleanor turn and gasp. Matt moved faster and stepped closer.

Lily apparently hadn't seen Matt; she was intent on the boys. Her voice was fierce as she said, "My papa is going to teach me how to shoot a gun. Then you'll be sorry for what you said."

Matt felt his heart warm at her words.

"Ha!" the oldest of the boys said. "You're lying. You're a girl. You don't even have a gun."

"It's true," Lily maintained, her chin lifted stubbornly. "My papa is the sheriff here. He'll teach me good. He'll let me use one of his best guns and I'll hit you in the head for sure."

"Lily!" Eleanor's shocked voice came from behind Matt.

The girl's face blanched. "Well, in the knee, at

least." Lily looked up at her sister. "That should be okay, shouldn't it? Just a little bullet. They'd still be able to walk."

He could tell the boys were nervous by the way they edged away from Lily. Of course, they were also retreating from that cat, which had raised up and hissed at them. Lily reached down and put her hand on the feline's back, but it wasn't clear if she was restraining the animal or preparing to send him forth in her defense.

Matt decided it was time for him to introduce himself to those boys.

"Are you visiting church today?" Matt asked as he put a hand on each of the boys. Both of them turned and looked at Matt in horror as he gave a firm squeeze to their shoulders. He saw them take note of his badge.

"We weren't doing nothing," one of the boys finally found the nerve to say and then added quickly, "Sir— ah, I mean—Sheriff—ah, sir."

"You were, too, doing something," Lily corrected him indignantly. Her face was no longer pale. "You were saying mean things to me about—" Lily stopped and sputtered. Finally, she looked down. "It doesn't matter. It's nothing."

"See," the oldest boy said defiantly.

"I still think an apology is needed," Matt said. "Gentlemen don't make ladies cry."

"Ha!" the same boy said again. "She's no lady. She was going to shoot us."

Matt nodded. "All the more reason not to make her cry."

Both boys shrugged and looked a little sheepish.

"Sorry," they muttered in unison.

"You're not going to put us in jail, are you?" the youngest of the boys asked.

"Not this time," Matt said, realizing as they stood there that they looked a lot like he and his brother, Luke, would have appeared at their age. Ragged shirts hanging out of worn jeans. "You boys have someplace to eat dinner after church?"

They stood there a moment before slowly shaking their heads. "We don't have much at home, except for the last of a rabbit we got in a trap. Our bullets are gone, and Pa took off to go hunting in the mountains some months past. Said he was going to come back a rich man. We thought he was fooling about the riches, but we don't know what happened."

"And your mother?" Matt asked, filing the comment about riches away for future contemplation.

"She died last Christmas," the oldest muttered. "Had a bad fever."

"Oh," Lily's voice came out in a long breath, and then she reached out to touch the arm of each boy. "Why, you poor things. I know how you feel. I'm an orphan, too—except for my sister, of course. Well, we're both orphans, I guess."

Matt thought Lily was overdoing it. After all, they had him to take care of them. But those two boys were lapping up the sweetness in her voice like they'd never had a kind word spoken to them until now.

Well, and maybe they hadn't, Matt admitted. He knew how life was around here. Theirs wouldn't be the first story of a mother dying. Or of a father wandering off—whether hunting for gold or a new unencumbered life for himself. They would likely never know.

"At least you both had sense enough to come to the church here," Matt said to the boys. They looked a little startled, as though they had shown up intending to steal the offering or some such mischief. But he looked over and saw the expression on Eleanor's face and knew he wouldn't press those boys to confess their intentions. It was better for everyone if the story was that they had come seeking honest help.

"Maybe you can make an announcement after the service," Eleanor stepped over and said to Matt, soft enough that no one else could hear. "Someone would likely take them in."

"What's your names?" Matt asked. "And how old are you?"

"I'm Tom. I'm ten years old," the tallest one said and pointed his finger at his brother. "He's John. And he's eight years old."

"Pleased to meet you," Matt said as he held out his hand. The boys looked at him suspiciously, but finally they both shook hands with him. "You look like sturdy boys. Maybe someone needs help mucking out their stables or herding sheep. Would you like that?"

"For money?" the oldest boy asked, his face serious.

"I reckon a little of it," Matt answered. He'd pay them himself if necessary.

Each boy's face lit up, but before they could agree Eleanor spoke.

"They need to be in school—now that one is opening," she said crisply. "And they need to be better fed than they are now. No one should be working them to death."

"But we—" Tom started to say, until Matt took a step closer to Eleanor.

"Boys that age need to be doing something or they get into trouble," he said in a low voice that wouldn't carry to anyone but her. "Doesn't mean they can't go to school, too. Besides, everyone out here has to earn their way."

"Even if they can't?" Eleanor said, the tone in her voice suddenly sounding defeated.

Matt looked at her more closely, but she had already turned away from him and was walking back to Lily with her shoulders slumped. Eleanor was no longer the proud woman who had walked by his side into the church. He wondered what was wrong. But right then, someone rang a bell. That was the signal that church was about to begin. He'd have to talk with Eleanor after the service was over. Of course, they needed to talk to the pastor together then and make an arrangement to get married soon. Maybe the pastor would have some wisdom to share on how they could make their marriage work, even if it was likely going to be only a short one.

Matt looked down and saw that the boys were still standing there, uncertain of what to do.

"You'll have dinner with us after the service," Matt said as he put a hand on each back and guided them into the church in front of him. He truly wished someone had done the same for him and his brother years ago. If they had, he might know more about how to build a family now.

He noticed Eleanor ushered the boys into a pew before she motioned for Henri, Lily and then Sylvie, all in that order, to slide in beside the new boys. It took a mother to know that it would make Henri's eyes shine to be included with older boys, and Sylvie smile, grateful to be tucked in safe between Lily and Eleanor.

One thing he knew for sure, Matt thought, was that his family needed Eleanor. She was a natural mother. And, he told himself a little smugly, she would make a very sensible wife. He had chosen well. Everything was going to work out fine. And then he remembered she had felt the need to talk to an attorney before she'd marry him. There might be trouble ahead after all.

Chapter Eight

The walls of the sanctuary were made of raw pine boards, and a cross made of tree branches had been fashioned for the front. The air still smelled faintly of fresh-cut wood. A lanky minister paced in front of the congregation as he spoke, but Eleanor couldn't concentrate on what he said. She kept wishing she had directed the children differently. She had not intended to sit beside Matt. She clenched her purse in her hands, grateful for the contract she had inside it. He would not be pleased with that document. She felt like a traitor just sitting beside him.

She glanced over at him. He'd taken time to shave this morning and his jaw was set, as always, at a determined angle. He had a faint bruise around the eye closest to her, but that was the only hint that things did not always go his way. He was a force all on his own. And she had felt like weeping every time she saw how heartless he was when it came to anyone who couldn't take care of themselves. He had been independent all his life and likely did not understand how other people might have difficulties.

She knew Lily fell into the category of those who needed help. Not that her sister couldn't dress herself. But in a place like Dillon, she would always require assistance. She couldn't chop wood for the stove. She couldn't carry a bucket of water for any distance. She couldn't even manage the slippery walkway now that she didn't have her customized shoe.

But all of that did not mean that Lily did not have something to offer others. She was imaginative and good-hearted. That should count for something, even in a rough town like Dillon.

Suddenly, Eleanor heard the pastor's tone of voice change and she was brought back to the sermon. She'd already caught enough words to know the man was talking about the need for everyone to know the gospel. She agreed with that.

"Over the past year," he said, smiling, "my heart has been increasingly drawn to the plight of the dockworkers in San Francisco. Many of the Chinese men who load and unload ships there have never heard about the love of Jesus."

Eleanor remembered what the lawyer had told her.

"So that's why I have arranged to move there and set up a mission," the pastor announced.

Eleanor nodded and the short silence was broken by a chorus of gasps.

"But—" several people in the church exclaimed and then started to talk at once.

The pastor held up his hand. "I've arranged for a

couple of local men to do the preaching for you while you look for a new minister. I'm taking the train out of here in a few hours. I was going to wait a few days, but I heard another storm is coming and I didn't want to get snowed in. They are expecting me in San Francisco. I know you will pray for me as I accept the new call to preach there. I will write to let you know how the ministry is going."

Eleanor felt the pew sway slightly as Matt started to stand up. She glanced over and saw the shock on his face. He turned and looked at her. "He can't be going. We need him."

"I knew he was leaving," Eleanor said, "but it's too soon."

Matt was right. The pastor couldn't be heading out now. That left only today for the ceremony, and she hadn't even talked with Matt yet about her contract. She had thought she'd wait until tonight when the children were all sleeping and they could sit by the stove and have a civil conversation. Surely, he would understand if she had time to explain.

There was such a clamor in the church that the pastor must have decided to forego the ending prayer. He stepped down from the pulpit so he could respond to the questions of the people who were already standing and making their way to the front of the church.

"Come," Matt said as he reached for Eleanor's hand. "We've got to talk to him before he leaves."

Eleanor turned to admonish the children. Five pairs of excited eyes were focused on her. "Everyone is to stay here. We won't be long."

She had barely finished the command when Matt was tugging her along, pushing his way through the press of people surrounding the pastor. When they stopped, still some distance from the minister, she reached up to adjust her hat.

"Surely, he's a reasonable man," Eleanor leaned closer to Matt and murmured. "He'll stay a few more days if we ask him."

Matt raised his eyebrow as he glanced down at her. "This is blizzard season. He knows if he doesn't get out today, he might be stuck here for weeks."

"That will give me time to talk to you about—" Eleanor started and then stopped. Matt's back was to her by now, and several curious women were watching her. Two older ladies seemed the most intent. One was clearly a ranch woman, her gray hair pulled back under a faded cotton bonnet, tiny wrinkles showing on her tanned face. The other one wore a stylish black hat that had a row of delicate pink roses embroidered around its brim. Her face was clearly tended with creams and shade. Eleanor knew enough about hats to know that the one this lady wore had likely been made in a millinery shop in some large city. Her face was as lovely as her headwear, and she smiled at Eleanor, muttering something about welcoming her to Dillon. She looked familiar, but Eleanor hadn't met many townspeople yet. Maybe the woman had been on the train coming here and they had passed once in the aisle.

"What do you need to talk about?" Matt prodded her, and Eleanor realized she'd trailed off in her comment to him. He was now facing her, his back to the women, and Eleanor didn't think he would like to discuss their private business in front of an audience any more than she would.

"I'll tell you later," Eleanor said and turned to give a slight inclination of her head toward the woman with the black hat, since she had been standing the closest. But she and her companion were both gone, folded back into the crowd. The other women from farther back remained, however, and Matt followed the direction of her nod.

"Good morning, ladies," Matt said as he dipped his head like a gentleman and smiled at them.

"I hope you all have a good day," Eleanor said smoothly to the women as she took Matt's elbow and turned him slightly. She lowered her voice so only he could hear. "I have to discuss something with you before we talk to the pastor."

"Oh, there's an opening," Matt said. He was tall enough that he could see over the other people gathered around the pastor. "We'd better take it."

With that, he put his arm around her waist, tucked her close to his side and then pulled her through the small crowd.

The pastor smiled at them both as they slipped into a space next to him and exclaimed, "Ah, the mail-order bride and our sheriff. What can I do for you?"

"We need for you to tie the knot for us," Matt said quietly, obviously trying to keep as many others from hearing as possible. "When can we see you?"

"No time like the present," the pastor said heartily. "I'm invited over to the Wellses' home to eat after church, and I don't want to miss that. Mabel is one fine cook."

"Thanks. We'll wait outside for the others to leave," Matt said.

"Nonsense," the pastor said, his voice suddenly booming as he addressed his congregation. "Don't leave, folks. We've got us a wedding to celebrate."

"Right now?" Eleanor thought she'd faint. She turned to Matt. "But we haven't had time to talk."

"It'll have to wait," he said grimly as he glanced down at her. "We have to do this now—we'd be unmarried for months before a new preacher comes to town. The gossip would bury us alive. And the children deserve better."

"The children—" Eleanor managed to gasp as she tried to stretch her head high enough so she could see over to where she'd left them sitting.

"Don't worry," Matt said as he gave a piercing whistle and waved an arm for the five to come closer.

"But Lily can't—" Eleanor protested.

"She can if she wants to bad enough," Matt said. "She's going to have to learn how to take care of herself from now on."

"No," Eleanor said firmly. "That's what I wanted to talk to you about." She opened the drawstrings on her black velvet purse. "I have a contract."

"A what?" Matt asked. The chatter of the crowd had grown so loud she was sure he could barely hear her.

Just then a boy's voice rang out with a note of command. "Let us through."

Tom and John, one on each side of Lily, finished

helping her to the front. The girl was grinning. "I'm the flower girl."

"Yes, indeed." Eleanor bent down to her sister's level. "I'm afraid you'll have to toss imaginary roses though."

"I know this isn't the wedding you planned," Matt said before he turned to face the other people in the church. "Give us some quiet, please. The bride needs to catch her breath."

The church went silent. But Eleanor noticed that the expectation in the eyes of everyone around did not lessen.

"What I need to talk to you about is my contract," Eleanor whispered to Matt. "The one I had the lawyer write up."

"I thought Wayne would explain all of that to you," Matt said, irritation in his voice. "When we say the vows, we are married. The other part—" His face turned pink, but he persisted. "It's no one's business what happens in the privacy of our bedroom."

Eleanor heard the soft gasps behind her but wasn't brave enough to turn around.

"It's about obeying," she said, thinking this would stop the bedroom speculation. "I don't want to obey in all things."

"What?" Matt said as he looked down at her in confusion. "What kind of a wife won't obey?"

The chatter behind them increased. It seemed people didn't know whether to listen for more gossip or repeat what they'd just heard.

"Just not in all things," Eleanor repeated. She didn't

have the nerve to look behind her, so she glanced down at her sister's sweet face. Lily was standing between her and the pastor, looking up at her with anxiety on her face.

"You don't agree to obey?" the minister asked, sounding perplexed.

"No, I can't," Eleanor said and then added, "I mean no disrespect."

The minister nodded vaguely.

"I think Matt needs to sign the contract, too," Eleanor added hesitantly.

"We can do that later," Matt said stiffly.

Eleanor glanced down and saw Lily looked ever more distressed.

"It will be all right," Eleanor whispered to Lily, but Matt must have thought she was talking to him.

"I guess it has to be all right," he said, a little stiffly. "We've got to get married now, whether you want to obey me or not. People will come up with all kinds of stories about us if we don't get down to it."

"I can explain," Eleanor whispered.

"Later, maybe," Matt said. She thought his expression softened somewhat, but she wasn't sure. Then he continued, "All I know is that if I say duck, you better do it. Someone could be shooting at you and I wouldn't have time to convince you to obey me."

Eleanor had no idea how to respond to that. She certainly didn't expect to be shot.

"So, you're ready then?" the pastor inserted, smiling smoothly as though their conversation hadn't just attracted more attention than it should have. The man looked out past Eleanor and Matt to the small crowd gathered. "Quiet so I can begin."

Eleanor reached up to adjust her hat. When she finished, Matt squared his shoulders and reached over to take her hand. She realized with a start that they had never held hands before—at least, not apart from the times when he'd kissed her fingertips—and it was comforting.

"Wait," Matt said as he reached for his pocket. He pulled out her parents' locket and draped it around Eleanor's neck. She reached up to touch the smooth oval. She had forgotten and was grateful he'd remembered.

"Thank you."

"We're ready now," Matt said.

The pastor quietly cleared his throat before speaking.

"Dearly beloved, we are gathered together here in the sight of God—and in the face of this company—to join together this man and this woman in holy matrimony." He paused and looked at Eleanor.

"Name, please," he whispered.

"Eleanor Marie Fitzpatrick," she answered.

The pastor nodded. "Do you, Eleanor Marie Fitzpatrick, take this man to be your holy, wedded husband, to love, honor and—ah," he stumbled. "Well, I guess that is sufficient. Do you?"

"I do," Eleanor whispered and felt Matt squeeze her hand.

"She does," someone close behind Eleanor shouted out, and there was a cheer. Eleanor could even hear the sounds of a woman sobbing, but before she could turn and see who it was, the pastor turned to Matt.

"And, do you, Matthew—ah—middle name?" the pastor asked.

"Prinz," Matt whispered. "My middle name is Prinz. My mother's family."

"Prince!" The sweet, reverent voice sounded from Eleanor's elbow, and she looked down to see the glow on Lily's face as she repeated, "He's a prince."

Eleanor shook her head slightly in an attempt to stop her sister.

Lily pressed her lips together, but her eyes still danced joyfully.

"Z," Matt said curtly with a quick glance at them both. "Prinzzzzz. It's my mother's—"

The pastor decided to begin again. "Do you, Matthew Prinz Baynes, take this woman, Eleanor Marie Fitzpatrick, to be your lawfully wedded wife, to have and to hold, through sickness and health, until death do you part?"

There was a collective gasp from the crowd, and Eleanor flushed. She could tell from the reaction that everyone here knew exactly why Matt had sent off for a mail-order bride. He was preparing for his death. Suddenly, everything was silent except for the sounds of the lone woman who was still sobbing. Eleanor wondered if she should have asked the pastor to take that word out of their vows, too.

"I do," Matt said quickly.

The crowd seemed to give a sigh of relief right along with Eleanor. They had made it through, and here was Matt gazing down at her fondly as though their marriage was completely normal.

Contentment hung in the air for a few moments, and then a man somewhere yelled, "Sheriff, aren't you going to kiss the bride?"

"Oh," Eleanor said, startled.

Matt grinned and bent his head to whisper, "We have to give them what they want, don't we?"

Eleanor meant to protest, but Matt was already teasing her lips into silence. The softness of his kiss deepened as his arms circled around her and pulled her close. Eleanor knew the kiss was for the people standing there wishing them well, but she longed for something more private and lasting. She realized her heart was in jeopardy. She was falling in love with a man who was going to ride out of town any day now and get himself killed.

Eleanor pulled back, shaken from the kiss. She had to get her feelings under control. She had been left behind by her father as a young girl; her grandmother had rejected both her and Lily in the ways that counted. Eleanor refused to love someone that she knew was going to abandon her. Whether he was duty-bound to do so or not would not lessen her pain when he didn't come back. And besides that, she had to remember Lily. She couldn't trust him with her sister's future, and a real marriage would do that.

Slowly, Matt let her go a few inches. She stepped back for a wider gap. Then she glanced up and was startled to see the bewildered expression on his face.

The pastor cleared his throat. "We should head back to my office so we can sign your marriage papers."

"Wait," a woman's voice called out. Eleanor turned

to see the black hat weaving its way through the crowd. The older woman she'd seen earlier was coming forward.

"What?" Matt breathed the word out as though it was choking him. He could see more of the crowd than Eleanor could because he was taller. She wondered if someone had a gun or something. Would Matt tell her to duck? She'd certainly obey if he did.

"What's she doing here?" he finally muttered.

"She?" Eleanor asked in dread. Maybe the threat was some woman Matt had been involved with earlier. Maybe he was already married and the woman was coming to claim her husband. How much did she really know about this man?

Eleanor reached up to grab Matt's arm. She wasn't about to let him go.

"Who is she?" Eleanor demanded, knowing the woman was likely in front of them by now, but she was staying focused on Matt's face. If she saw a welcoming smile cross his lips, she'd—

"My mother," Matt whispered softly. "It's my mother."

"Oh," Eleanor gasped in astonishment as she let go of his arm so she could turn. "Your mother!"

"I told you I had one," Matt muttered.

There stood the woman in the black hat. No wonder the face looked familiar. She could see Matt's blue eyes, and something about the shape of the eyebrows was the same, too.

"I brought the family Bible for you to sign," the woman said sweetly as she held out the large book that they'd just seen at the family's ranch house. Matt had obviously forgotten to bring it back with them. "Your father and I signed it at the same time we filled out our marriage documents with the pastor who married us. It's tradition to do it then."

The woman was looking at Matt, but Eleanor guessed he was too shocked to reach out and take the offered book. That didn't seem to discourage his mother though. She only lifted it a little higher.

"You've grown some," Matt's mother said, and Eleanor stood closer to her husband since she heard a growl starting in his throat that reminded her of that wildcat when the beast thought someone was ready to shoo him away.

Lord, help us, Eleanor prayed, and for the first time in years, she forgot about the many times her prayers had languished without an answer. She was no longer keeping score. All she knew was that she needed God's assistance. And she needed it now. Matt looked capable of breaking the tenuous bond he had with his mother, and Eleanor knew that would be a mistake he would regret.

Matt managed to stop the word that had been climbing up his throat and demanding to be let out. Not that long ago, he would have uttered that word with no regrets. But he was standing in a church—and talking to his *mother*. He'd never thought to see her again, and yet here she was.

Finally, he managed to say something else. "You

would know how tall I am if you'd bothered to write me even one letter over the years."

The whole church had grown absolutely silent by then, but Matt barely noticed. He figured he had scant privacy in this town anyway.

"I didn't think you would answer me if I did write," his mother finally said, so soft he could barely hear her. "I heard you were very angry with me, and I couldn't blame you for it."

The misery on his mother's face stopped Matt cold. He didn't know what to say, but for some reason, his gaze moved to his new wife. Eleanor looked up at him with compassion in her eyes and inclined her head encouragingly.

"I was spitting mad," Matt admitted, turning back to his mother. "But I would have welcomed a letter. I worried about you. Wondering if you were alive—if you had enough to eat and a warm place to stay."

"I was fine," his mother told him, her voice stronger. "I got work in Denver. Of course, there wasn't much of a town there at first, but I took in laundry for the mine owners until a few families decided they needed a teacher for their children. Then I asked for that job."

Matt was startled by that revelation. "But what about Mr. Blackwood? What was he doing? Certainly, you shouldn't have had to work a washboard." That was hard labor, he thought indignantly. Even his father, with all the man's faults, would never have asked that of his mother.

She didn't answer him but looked over his shoulder

at someone who must have been standing there the whole time his mother had been talking to him.

Matt felt a growing unease and knew that something was wrong, but he was not able to see who his mother was so intent upon, and he hesitated to turn around. He feared he would see the man who had lured his mother away from her family all those years ago. He prepared himself for the sight but was shocked when he swiveled and the face greeting him was a younger version of what he expected.

"Ethan?" Matt asked in surprise. He had not seen the oldest of the Blackwood brothers in a decade, but he still recognized the way his eyebrows were in a perpetual arch and the dark hair on his head shaped itself into a downward arrow at the top of his forehead. All of the Blackwood boys had those same, intense features, but Ethan was the only one with eyes the color of a spring meadow.

"It's me, all right," the man said without much enthusiasm.

The facts tumbled through Matt's mind. He had known he would have to face the Blackwood brothers down, but he hadn't expected to meet up with one of them in church. Like always, he'd left his gun back at the jail with Jacob. He had a knife strapped to his ankle, but he had no way to grab that in a hurry.

"I'm not armed," he mentioned as casually as he could to the man in front of him.

An ironic smile flitted across Ethan's face.

Surely, he knew this was not the place for a fight anyway. There had to be forty people in the church right now, and any one of them could be hurt if Ethan started to fire bullets around.

"Don't worry," Ethan muttered. "I'm not hunting."

Matt could not afford to trust the other man on that, so he turned slightly until he could see Eleanor. "Take the children and go to the back of the church."

"I—" she started to protest. He willed her to obey.

"I'll do it for the children," she finally said softly as she reached for Lily, nudging the girl toward her and directing with a glance the two boys who had come up front with Lily. She then headed toward the opening Henri and Sylvie had found in the gathering and herded all of their children away from the confrontation.

Matt breathed easier once they had all disappeared into the crowd. She hadn't obeyed him, but at least she'd used good sense. He noticed that others had also taken the measure of the situation and stepped back.

"I heard you were looking for me and my brothers," Ethan said, laying it right out there.

Matt nodded. "I have some questions I want answered."

Ethan squared his shoulders.

By now, they were the only two standing at the front of the church. Even the pastor had put some distance between them and him.

"Your mother asked me to bring her here today," Ethan said. "Fact is, I brought her up from Denver some time ago. She's been staying with my mother out at the ranch."

Matt couldn't have been any more astonished than if Ethan had stood there and confessed to shooting down a dozen innocent people. "I don't remember your mother being that forgiving."

In fact, Mrs. Blackwood seemed to always have been yelling. Looking back, he supposed she was mostly chastising her own boys, but her voice was strong enough to make any child within hearing distance cower. He and Luke took pains to avoid her when possible.

"Things aren't always as they seem," Ethan said quietly.

"Tell me how they are, then," Matt said, annoyed that this Blackwood boy didn't seem at all worried about what Matt would do. Of course, Ethan had always been the cool one of the brothers. According to Luke's letters, the twins were the ones who usually charged into trouble, dragging the three middle boys with them. Come to think of it, Luke had mentioned the Blackwood brothers a fair amount in his letters.

Ethan gave a scant smile. "My father didn't exactly run away with your mother like we all thought back then. He was sick—dying, really—and she drove him down to the doctor at Fort Hall in Idaho. Turns out my father had asked my mother to do it and she refused. She said she didn't believe anything was wrong with him. Thought he was making up the stomach pains."

"Well, why didn't my mother say what she was doing?" Matt demanded. "People would have understood. She should have left a note, at least."

"She says she did," Ethan said and then continued, "I don't think she knew how long the trip would take. Anyway, she got him there and stayed with him until

he died. By that time, over a month had gone by." He
paused. "Remember when you took me and my brothers out hunting and we were gone all day, looking for
a herd of antelope?"

"Of course."

"Well, it seems your mother came back that day to
tell my mother that my father had died," Ethan said.
"My mother never told us boys until a few months ago.
Said she was ashamed she hadn't believed him when he
said he was sick. Apparently, your mother went back
to your place and your father told her to leave. Said he
didn't want her after she'd spent a month with another
man. Never mind that my father was in no shape to be
a threat to any woman's virtue on that trip."

Matt stood there for a long minute. "My father did
that?"

Ethan nodded. "I figured he hadn't said any more
to you than my mother had to us boys."

"And my mother just drove away," Matt finished the
story. "Not even bothering to write."

"She said she wrote a couple of letters at first," Ethan
said. "Then she gave up. Figured you were all mad at
her."

Matt turned to look for his mother and noticed she
was gone. Only a few hearty churchgoers remained at
the back of the room. His eyes roamed over them until
he found who he was looking for. The mauve figure
sitting in the corner was Eleanor. She seemed to shrink
back into the pew when he saw her.

He frowned as he walked over to his wife. "You
heard all that?"

"Most of it," she said hesitantly. "I sent the children out with Mrs. Wells. I wasn't sure you'd want them to hear—"

"Nothing is like I thought," Matt admitted as he stood there. "At least you've been honest with me."

Eleanor flinched and her face flashed from pale white to blushing pink, right before his eyes. Then he saw a resolve come over her.

"I didn't write the letter," she burst out, the words tumbling over each other. "The letter you got at first, answering your ad. That wasn't me."

Matt felt a headache coming on, so he sat down. "I think you better tell me the whole of it."

"I didn't want to get married," Eleanor said, talking fast as though she was determined to get it all said. "I would never have answered your ad. Mrs. Gunni and Lily were the ones who wrote to you."

"You don't want to get married?" he asked, grasping the most important thing she'd said.

"I didn't then," Eleanor said. "But now, I—"

"It's too late," Matt said suddenly, even though he knew it wasn't. They hadn't signed the papers. But he wasn't going to let her leave. "We just said our vows."

She cleared her throat. "What I was going to say was that now I feel differently."

"Enough to stay married?" Matt asked, surprising himself at how much he cared about her answer.

"Yes," she said. "Enough to carry out our agreement."

"Oh," Matt said. He felt like he'd been punched in the gut. Of course—their agreement—she expected in a few months that she'd be a widow and not have to worry about being a wife.

Then he heard the sound of a man clearing his throat and looked up to see Angus Wells standing there looking shy.

"I've come to invite you to eat with us today," Angus said. "We have asked the pastor over and a few other folks. Mabel put a big beef roast into the oven this morning. She's got potatoes, green beans and corn bread to go with it. That and two thick apple pies."

"Oh, but there's so many of us," Eleanor stood and protested slightly. "Are you sure?"

"Mabel sent me, and she knows how many there are of you," Angus said. "She was counting on them two boys, too."

Matt saw Eleanor standing there in indecision. She clearly wanted to go but looked at him as though he would deny her something as simple as a friendly meal.

He managed a wry smile. "If we go back to the jailhouse, it's eggs and bacon again. Once in a while, we have some red beans, but we don't do much real cooking there. The stove's not up to it."

"Mabel's a good cook," Angus assured her. "And she'll count it a party since you just got married."

Matt watched as Eleanor relaxed and finally nodded at him.

"We are pleased to accept your invitation," Matt said to Angus. "We have to sign our marriage documents first—and the family Bible—but we'll be there as soon as we can."

Matt was aware of Eleanor as she sat back down next to him on the pew.

Angus nodded to them both and announced as he was turning, "Mabel invited your mother, too, since she's the new schoolteacher. Be good for the children to get acquainted with her."

Matt opened his mouth and then closed it again. He had nothing to say about his mother. Not until he thought through all Ethan had told him. In the meantime, he offered an elbow to Eleanor so they could stand.

"Shall we gather up the children, Mrs. Baynes?" he asked her in a whisper. "They should see us signing all those documents. I'll go find my mother and retrieve that Baynes family Bible so we can make it official."

Eleanor nodded as they both stood. Matt kept them standing where they were for a minute.

"I'm willing to sign whatever legal document Wayne drew up for you as well as everything else," he said. "I just want to be sure we're well and truly married."

He never wanted to strike a black line through their wedding registry in the Baynes family Bible, like his father had done when his mother left. "We have to consider that I might not die. Are you good with being married a long time, then?"

"I would certainly never want anyone to die," Eleanor retorted in convincing tones and then fluffed up her hair suddenly, like a mother hen would her feathers if any chicks were threatened.

It wasn't the answer Matt wanted and he was uncertain what it meant. But they were standing so close that he just naturally reached up and traced her cheek. Her skin was soft as one of those feathers he'd imagined. And he could feel the tremble that went through her at his touch.

She was not indifferent to him, then, Matt thought with more satisfaction than was probably wise.

"We better be quick about the signings," Eleanor said then in a breathless voice, stepping away slightly. "The pastor is in a hurry."

"It won't take us long," Matt assured her. He was already seeking the clergyman. He did not know how Eleanor thought. But then, of course, he had not known her long. Maybe he just needed to refuse to look beyond today.

"There's your mother," Eleanor whispered as she nodded her head to the left. He could see that black hat. And he noticed his mother was dabbing at her eyes with a lace handkerchief that had a rose embroidered in the corner.

He gave an inward sigh as he walked in that direction. He had never intended to make any woman cry and that included his mother. He glanced back at Eleanor. Regardless of her ultimate plan, at least she wasn't outwardly weeping at this wedding.

He studied her more closely. She didn't even look distressed. What she seemed was jittery. Like she wasn't quite sure what to do. He could live with that, he decided. After all, he wasn't sure what to do either.

Chapter Nine

Eleanor was seated just left of her new husband at the Wellses' cloth-draped kitchen table. Mabel Wells had announced before they sat down that her dining table was a place for harmony. Then she lit the kerosene lantern that hung over it.

In that warm glow, peace did seem possible. Eleanor noticed how quiet Matt's mother was as she sat across from them. Sylvie's chair was pulled close to the older woman. Through most of the meal, the young girl sat there with wide eyes, clutching her doll and staring at her grandmother with the same fascination that she had previously reserved solely for her precious Dolly. Eleanor wasn't sure if that was good or bad, not when Matt seemed to hold himself aloof from the woman. But then, perhaps he was just striving to obey Mrs. Wells's request. Difficult questions could wait.

"More apple pie anyone?" Mabel Wells offered graciously as she held the last of the second tin up. Everyone had already had a piece, and the two boys, Tom and John, had already accepted pieces twice.

"I couldn't eat another bite," Matt said to her. "I don't know when I've last had such a good meal."

Mabel's face flushed with pleasure and she smiled at them all. "You'll remember I have a standing offer with the jail to prepare any last meals needed for the prisoners."

Eleanor gasped. What kind of prisoners did they have that needed a traditional last meal?

"She means the prisoners that are being set free," Matt said quickly, obviously understanding the turn her mind had taken. "We send any serious criminals down to the territorial prison near Fort Boise on the Snake River. We haven't had any of those lately. And Dillon has a policy that prisoners who have been in our jail for three days or more get a special last meal before they are released. And it's all thanks to Mabel. Most lock-ups don't last any longer than the three days."

Eleanor nodded in relief to their hostess. "I understand. That's very kind of you."

"A bit of simple kindness like that can make a man turn his life around," the minister added as he forked up the last of his pie. "And Mabel puts out a feast for them—especially the ones who don't have family around."

"I want to do it," Mrs. Wells said. "I tell myself maybe someone is doing the same for my son somewhere out there." She looked over at her husband. "We pray for our Phillip every day and ask the good Lord to look out for him. But I sure wish that our boy would let us know where he is."

Angus nodded. "We miss him. It's been nigh on ten years now since he left." He glanced at his wife. "And my missus has gotten quite the reputation for her last-day meals. Over the years, the deputies have told me that there are men who ask to stay the third night just so they can earn one of her special suppers."

"That's so thoughtful." Eleanor was touched at what this couple were doing for their community.

"We haven't had much crime—not since the children and I have been here anyway," Matt added.

Angus nodded. "The whole town has been on its best behavior for the sake of the little ones."

"It sure makes my job easier not to have to keep prisoners right now," Matt said. "It wouldn't be suitable with the children there."

Eleanor looked over and could see Matt's mother frowning.

"It's not suitable for you, either, to be subject to that kind of a rough element," Rose Baynes finally said to Matt. "I don't think I like you being the sheriff."

Eleanor scrambled to think of something to say to take the tension out of Matt's face, but she couldn't. Not even when she could clearly see the muscle along his jaw tense up. Mabel was right to not allow dissent at the table.

"Being a sheriff is good, honest work," Matt finally said, obviously struggling to keep his voice even. "We can't all be gentlemen scholars wearing a suit every day and drinking tea with our bankers. As much as you wanted that for me, it was never the life I chose—not that you stayed around long enough to know what I was going to do with my life anyway."

Everyone was silent for a minute.

"I'm sorry," his mother finally said quietly. "Of course you need to live the life you choose. I had just hoped—" She didn't finish her thought, but Eleanor figured everyone knew what she meant. The woman had hoped for more success for her oldest son.

"It takes a strong man to be a good sheriff," Eleanor said, defending Matt. It was true, too. Not many men would risk their lives to go after outlaws. Even the last sheriff had left when the job became difficult.

No one said anything after that, but Matt reached over and took hold of Eleanor's hand—the one she had lying in her lap. He curled his fingers around it and gave a squeeze. He did not look at her and she appreciated it. She liked that he held her hand in private, with no one being the wiser.

"No point in letting this pie go to waste," Mabel said then with some forced cheer in her voice as she looked at Tom and John. "You boys look like you could each use another piece."

"Yes, ma'am," they said in eager unison.

Mabel turned to Matt's mother then and smiled gently. "I wanted our son to be a clerk in a general store. His uncle owned the place and we figured he might someday be able to buy it. Then he'd be secure. He didn't want that, though, and we had a fierce fight about it and he left." She stopped as though the recounting pained her. "Now I don't know where he is or even if he's alive. I should have just let him make his own choice."

"I'm sure he's all right," Eleanor said encouragingly as she reached across the table to pat the older woman's hand.

Mabel blinked back some tears but nodded. "I have to trust that he is."

Everyone sat there for a few minutes, and finally, the minister said he needed to see about catching that train. Matt added that it was time for his family to leave, too, since they needed to move everyone into the rooms over the bakery.

"I took the reverend's trunk down to the train station before church," Angus said, and then he turned to Matt. "But we better get to moving your things before the storm hits. The wind goes through that jail until you like to freeze to death in there. I've seen a few times when enough snow blew in to turn the floors white."

"Oh." Lily sighed and then said softly from her place near the end of the table, "Those poor prisoners."

"Well, crime doesn't pay." Matt met the eyes of every child at the table. "You all need to remember that. Jails aren't meant to be comfortable."

Eleanor thought John flinched like he might have contemplated doing something he shouldn't have. But his older brother, Tom, said, "Yes, sir," as he nudged his younger brother to give a mumbled agreement.

"Ach, but you are good boys," Mrs. Wells said to their apparent astonishment. "I can tell that already. You won't end up in any old jail."

Eleanor bit her lip and didn't say anything. She could

tell the older woman was giving those young boys encouragement to live up to her expectations.

"Seems to me that the lady is right," Matt added his voice to Mabel's. "You both have what it takes to be good men."

The brothers sat up straighter in their chairs.

"Maybe even what it takes to be princes," Lily added in her sweet voice with a sweeping gesture of her hands.

The boys looked alarmed at that prediction until everyone chuckled.

"Well, you do have choices," Mabel announced. "Doesn't hurt to at least be a gentleman."

Before long, everyone was bundled up and ready to open the door. They knew they'd face cold winds as soon as they stepped outside the Wellses' home.

Eleanor touched Matt's arm and drew him aside.

"Your mother shouldn't be driving out in this kind of weather." Eleanor already knew the one decent hotel in Dillon was full for the week. Men were always welcome to bed down on the floor of the saloon after it closed—or pay for a room upstairs—but that would hardly do for Matt's mother.

"I thought Ethan would be waiting to take her back," Matt said and then turned to his mother. "Are you meeting Ethan?"

She shook her head. "I told him to take Mrs. Blackwood home after church. I plan to rent a buggy from the livery. I can certainly drive myself out to their ranch."

"Not if it storms," Matt said, a scowl settling on his face. His chin was angled in what Eleanor could only conclude was stubbornness.

"There's no snow yet," Mrs. Baynes replied. Her chin mirrored Matt's by now. "I have no intention of spending a night in that jail of yours."

They glared at each other.

"Of course you won't do that," Eleanor said to Matt's mother as she stepped forward. "You'll stay with us."

"What?" the older woman exclaimed.

"What?" Matt echoed a second later.

"We have room," Eleanor assured them both. "Mrs. Baynes can have one of the beds in the girls' room. We'll make up a place for Sylvie to sleep on the divan. And Lily and I will share the other bed—"

"What?" Matt's mother objected, sounding astonished.

"What?" his protest followed like before.

"But you can't sleep with me," Lily leaned closer and said as though something was terribly wrong. "You're married. You have to sleep with your husband. That's the way it works. That's how you know it's True Love."

"Ah," Eleanor said as she knelt down to her sister's level. "True Love is in the heart. We'll talk about it later. But it's fine for us to keep sharing a bed for now. We're sisters. That's True Love, too."

Lily continued to look skeptical.

Eleanor glanced over and met Matt's gaze. The next thing she knew he was bending most properly toward her and offering her his hand to help her rise.

"Thank you," she said as she took his outstretched hand and let him pull her upright.

"My pleasure," Matt murmured softly as he then dipped his head farther and gave her a perfect gentleman's kiss on the top of her hand. She didn't have her gloves on yet and she felt the impression of his warm lips all of the way down to her toes.

"Ahhh," Lily gave a delighted sigh. "He's a Prinzzzz."

Matt chuckled and Eleanor smiled. It was clear Lily's world was righted once again.

"He is that," Mrs. Baynes added in a crisp, proud voice. "Takes after my side of the family, he does."

Eleanor noticed the two boys, Tom and John, standing there with their mouths open and their eyes horrified.

"We won't have to do that, will we?" the oldest brother asked. "The kissing thing."

"No," Eleanor assured him.

"Only princes do it," Lily said self-righteously, adding her bit of knowledge to the conversation. "Not little boys."

Eleanor saw the younger brother, John, frown at that, as though he couldn't decide if he should be insulted or relieved.

Matt settled it for all of them when he announced, "Time to check that everything is buttoned up and gloves are on. We're going out into the cold."

There was a scramble to obey. Then Eleanor and Lily trailed at the end of the line as Matt led their family down the boardwalk to the jailhouse. The man should have been a general, Eleanor thought. The boys just naturally followed him. She glanced down at Lily. She was becoming more adept at moving along beside her. Her sister still needed to lean on Eleanor, but Lily seemed to have more strength on her own.

It reminded Eleanor that she still had to talk to Matt about the contract hiding in her purse. She wanted to do it in private, though, and with all of the moving that needed to happen, it might not be today. She was already regretting that his Sunday was disturbed when he had so much on his mind.

She bit her lip in worry. She wondered if he was thinking about the Blackwood brothers.

Matt never would have thought he would spend his wedding day carrying trunks up and down stairs and sweeping floors. And, after a couple of hours scrubbing ovens and moving flour bins, he would have been horrified if he had known he'd later spend the only wedding night he was likely to have alone in a big bed that smelled faintly of lemon. Eleanor had graced the four-poster with sheets from the trunk she'd brought from her grandmother's house. There were even two pillowcases that she'd embroidered. He decided it truly was a bridal bed—or would have been if the bride had chosen to join him.

He smiled at his wit, but he knew Eleanor was right. It didn't make for restful sleep though. He tossed and turned for a couple of hours before he realized he was never going to doze off. Finally, when the night was so dark that he guessed it must be midnight, he got up and looked out the window of the room. The whole town of Dillon should be locked down by now. A faint light shone from inside the saloon though. And he thought he heard sound coming from that direction. It might be wind rattling some shutters or it could be trouble.

Since he wasn't getting any sleep, Matt figured he might as well check on the town. He got dressed, shrugged into his sheepskin coat and pressed his hat down on his head. He buckled on his guns, then gathered up his boots and slung them over his shoulder. He'd wait to pull those on when he got downstairs in the bakery. There was no sense waking anyone up when he left.

He silently made his way down the inside steps until he reached the first floor. He leaned against the counter while he pulled his boots on and then walked over to open the door before stepping outside. The air was heavy, but there had been no snow. It felt like a blizzard was still coming though. A man who worked cattle as much as he had could always tell when a storm was rolling in. There was a certain jumpiness right under a man's skin.

He made his way down the boardwalk and the only sound he heard was the crunch of his footsteps on snow that had become crusted when the bit of a thaw they'd had was followed by freezing temperatures.

When he got to the saloon, he listened for sounds of trouble. There were none, but he pushed the door open anyway. He didn't think the owner ever locked the place; he probably didn't even have a key. Once inside, Matt stood there and looked around. The lamp that was sitting on the bar was turned down low. Most of the large room was in shadows. He could see dark shapes where men were curled up in wool blankets and lying against the outer walls. One or two of them were snoring.

His only welcome was a low hiss from the throat of that tomcat. The beast appeared to be slinking around the edge of the bar, no doubt coming out to see who had disturbed his rest. He was a better guard dog than a cat had any right to be.

"It's okay, Whiskey," Matt whispered.

The tom clearly didn't take his word for it and kept coming.

"Somebody need a shot of whiskey?" a sleepy question came from behind the counter, and before long, Matt saw the bartender pull himself up and squint out into the darkness.

"That you, Sheriff?" the man said a little louder. Then he straightened fully and slapped his hand down on the wooden counter in front of him. A few glasses rattled and the man bellowed, "What in tarnation are you doing here? On your wedding night?"

"I'm doing my rounds around the town," Matt said, keeping his voice low so as to not wake anyone else. "It's my job, you know."

"Not on your wedding night, it's not," a second protest came from the corner of the room where a blanket was rolling around with a substantial man inside it. That someone sat up. Matt recognized the shepherd who ran a small herd out by the Blackwood place.

"Who's tending your sheep?" Matt asked the man.

"My sheep are bedded down in a safe place," the man retorted. "Which is more than I can say for you. So, where's that bride of yours? It's not good to leave a bride alone on her wedding night. She might take offense."

Matt looked around and saw that a half dozen men were waking up and staring at him. Their hair was wild and their eyes full of curiosity.

"Don't tell me she kicked you out of the house already?" a querulous voice finally asked.

Before Matt could defend himself, another man responded as he sat up from his place on the floor and stretched his arms.

"I certainly wouldn't be standing here in the saloon, waking up innocent men from their sleep, if I had a new wife at home on a night like this," he said, clearly disgruntled.

"He ain't got himself a home," someone else offered. "He lives in that jailhouse, remember? Maybe that's the problem. He can't be too cozy with his new wife in a place like that. Not with Jacob there."

"And the children," another man said. "That wouldn't be fitting."

"My mother is with us, too," Matt added before he could think of whether it was wise to encourage them or not.

By that time, the bartender had turned the lamp up and muttered, "I better put some coffee on."

No one spoke for a minute, but Matt knew the conversation wasn't over. "I moved my family into the rooms above the bakery this afternoon," he finally added. "Not that it's anybody's business."

The bartender gave a long, low whistle as though

he'd just understood what Matt said. "You mean, your mother's there, too?"

Matt nodded. "Haven't seen her since I was twelve years old."

"That's why you're here, then." The bartender nodded like it finally made sense to him. "I would be here, too, if I was in your shoes."

"And I am the sheriff," Matt said, trying to lighten the conversation. He didn't want these men to feel sorry for him. "I'm responsible to check and see if anything is happening in Dillon. I do that all the time. Nothing different about tonight."

"Well, you're always welcome here," the bartender said as he gave the men a warning look. "Isn't that right?"

"That sure is," the shepherd said as he stood up and patted Matt on the back. "We men need to stick together. Women shouldn't tell us what to do."

"No one has actually told me anything," Matt said in the interest of fairness.

"I heard your bride wants to wear the pants though," a grizzled old man offered. "She doesn't want to obey. What's the world coming to when a wife won't obey her husband?"

"You ever been married?" Matt asked the old man after he finished speaking.

The man nodded his shaggy head.

Several of the other men looked at the old one and nodded their heads, too.

"The wives never have obeyed," one of the men finally said. "If you'd been married, you'd know that."

Everyone was silent for a minute.

"Not that they announce the fact that they won't obey in front of the whole church at their very own weddings," the man continued. "My wife sure didn't. Someone should give them all a talking-to—that's what I think. Wives need to know their place."

Matt didn't like the way the men in general were scowling, so he added. "I'm going to teach my wife how to shoot a gun."

He heard a collective gasp.

"When?" the bartender asked.

"Soon as she wakes up and has breakfast," Matt announced.

He could tell the men would walk respectful around her after this, even if he was gone looking for the Blackwood brothers.

The questions had come to an end, and it appeared as though the bartender had forgotten about his offer to make coffee. Most of the men were lying down with their bedrolls now anyway. He didn't even want to know where their wives were. He hadn't realized any of them were married. They'd probably left home in search of riches and didn't want to go back empty-handed.

"I can lend you a blanket," a man offered suddenly. "I have me an extra one."

"We don't even allow mothers in here," another one assured him.

"I'm obliged," Matt said. "And my mother's not so bad. She's just—"

The shepherd put up a hand. "No need to explain. We all have mothers, too."

Matt nodded as he took his borrowed blanket and wrapped it around him until he was trussed up tight. He doubted he would sleep for more than an hour or so. He noted right off that there were no womanly smells in this place. Sour whiskey and old men. That's all his nose identified. That is, until that tomcat came up and stared straight at him. That beast smelled like wet fur.

Matt turned his back to Whiskey and faced the wall. He and the cat would take up their battle on another day. At the moment, all he could think of was that empty bed upstairs at the bakery and his new wife, Eleanor. He went to sleep with a smile on his face. She sure was something.

Chapter Ten

Eleanor had her hands filled with dough as she looked out the bakery kitchen window and watched the pink start to wear off the morning's sunrise. She'd woken up early—aching in every part of her body, obviously due to yesterday's move—but she felt too excited to lie abed until the others were up. She didn't want to consider that her enthusiasm for the day was partly due to her wedding, although she'd lain awake most of last night thinking about the unnaturally fast ceremony.

She wished now that she'd had more time to spin her vows out so they hadn't sounded so abrupt—especially the part about refusing to obey her husband. The minister had said it was enough for the ceremony to be official, and they had signed all of the documents, but she wasn't sure if they were really tied to each other. She wondered if she should try to see the attorney again and ask him, although she knew Matt would not like that.

She couldn't help but note this morning when she first stepped out into the parlor that the door to the big bedroom was closed—which must indicate Matt was still sleeping—which had to mean he had no troubling questions keeping him awake.

And if he was that calm about the wedding, she would be, too, she decided. Besides, all of those tumultuous feelings from last night could have been because she was getting ready to open the bakery. That was nerve-racking, also. She'd do no business today, but she was preparing enough to become familiar with the ovens and the routine she planned. Currently, she had six loaves of French bread rising on the counter and she'd soon finish this bowl of shortbread dough and would set it to chill so she could cut it into squares while the bread was baking. She'd already slipped a coffee cake into the oven a half hour earlier to test the ovens. She'd heard the main door open while she was in the kitchen so Matt must have slipped outside.

And that was just the beginning. Before the morning was over, she planned to make a batch of croissants, another six loaves of French bread and dozens of apple fritters. She would make the fritters small so she could take them over to the saloon and offer them as free samples. Men seemed to love those fritters, and she figured that single men would be good customers when her bakery opened tomorrow.

Eleanor was feeling pleased with herself for making some business plans when there was an awful pounding on the door of the bakery.

"Goodness," she gasped as she tugged her apron off and rushed toward the sound. Someone must need something urgently.

She had rounded the main counter when she saw through the big square window that a buggy and team were hitched to the post out front. She opened the door and was surprised.

"Ethan!" she exclaimed. The old neighbor of Matt's was there, looking cold and distraught. She stepped aside so he could enter. "Please, come in. No point in standing out there freezing."

The man entered and swept his hat off. "Sorry, but I think something has happened to Mrs. Baynes."

"Matt's mother?" Eleanor asked, and when he nodded, said, "But that can't be. She's sleeping upstairs."

Ethan looked stunned. "Matt knows about that? I never expected her to be with you. I figured she had taken a wrong turn coming back to our ranch and was lying in some ditch along the way. Only I didn't see her on my way here. I stopped to see if Matt would help me search. I wasn't sure he would, but I thought he should know she didn't get to the ranch last night."

"I'm sorry. We should have sent word," Eleanor murmured. "Matt didn't think it was safe for her to drive out by the time we finished eating yesterday. She sat with Sylvie and Lily while the rest of us moved into our quarters on the second floor here."

"Well, he was right about the storm," Ethan said, calming down. "It hasn't snowed much yet, but it's getting cold and it could start any minute. I'm just glad she's somewhere warm."

"Probably too warm," Eleanor said with a smile. "I tucked Sylvie in bed with her this morning. Mrs.

Baynes wanted to cuddle the girl. I'm sure they are both very toasty by now."

"Mrs. Baynes would like that," Ethan said. "She's wanted to be closer to her grandchildren ever since she got here a week ago. The only reason she didn't speak to Matt earlier was because she was nervous about his reaction and didn't want him to poison the children's minds against her."

"Oh, he'd never," Eleanor protested and then remembered her manners. "Matt might be angry, but he's a fair-minded man. Please have a seat."

Ethan nodded, but made no effort to sit down. "I told her that."

Eleanor motioned again. "We have perfectly good chairs and even a table."

"You're right. I could use some time to thaw out," Ethan agreed as he sat down. "Something sure smells good."

"That's the cinnamon coffee cake," Eleanor informed him as she turned toward the kitchen. "It's ready to come out of the oven. I'll cut a piece for you, too. I always have mine with a cup of tea—if you'd like some? Or I could make up some coffee—I know that's what Matt would prefer."

Eleanor waited.

"I don't want you to go to any extra trouble," Ethan finally said. "I'll be happy with a cup of tea, since that's what you're drinking."

"I have sugar and some lemon juice. Would you like either with your tea?" Eleanor asked.

"Just plain is fine," Ethan answered. "I'm not much for fancy food."

Eleanor smiled. Matt was right that the men around here were conservative in their tastes. "You're sure you don't want coffee? It won't take but a few minutes to make some."

Ethan shook his head. "It'll do me good to try something new."

"I'll be right back with tea and cake, then," Eleanor said, already continuing back to the kitchen. She looked back after she walked around the counter. "Please, find a table and draw up a chair. The front window makes a good place to sit."

When she came back from the kitchen, she had a tray displaying tea served in her parents' French cup-and-saucer sets and two small plates, each with a slice of coffee cake. Ethan appeared to have settled into his chair comfortably and was basking in the sunlight. He'd set his hat on the chair beside him.

Eleanor set a cup of tea in front of Ethan and a plate with coffee cake beside his right hand. Everything was very properly placed. It wasn't until she'd sat down that she noticed several rumpled, unshaven men were staring through the window at them.

"They must smell the coffee cake," Eleanor muttered as she lifted her cup. "I know it's been some time since anything came out of this bakery."

But as she turned and looked more closely at the faces outside, she decided it wasn't surprise that she saw. In fact, it looked like dawning horror. And they were all staring at Ethan.

246 Montana Mail-Order Bride

"It's me drinking tea," Ethan said calmly when he apparently noticed her puzzlement. He held his cup aloft and saluted his audience. "And doing so out of this precious china cup."

Eleanor saw at once by the reaction of the men outside that he was correct. "Matt was right. He told me that people here wouldn't want tea, even though this is hardly a luxury blend. It doesn't have rose hips or orange peel or even mint. I put in a little lemon flavoring, but that is hardly noticeable."

Ethan finished taking a long sip of the tea. "It's surprisingly good."

"You think so?" Eleanor asked eagerly. "It's what I plan to serve when I open up for business. I figure the ladies would enjoy a cup of good tea with a pastry in the morning."

Ethan set down his cup and arched an eyebrow. "The ladies in Dillon who can afford to pay for tea and pastries likely don't come out much in the morning."

"Matt explained all of that," Eleanor said firmly. "I plan to serve everyone in my establishment, saloon girls, too, and they can come in the afternoon if that suits them better."

This time, when Ethan lifted his teacup, he saluted her.

"Spoken like a forward-thinking woman, Mrs. Baynes," he said.

"Oh," Eleanor gasped and then sat back in her chair. "You are the first person to call me Mrs. Baynes."

"Congratulations, then, on the wedding," Ethan added.

Eleanor stared at him. He'd been the first to say that to her, too. Then she realized it was probably because he didn't know. "Matt doesn't expect the marriage to last long. Not when he feels duty bound to go after your brothers."

Ethan set his teacup down gently on the saucer. "I've heard he plans to do that. But he's wrong. My brothers weren't even in the area when Luke and his wife were gunned down."

"How do you know?" she asked, hoping he could know.

"I was there that day," Ethan said. "I was riding over to tell Luke his mother was out at our place. I didn't want to just take her there with no warning to him. I didn't see the men shoot Luke and Adeline, but I heard the shots before I got to the top of the rise. By the time I spotted those men they were running toward that old mine. There were two bodies beside the house and I knew those men were responsible. I fired a shot at the one in the lead, hoping to wing him. I saw him flinch, so I think my bullet did some damage, but before I knew it, they were racing to their horses, and then they were gone."

"And you told no one?" Eleanor asked.

"I didn't recognize the men, and that's what I told the sheriff who was here at the time," Ethan said. "I didn't know Matt took the job until recently."

Eleanor searched his face for the truth, but she wasn't sure. "If they killed two people already, why didn't they just shoot you? You were only one, and they were many."

"It was because I had my rifle." Ethan held her gaze as though he knew he had to convince her he was honest in this. "My bullets could hit them, but I was too far away for the bullets from their pistols to hit me. They were right, too. I had it in mind to just mow them down as I rode down that hillside."

"So, they just got away," Eleanor concluded.

Ethan nodded. "I would have ridden after them, but when I got closer to that mine, I could hear the sobs of the little girl. So I had to stop and tend to the children. I put the both of them up on my horse and took them over to another neighbor's place. We didn't even go into the house."

"But there were footprints," Eleanor protested.

"Later, I took Mrs. Baynes over," Ethan said. "I had gone back and buried the bodies and made a rough cross to put over them, but she wanted to add some flowers. Of course, we couldn't find any fresh ones this time of year, but my mother had some dried flowers. I drove Mrs. Baynes over in the buggy."

"Do you know who those men are?" Eleanor asked and then added silently, almost in a prayer, *God, forgive me, but I hope they're already dead. That way Matt won't have to go after them. Please, Lord. And if they can't be dead, have them already arrested.*

"No, I don't know who they are," Ethan admitted. "But my brothers have some ideas."

Eleanor saw that the men staring through the window had shifted their positions and were now gaping at something down the street.

She turned back to Ethan. "Are you going to tell all of this to Matt?"

"I plan to," Ethan said and then added a little wistfully, "I would have told him sooner, but I didn't know he was in town. I thought the old sheriff would tell Jacob, but he didn't. You know, Matt and I used to be friends. He was a few years older and I looked up to him. He helped me with my brothers. None of us knew what to do with our grief, but we all liked Matt."

Eleanor nodded. "He thinks you'd shoot him down in a heartbeat."

They were both silent for a minute.

"Half of what people say about my brothers isn't true," Ethan finally said.

"That still leaves half that is." Eleanor turned her head so she could see over Ethan's shoulder. The front door of the bakery was being pushed open.

"It's freezing out there," Matt said as he stomped into the shop. He closed the door behind him and looked around.

"Ethan?" Matt finally asked. Eleanor knew he could see only the back of his old friend's head.

Ethan stood and then turned around. "I came to see you because I was worried about your mother."

"She's with us," Matt said.

"That's what Eleanor told me," Ethan admitted and paused for a minute before sitting back down. "I was cold, so your wife invited me in for something hot to drink."

Matt grinned. "I heard it was tea."

Eleanor looked at the men outside the window and

glared. To a man, they stared at their toes like little boys who'd been scolded. Clearly, they had been the ones to gossip.

"Tea is good for you," Eleanor said firmly as she stood up. "It's not like I'm serving hemlock."

"No, it's not," Matt agreed politely as he sat in the chair she'd just left. "And, if you still have some of it left, I'd enjoy trying it."

"You would?" Eleanor asked in surprise. "Why, that would be nice. I'll just get you the other cup and saucer I have."

"That's right," Matt said. "You have the three sets from your parents, but we can use the cup-and-saucer set left from my family. That would let you serve a full table of four people at a time."

"The dishes from your family belong to your mother," Eleanor said. "I'll not deprive her of them. When I get some money ahead in the bakery, I'll add a few more sets. Tea always tastes better in a china cup. I doubt I'll have that many people taking tea here at the beginning of my business."

"You have to have faith, Eleanor Baynes," Matt said, a boyish look on his face.

"Oh, you," Eleanor sputtered and then smiled. She found she rather liked being teased. She started walking to the kitchen and then turned back. "Be sure and let Ethan tell you about what he knows from that—that day." She didn't want to be more specific.

Matt nodded, suddenly serious. "And I plan to take you and the children out shooting this morning."

"The storm could come any minute," Eleanor protested. "Can't it wait?"

Matt shook his head. "I won't rest until I've done it. I don't expect any of you to be crack shots, but you all need to be able to defend yourselves."

"Even Lily?" Eleanor asked.

"Especially Lily," Matt confirmed.

"You remind me of your brother," Ethan said. "The way he used to fuss over his wife and kids."

Eleanor watched as Matt grew serious and turned to look at Ethan. "You have something to tell me about that day when he and his wife were killed?"

Ethan nodded. "I told the old sheriff what I saw and I have not been off the ranch since then, what with the blizzard and all. I did see the men who did the shooting—I didn't recognize them and don't have much of a description since I was pretty far away, but I do know they weren't my brothers."

Matt seemed to relax as he sat there, and Eleanor walked into the kitchen and closed the door. She needed to get busy if she was going to go with Matt later this morning to practice using a gun. She wanted to take some apple fritters down to the saloon so she'd have customers tomorrow. And, she'd make sure to tell the men she'd offer free coffee with the treats. What man could resist that?

Matt could scarcely resist the temptation to kiss his wife. *His wife!* But he didn't want to throw her aim off, so he merely curved his arm around her shoulder and pulled her close enough that her dark curls were tickling his chin as he helped her position his rifle. "You see the old tin can on the downed log by the tree?"

The children were all sitting on a log far behind them.

"Yes," Eleanor admitted, her voice muffled by the wool scarf he'd insisted she wrap around her neck.

"Now, pull back easy on the trigger," he said, and he felt her nod. "A little more."

The blast of the gun made her jump, and her head hit the bottom of his chin hard enough to bring tears to his eyes.

"Did I hit it?" she asked, her voice shaky but eager.

"No," Matt admitted. The tin cup was still there. "But I saw a rabbit run out from under the bush to the side. He's probably miles away by now."

"I scared him," Eleanor said with regret. "Poor thing."

"He likes to run," Lily called out from where she sat, to assure her sister. "Don't worry. All bunnies like to run."

Matt turned around to look at the children.

"Can I be next?" Henri asked from his perch.

"After I explain what to do if someone is shooting at you," Matt said. That rabbit had reminded him that bullets didn't always find their target. No one was likely to challenge any of the youngsters to a duel, but they might certainly shoot them by mistake.

"Is someone going to shoot us?" Lily asked, and Sylvie began to cry.

Tom and John, who were each on one end of the log, sat up straighter. They had both informed him that they had already shot a rifle, so they didn't need a lesson. But they were apparently reconsidering if Matt thought someone might shoot at them.

"Of course not," Eleanor said as she gathered up her skirts and rushed to the log. "I don't want any of you children to worry. No one will be coming after you."

"Those bad men might come back," Henri said softly.

"Otis Finch wanted to get me," Lily added.

"Well, yes, I suppose," Eleanor said, clearly torn between acknowledging their fears and assuring them of their safety.

"The children need to know these things," Matt said to Eleanor as he walked over to where she stood and waited. She finally nodded.

"We need to have a signal for what to do," Matt said as he crouched down until he was eye level with the children. "If there's a bad man with a gun around, and I say the word, I want each of you to fall to the ground until you're flat as a pancake."

"What if there's snow?" Sylvie whispered. "Or mud? I'm not supposed to get my dress dirty."

"It won't matter about your clothes," Matt reassured her.

"What's the word?" Henri asked, a frown on his face. "It can't be hard to remember or Sylvie will forget."

"I will not," the little girl protested.

"It should be something we can all remember," Matt said. "Something simple, but something that the bad man won't recognize, so he won't know what we're doing."

"Whiskey," Lily said. "For the kitty."

"I don't think it's proper," Eleanor said as she looked at him. "We can't have them going around talking about alcohol."

Matt nodded. "I know, but I think it would work. It would confuse any man with a gun. And some men would decide they wanted a drink just from the word alone."

"All right, then," Eleanor said, obviously reluctantly. "If you think it's best."

Matt grinned. Maybe she was going to obey him sometimes after all.

"You would fall to the ground, too?" he asked just to be sure.

"Yes," Eleanor said.

Matt felt proud that he had his family behind him on this. As he looked around, though, he saw a lot of red noses. "Maybe it's time to go back to the bakery and warm up. We'll have more lessons later."

"I'm going to put the apple fritters on to fry, too," Eleanor announced. "I've made plenty, so I can give away for samples and still have enough for us, too—as a reward for how hard everyone worked yesterday."

"I didn't work," Sylvie confessed anxiously. "Lily didn't either. We just sat and talked to Grandma."

"We all did what we could," Eleanor said with a smile. "That's all that counts. So, of course, you'll both get apple fritters, too."

Then she looked at him like she was challenging

him, but Matt couldn't understand why. He certainly wouldn't object to apple fritters.

"We don't judge everyone by the work that they can do," Eleanor said then.

"You're worried about work?" Matt asked.

"No, I'm worried about judging people and throwing out anyone who can't do what everyone else can," she said with an intensity that surprised Matt.

"Who's doing that?" he asked.

She didn't answer him, though, and turned away before he could question her again.

"The apple fritters will be ready shortly," she announced as she stomped down the slope, clearly headed back to the bakery.

"Come, children," Matt called. "I'll take you back to the—" Suddenly that word didn't seem right. "I'll take you home."

Faint smiles lit all of their faces, from Tom, the oldest, to Sylvie, the youngest. He could see they were all pleased as they could be. And, he had to admit, it felt good to have a home.

They walked together and just before they got to the door of the bakery, he stopped.

"I'll need to go do some sheriff duties," Matt said. "I'll be back in a few hours, so save a few apple fritters for me."

With that, he went off to see what was happening in the jail. Jacob was out when Matt stepped inside the place, so he put a few more pieces of wood into the stove and decided to wrap up in a blanket on his cot until everything warmed up. He closed his eyes so he could concentrate on all that Ethan had told him. He'd looked for signs the man was lying, but he'd seen none. If Ethan was right, Matt's job had just gotten more complicated. He needed to find the Blackwood twins so he could press them to tell him who the outlaws were who had shot his brother and sister-in-law. According to Ethan, the twins were up by Helena and he'd sent them a wire telling them what had happened and asking them to contact him. He hadn't heard back, but he knew the outlaw world was a small one.

Matt stretched out so he could think better. He hadn't gotten enough sleep last night, what with his nerves and the constant snoring of the other men sleeping in the saloon. He was beginning to see why so many fights broke out there. Too many men were crammed together with no other place to go. He thought about what Ethan had told him about his brothers, but he didn't know what to make of it, so he started wondering how women put up with men. That led to him considering whether his new wife was likely to tolerate him much longer. He couldn't figure her out. She seemed half-mad at him sometimes, but she never came out and said what was bothering her. He thought about that for a minute, but nothing useful came to mind. And before he knew it, he was nodding off.

An hour or two later, Matt was awakened by the slamming of the door. He rolled over and squinted. "Jacob. That you?"

"Who else would it be?" his deputy asked irritably as he took off his hat and hung it on a peg by the door. He then took off his coat.

Matt sat up and yawned. "As far as I know, it could be anybody. How are things going out there? Something wrong?"

"I don't know," Jacob said as he reached up and self-consciously rubbed his hand over his head. "I was over at the barber shop, getting my hair cut. He got it too short and I look like an owl."

"Nothing wrong with owls," Matt muttered as he scrutinized his deputy. "But that hair of yours will grow out before you know it."

Jacob just grunted and then was silent for a minute. "Some excitement over at the saloon. I think a new lady is joining the establishment, if you know what I mean."

Matt nodded. He knew what his deputy meant. "As long as she's willing."

"They say she's wonderful," Jacob muttered. "Sweetness itself, I heard one man say."

"Well, that will be a good change for the men," Matt said as he walked over to the desk. "Want some coffee? I'll put on a pot."

"We probably don't have time," Jacob said. "I heard men are flocking to the saloon from all over. I think there will be a fight. Charley mentioned something about having to use his fists to get some of the woman's fritters."

"What?" Matt lifted his head. "What did you say?"

"I've never heard a woman's anything called *fritters*," Jacob acknowledged. "So, I might have heard wrong."

"No, you haven't heard wrong." Matt slammed his hat on his head, slipped on his gun belt and shrugged into his coat, all in less time than that gray tomcat took to slip out the open door. He even beat the beast across the street to that two-story saloon.

There was so much noise when he stepped into the saloon that no one even seemed to hear the door slam behind him.

"Hands up," he drew his gun and yelled. "You're under arrest."

It was instantly silent as a graveyard. Everyone stood where they were and turned their heads toward him.

"Sheriff?" the bartender asked tentatively. "That you?"

"Who else can arrest every man here unless they stand away from that woman?" Matt demanded to know.

The ragged group of men slowly backed away from the counter. Half of them had white flecks in their beards. The others had something small clutched in their meaty fists. They all looked guilty.

As the men peeled away, Matt began to see a piece of mauve skirt and then a dark curl. Finally, he saw all of Eleanor. Her hat had been knocked sideways, her hair was in disarray, her skirt smudged and rumpled. In her hands she held an empty platter with nothing left on it but grains of sugar.

"What were you thinking?" Matt demanded of his bride.

"I was handing out samples so the men would know how good my apple fritters are," Eleanor admitted meekly. "I brought three dozen, but it wasn't enough."

"You could never bring enough," Matt said as he took two steps closer.

A heavy muttering from the men on both sides of him made Matt pause.

"You better not touch her," one man said menacingly.

"She's the kindest woman I've ever seen," another man said in reverent tones.

"She might be married to you, but she doesn't need to obey you," the bartender added. "We all heard those vows and we're on her side."

"I'd die for her," yet another champion intoned.

Matt holstered his guns and lifted his hands to show they were empty. "I just want to see that she has room to breathe."

The men around nodded. Matt figured it was hard to argue with that.

"Are you ready to go home?" Matt asked in the sweetest voice that he had. It sounded a little sickly, but no one could accuse it of being demanding.

Eleanor nodded. "Please."

With that, she walked toward him and he ushered her forward.

As he opened the door, Eleanor turned to the men and announced loudly, "The bakery opens at eight o'clock tomorrow. There will be more apple fritters and some French bread for sale. Come for breakfast!"

The men cheered as Eleanor stepped outside. Matt followed her.

They'd walked side by side down the boardwalk for a few yards before Eleanor looked over at him and grinned. "They don't eat breakfast, do they?"

Matt chuckled. "They will tomorrow morning. I'd brew a big pot of strong coffee though. They'll need it."

"Maybe they'll go to bed early tonight," she said.

"I wouldn't count on it," Matt said as he took her arm and they continued on to the bakery. "Next time you want to give away samples, though, I'd try handing some out after church on Sunday."

"There might not even be church for weeks, since the pastor left yesterday," Eleanor protested.

"He said he'd arrange for someone to preach," Matt said. "But I don't know the final details."

He glanced over at her. She'd taken her hat off altogether and was letting her dark curls blow this way and that in the cold wind. Her gray eyes snapped with amusement now that she'd escaped from the saloon. Her cheeks were warm and her lips just as inviting.

"Wait," he said suddenly, and she stopped to look up at him. A single snowflake fell on her face.

He bent down and kissed her lips. Then he kissed them again. The white breath from Eleanor met the white air from his own mouth until a small cloud formed around them in the frigid temperatures.

"I meant to wake you with a kiss," Matt said. "But I didn't want to disturb Lily."

"She would have loved that," Eleanor smiled. "She would have thought you were a fairy-tale prince."

Matt acknowledged that truth with a nod. "I might not be a prince, but I am very glad you married me yesterday, Mrs. Baynes."

Eleanor's cheeks turned a pretty pink. "Thank you."

The snow started to come down faster as they hurried back to the warmth of the bakery. By noon, the streets were covered with an inch of snow. While Eleanor put more loaves of French bread into the ovens, Matt sat at one of the bakery tables and had a cup of coffee with Ethan. They'd already talked to his mother and arranged for her to stay with Eleanor while Matt was gone for a few days.

"I'm hoping you will ride with me over to Helena," Matt said to the other man. "Help me look up your brothers so I can talk to them. They likely know the men we're looking for."

Ethan nodded. "There's a few people there who will point me in the right direction." He paused and then added, "You know, my brothers, not even the twins, are bad men. They just got off to a bumpy start. I'm trying to find a way to help them."

Matt nodded. "I felt the same about Luke. I did too much for him because he was always sickly—now I wonder if I made him think life was somehow easier than it really is. I've decided it does no good to coddle people."

Ethan eyed Matt for a minute as though debating about saying something. "Do you think he had something to do with the gold?"

"I've wondered that, too," Matt finally admitted. "He was a decent man, but he never learned to be responsible. I should have made him do more for himself. I ruined him for life by stepping in when he had trouble. And all the while, I thought I was being a good brother."

They were both silent for a minute.

"This last year has been a hard one for all the ranches

around here," Ethan said and then, almost apologetically, added, "I'm sure he wasn't the only man tempted to take some easy money."

Matt took another sip of his coffee. If someone was going to put the ugly conclusion into words, he felt it was his duty to do so. "Do you think he was in on the robbery itself, or did my brother just offer the outlaws a place to hide their gold?"

Ethan thought a moment. "I'm guessing he only went as far as giving them a hiding place. Most likely they were in a hurry. Luke wouldn't be up to robbery, but I can see him giving desperate men a place to conceal something. They likely threatened him, and a man with a wife and children can't refuse armed men much. And they might have offered him some of the gold. What choice did he have? He never was as good as you were with a firearm."

"I suppose so," Matt agreed.

They sat quietly then, drinking their coffee, until Eleanor brought out a plate of shortbread, each square impressed with a fork tine, and set it on their table before going back into the kitchen.

"You're a blessed man," Ethan said as he pulled a piece of shortbread off the plate and used it to salute him. "She's pretty and she can cook."

Matt nodded. "I'm blessed, all right."

"Be sure she knows you feel that way," Ethan advised. "Don't be like our fathers. Too proud and bullheaded to appreciate their wives. Couldn't even say a simple thank-you to save their lives—neither one of them."

Matt nodded, but inside he was fretting. He still wasn't sure what Eleanor wanted. He'd have to figure it out pretty soon though. He was beginning to think it was possible that he wouldn't die as he sorted out his brother's murder.

"We'll leave from the ranch, if that's okay," Ethan said before walking to the door a few minutes later.

"I'll be there as soon as possible," Matt assured him.

Ethan pulled up his collar and stood in the open door. "Dress warm. It's coming down hard."

"My horse is used to bad weather." Matt stood up. "I can at least get to your place before dark. We can leave from there tomorrow."

"See you then." Ethan exited fully and closed the door behind himself.

Matt watched from the window as the man un-hitched his team and climbed into his buggy.

As Matt turned around, he heard Eleanor moving in the kitchen. He wondered how long that storm was going to last. Not that it mattered. He was heading out as soon as he got his bedroll packed and his horse saddled.

He walked toward the kitchen. He might as well tell Eleanor now that he was leaving for a few days. Of course, she probably already suspected that. He'd make it a point to thank her for all she was doing, too. Ethan was right. Regardless of how long his marriage lasted, he wanted it to be different than the union his parents had.

Chapter Eleven

Eleanor was still fretting the next morning about the way Matt had so easily said goodbye before he left on his mission to look for the younger Blackwood brothers. Oh, he'd thanked her very prettily for the coffee and shortbread yesterday afternoon. Then, before she knew it, he had his hat tied down with an old bandana, his sheepskin coat buttoned to the top and, in his arms, a double roll of blankets that were ready to tie behind his saddle. He held his rifle along one side, too.

"You're going now?" she'd asked in shock. "The storm is coming. You'll freeze to death out there."

"I'm spending the night on the Blackwood ranch," Matt said easily, although he could not have named a place that would have surprised her more.

"You're safe there?" she asked.

"Of course," he said. "The Blackwood boys might be halfway to outlaws, but they are honorable men in their own way. Besides, they're not even there—just Ethan and their mother."

As he talked, Eleanor realized she was totally unprepared for his leaving. She knew he had said he'd go after the killers, but it had always seemed to be something far in the future, not something that would hit her with any force when it happened. But it did. And that was when she knew her heart was breaking.

He bent to place a kiss on her cheek. "I already said goodbye to the children."

Eleanor thought she heard the faraway sounds of sobbing. That would be Sylvie, and maybe even Lily. Soon it might be her, too.

Suddenly a chaste kiss on the cheek was not enough, and she put a hand up to bring his head down so she could give him a fierce kiss on the lips. He seemed stunned.

"You better not die out there," she commanded quietly. "Even if the Blackwood brothers didn't kill your brother, someone did."

He gave her a slow smile. "I'll be careful."

"Promise?" she asked.

He nodded and started walking to the door of the bakery. He'd barely closed it before she heard him whistling.

She'd spent the rest of the day baking bread, apple fritters, donuts and a sour cream–raisin pie for Mr. Lunden. She was tired that night but was restless, trying to get comfortable on the bed with Lily. Before they said good-night, Henri had asked why she didn't just sleep in the big bed since Matt wasn't there. She had barely been able to step away from the boy before she started to cry.

And then this morning, she was late by fifteen minutes in opening the bakery and had two dozen customers waiting to come inside and grumbling about the cold. She gave everyone free tea or coffee and managed to sell all of the donuts and fritters. Then she sold every slice of French bread that she had left from yesterday. She toasted it and served it with butter and a cinnamon-sugar sprinkle. The men declared they loved everything, and they tipped her generously.

It was late morning before she took the new loaves of French bread out of the oven and slipped another pan of shortbread in. Eleanor frowned as she considered the amount she'd made. The sweet seemed to disappear when the children were around. She didn't have the heart to scold them, though, since none of them were accustomed to having an abundance of food around.

"Mama," Sylvie shouted, sounding excited. Eleanor could hear the little girl scampering down the stairway from the rooms upstairs. "Lily sees—" The toddler started waddling toward Eleanor. "Lily sees—" She stopped for air and then looked behind her to where Lily was standing. She, too, was beaming.

"I see Mrs. Gunni coming down the walkway from the train station," Lily announced. "I was looking out the window, hoping she'd come—and poof, poof—there she was."

"Like in a fairy tale," Eleanor finished her sister's thought.

"Yes," Lily said as she used the rails on the counter to pull herself over to a far table, where she sat down, still looking very pleased with herself. "Can we have tea when she gets here?"

"Of course," Eleanor said as she wiped her hands on her apron. "I've already got some hot water heating."

By that time, Eleanor could see Mrs. Gunni out of the bakery window. The woman was holding her hat on her head and slowly crossing the street, the wind blowing her skirts around. She turned to look behind herself twice as she made her way to the bakery, and Eleanor had reached the door as the other woman reached the few steps leading into the shop.

"You're here," Eleanor called out happily as she opened the door. A few stray snowflakes landed on her face, but that hardly signified. Her friend had arrived.

Mrs. Gunni looked up and grinned, her hand still holding her gray hat in place. Strands of her auburn hair blew across her face, almost obscuring it. That was, Eleanor told herself later, the only reason she didn't see the bruises right away.

"Oh, dear," Eleanor said as she helped her friend inside the warm bakery. Then she was hugging the other woman.

Lily had stood when Mrs. Gunni entered the room, and before Eleanor knew it, her sister was enclosed in their embrace, as well. The rails along the counter had helped her.

Within a minute, they were all crying. Eleanor finally pulled back enough to study her friend's face. There was a faint bruise above her right eye and another along her left jaw. Her forehead sported a deep cut that was barely healed.

"Did Otis Finch do this to you?" Eleanor whispered quietly, glancing down at her sister. She didn't want to upset Lily, and Mrs. Gunni must have agreed because she nodded but did not say anything.

Finally, the other woman formed the words without speaking. "I worry Otis might have followed me here."

"No," Eleanor gasped, forgetting the need for silence.

Mrs. Gunni's only answer was to look nervously out the window.

"What's wrong?" Lily's sweet voice rang out as she stepped away from their hug slightly.

"Nothing," Eleanor said quickly. "We just need to be vigilant."

Lily frowned. "What's that?"

"We need to keep our eyes open and be sure there are no bad people around," Eleanor finally said.

"You mean people like when Tom pulled my braid this morning?" Lily questioned.

"I'm not talking about other children," Eleanor assured her. "You just need to keep watch."

Lily nodded uncertainly.

"And in the meantime," Eleanor continued brightly, "we're going to have a cup of tea with our good friend here." She looked at Mrs. Gunni. "Would you like something more substantial? I can fry you a couple of eggs or make a bowl of oatmeal. I'm afraid we haven't done much shopping except for what we need to make items for the bakery."

"I'd like an egg, if you can spare it," Mrs. Gunni said

and then gave a big smile. "Imagine having enough eggs to just have one when you want."

"We're blessed," Eleanor agreed. "The two children, Sylvie and Henri, are such dears, and their parents left them a bakery and a ranch farm. The neighbor who is looking after the place brings eggs into town every week."

Mrs. Gunni closed her eyes. "Remember when we used to pray for enough money to buy an egg?"

Eleanor realized then just how many prayers of hers God had answered. She felt a warmth within herself. God really did care about her. He'd brought her safely to Dillon. He'd helped her muddle along with her marriage to Matt. So far, her husband was still alive. Lily was thriving. They had ample food to eat. She had two new children to love. She had much to be grateful for—except that she might not be able to keep any of it. She had to gather her courage and talk to Matt about Lily's future. She couldn't settle in here until she knew that she could trust him with Lily. The thought no sooner crossed her mind than the sky outside clouded over and the bakery was filled with shadows.

"I'll light a lamp," she said. "Then I'll see to the tea and the fried egg."

"There's no hurry," Mrs. Gunni said. "I'll just sit here and talk with Lily."

Eleanor nodded her head and went back to the kitchen.

Matt was so cold he could no longer feel his ears. He was riding his horse into Dillon and he'd tied his old bandana around his hat, but the snow had gotten the fabric wet and the rag had almost frozen to his face. The air had an unusual heaviness to it, like the sky couldn't decide whether to keep dumping down snow or switch to pouring rain. It was a miserable day. Matt was not disheartened though. He glanced back.

"Doing okay?" he asked.

He got four angry snarls in response.

"I guess not," he said, sounding very carefree, even to his own ears.

The four men right behind him only glared. They had their hands tied to the horns on their saddles, and six men behind them were prodding them along.

"Get a move on," Ethan shouted out.

Matt hadn't recognized the names of the four men who had stolen the gold, but he knew the Blackwood brothers who were bringing the lot of them to justice.

The boys, as Ethan called his brothers, had ridden up to their mother's ranch this morning with the outlaws all trussed up. They claimed the four men were responsible for the murders of Luke and Adeline. Apparently, the Blackwood boys had heard rumors even over near Helena that they were being blamed for those shootings, and they took exception to the accusations since they had never, they proclaimed, shot a woman, and they did not want anyone to think they might do so in the future.

"No one will marry us if they think that," one of the twins explained. "We had to do something or we wouldn't be able to court any decent woman around."

Matt saw their logic. And the four outlaws were so

spitting angry that they confessed to more than the killings, in an effort, Matt assumed, to impress upon the Blackwood brothers that they would be wise to release them. So far, none of them seemed to be tempted to do that.

Matt was glad he'd gotten his family moved over to the bakery. He would not have put these outlaws in the jail if the children were still there. The sky darkened further as they all rode close enough to see the town in the distance. Matt resisted the urge to race home, but he did head toward the one street.

Finally, he could see Eleanor standing on the narrow porch of the bakery. Wind was whipping her skirts around, and her hair had escaped the bun she kept at her neck. At first, he thought she was turned to watch him come into town, but then he saw she was looking in the opposite direction, toward the saloon.

"Lily," Eleanor called, and he could faintly hear it. Where had the girl gotten to, Matt wondered, and then he saw her crawling up the side steps to the saloon, chasing after that old tomcat, Whiskey. She was almost to the top of the stairs and would be on the balcony soon.

"What a fool thing," Matt muttered. The girl could fall. He urged his horse to go faster. Within seconds, he saw that an arm was attached to Whiskey and that the cat seemed to be struggling to escape someone who was lying flat on the roof and leaning over to dangle that cat above Lily.

Matt saw movement on the boardwalk and realized Eleanor was running toward her sister. His horse got there first, of course, and Matt was in front of the saloon, looking up, when a man with a black, flapping coat stood up and held Lily high. No one seemed to be stirring inside the saloon or on the street.

"What do you think you're doing?" Matt yelled to the man as he walked closer to the building. He could tell the brute was using Lily as a shield, even as he had a gun pointed at her head.

"She's going to fly," the man shouted as he lifted Lily even higher. "She's going to be healed, and then she can fly. Her aunt won't be able to hurt her anymore. I tried it with the cat that limps, but he wouldn't let go of me so he could fly. But Lily can—she just has to believe it—then she'll be cured."

He set Lily down on the roof and huddled behind her.

"Easy now," Matt called out. He could see that Lily was turned and looking at the man in fear. Matt didn't want to panic him by bringing out his gun, but he needed to get off a shot somehow.

Lord, help me, Matt prayed silently before calling out, "Lily."

Matt knew when she turned and looked down enough to see him.

"Papa," she called in terror. "Tell him I can't fly."

"Quiet," Otis yelled. "Or I'll shoot your precious papa."

The man waved his gun around and finally fired, the bullet hitting the ground a few feet away from Matt.

He could tell that Eleanor was standing beside him now.

"If she wasn't trying to rescue that cat," Eleanor muttered, "she wouldn't have gone near those stairs. And she wouldn't be in trouble now."

"Then, she wouldn't be our Lily." Matt turned slightly so he could slip his gun out without the man seeing it. "She always does the right thing. She's a good girl."

"You like her, then?" Eleanor asked hesitantly.

"I love her," he answered. "I'm her papa. She can always count on me."

"Oh," Eleanor said, emotion clear in her voice.

Matt knew something important had happened here, but he didn't have time to figure out what it was.

"It's time for you to back away now," he told Eleanor in a low voice. "I know it's hard for you to obey, but you need to go back to the bakery where I know you're safe."

"I'll obey," Eleanor whispered and quietly slipped away.

Matt waited for her to be out of the line of fire and lifted his gun. The other man was likely to shoot back, but there was no other way to do it. Time was running out.

He had to get Lily away from Otis a little bit so that he could wound the man in the shoulder. Matt took a deep breath.

"Whiskey," he bellowed as loud as he could. He saw Otis screw up his face in puzzlement at the same time that the old tomcat rose up and sank his teeth into the man's back. In the commotion, Lily twisted enough to fall away from the man as he looked down to the cat. She stayed down.

"Drop your gun," Matt shouted.

Otis didn't do that. Instead, he raised his weapon to take aim at Matt.

Matt shot him as he knelt there with his mouth open. The bullet hit the man's shoulder, and he shouted in pain.

"What did you do that for?" the man called out querulously. "I was only trying to help Lily fly."

"Lily doesn't need to fly." Matt was already bounding up the steps to the girl. He could hear Eleanor's footsteps right behind him. When he got to the roof, he saw that Otis was sitting down and crying.

"It hurts," the man said as he cradled his arm.

"You'll live," Matt said as he bent down to collect the man's gun. Then he went over to where Lily lay flat out on the roof.

"I made a pancake," she announced proudly.

"You did it perfectly," Matt agreed as he crouched down to help her sit up.

The girl beamed.

Then Eleanor came up to them and knelt down to gather Lily to her.

Eleanor kissed her sister on the head and then looked over at Matt. "You risked your life for Lily."

"She did the important piece on her own," Matt said with a wink to his new daughter.

"I made a perfect pancake," Lily informed Eleanor.

Matt looked up and noticed a dozen people had come rushing up those steps. Jacob was already putting handcuffs on Otis.

Tom and John crowded close to Lily and asked if

they could take her down from the building. Henri picked up the old tomcat and got ready to carry him down, too.

"That would be helpful," Matt answered all of them. "Although I'm not sure Whiskey needs your assistance."

"He helped win the fight," Henri explained. "And that white cat is waiting for him down on the street, so I think he wants to be carried—like a hero."

"Maybe so," Matt agreed. He wondered if that meant the white Persian cat was willing to be friends with Whiskey. Maybe so. Females of all species liked a warrior.

Before Eleanor knew it, she and Matt were the only ones sitting on the roof. The sun hit them, but it was still chilly. The crisis was over, but neither of them made any move to stand.

"I feel like that broken-down tomcat," Matt finally said softly.

Eleanor looked at him and saw his eyes shining with affection. She didn't know if it was love and she was afraid to ask.

"I don't have much to offer," he finally said. "But, at least, I didn't die."

"I noticed," she replied with a slight grin.

"I don't care if you don't obey me," Matt added quickly.

She smiled at that. "I was only worried about Lily."

"Why?" he asked.

"The only two men who proposed to me both wanted to send Lily away. One even said that if I was married, my husband could send my sister to some institution without my agreement." She looked at Matt. His hair was rumpled and he'd lost his hat. He still had that bruise above his eye. "But you risked your life for Lily."

"Of course," Matt said, and she felt like he was saying his vows all over again. "I'm her papa. You don't have to worry about me sending Lily away. All I want is for her to have the best of what life has to offer." He stopped then, for a moment. "I worry sometimes that I helped my brother too much and it made him weak. Ruined his life in some ways."

"But you were only trying to help," she assured him.

"I don't want to make the same mistake with Lily," he said.

"You won't," Eleanor said. "Lily likes fairy tales, but she's got good sense. Except for when she's, well—too imaginative."

"There's nothing wrong with believing in True Love," Matt declared as he glanced down at her.

"In fact—" Matt cleared his throat. She smiled as he ran his fingertip across her cheek. Then he reached over to pull her hand toward him and kissed her palm.

"In fact," he continued, "I think I believe in True Love, too."

He stood and assisted her in standing.

"Do you?" Eleanor said.

He nodded. "Now that I'm not going to die, I wonder if you'd be my wife."

"I already am your wife," she said.

"I mean for real," he said softly.

Eleanor nodded. "I would be honored."

That's when he bent down to kiss her. She savored the feel of his lips on hers. This was her husband. Her True Love. She knew in her heart that a good life was spreading out before her.

Epilogue

Months later, during the usual afternoon lull at the bakery, Eleanor stood at the counter, taking a moment to arrange a tall vase of roses. She'd been right that the spindly bush out front would green up and bear beautiful, deep pink flowers. She hadn't realized they would have a soft white edge though. She leaned close to the petals to smell their fragrance.

The door opened, a tiny bell rang and Eleanor looked up.

"Is everyone here?" Mabel Wells asked breathlessly as she marched inside, looking as excited as the day she and her husband had publicly offered to take Tom and John into their home as family. Both boys were with her now.

"Let me call them," Eleanor said and proceeded to shout out names. "Matt. Mrs. Gunni. Lily. Henri. Sylvie."

Until last week she would have called for Matt's mother, too. But she was not living with them now that the town had added two rooms to the school for use by the teacher. She did come over every Sunday for dinner, though, and she and Matt were working through their feelings about the past.

Matt arrived first, stepping out of the kitchen. His hair was tousled and he had a streak of grease along his forehead. He'd come to town to fix one of the ovens and had declared earlier that the gauge on it was more cantankerous than the worst stubborn cow in his growing herd. Matt had turned in his star after the outlaws who murdered his brother had been sent down to the prison in Utah Territory, and he spent his days running cattle on the land his father settled years ago. That is, he ranched when he wasn't helping with Mrs. Baynes French Bakery.

Some seconds later, Mrs. Gunni followed Matt out of the kitchen, wiping her hands on her apron. She did half of the baking and waited on customers when Eleanor was at the ranch. She and Eleanor had fixed up the rooms beside the pantry, and Mrs. Gunni lived there—with what she called a small boarder. She'd made a place for Whiskey on the back porch, and last week, he'd brought the white Persian cat and their new kittens there. Mrs. Gunni put a large bowl of milk out every morning and told those who asked that even Whiskey agreed the saloon was no place for little ones.

Lastly, Lily, Henri and Sylvie made their way down the stairs. It took some time because both Lily and Sylvie sat down and scooted to the bottom. Eleanor suspected Sylvie could manage the steps fine, but the child wanted to pattern herself after her new older sister. Henri, being good-hearted, was left to carry Dolly down.

By the time everyone was assembled, Mabel was looking out the front window.

"He's coming," she announced.

"Should I go help him?" Tom asked.

Mabel shook her head. "No, it'll only make him feel old. My Angus can manage a small crate like that."

"A crate," Lily squealed as she reached the last step. "Is it for me?"

"Did it come?" Eleanor asked. She turned slightly and looked up as Matt stepped close to her and put his arm around her shoulders. Both of them turned to each other every chance they had.

Mabel walked to the door and opened it with a flourish.

"It came?" Matt asked as Angus walked inside.

The other man nodded and set down the wooden box on the floor. "Addressed to Miss Lily Fitzpatrick, in care of the sheriff's office in Dillon, Montana Territory."

"I'll get a hammer to open it." Matt stepped away and went behind the counter to pick up the tool. He used the tongs to lift up the boards on the top of the crate.

Eleanor walked over to stand beside her husband and look down at the box. This was a big moment for all of them. Matt had shown Lily that no one loved her more than her new papa. Not even a prince could compare. Mr. Lunden was looking into the finances of their grandmother, but Matt decided they couldn't wait for the months it would take to settle their claim on the deceased woman's house. Instead, he used part of his savings to have his Chicago friend track down Lily's old shoe and take it to the cobbler who had made it years ago. That craftsman used the old piece of footwear as a pattern for a bigger shoe that would last Lily for many years.

Everyone was silent as Matt pulled the new black shoe out of the box.

"Shall we?" he turned to Eleanor and asked.

She nodded. She had torn up the contract about obedience after Matt saved Lily's life. But he always considered her opinion. She never doubted that Matt loved her and her sister. They—along with Henri and Sylvie—were a family.

Matt walked over and knelt when he reached the stair where Lily sat. He held out the shoe.

"Fit for royalty," Matt said as he slipped it on her foot.

"I feel like a princess," Lilly cooed, a tear streaking down her cheek as she cautiously stood up until her back was not bent. She did not waver at all. She glanced over at her sister in triumph.

Eleanor held her breath while Lily took her first step. And then another. And one more. "It works."

Lily nodded, clearly speechless by now.

Clapping and congratulations burst forth from everyone there. Lily was the center of attention as she walked around in the bakery.

Meanwhile, Eleanor held her hand out to Matt. "Let me help you up this time."

Matt took her hand and rose to his full height. Then

he opened his arms and drew her close to him. "I have to say, wonderful things come in on that train."

"Hmm." She snuggled closer.

"I love you, wife of my heart," he whispered softly as he gazed into her eyes. "Who knew I'd find True Love with a mail-order bride?"

"The same little girl who knew I'd find my happily-ever-after," Eleanor said with a smile.

He grinned and then bent his head to kiss her.

* * * * *

LOVE INSPIRED

Stories to uplift and inspire

Fall in love with Love Inspired—
inspirational and uplifting stories of faith
and hope. Find strength and comfort in
the bonds of friendship and community.
Revel in the warmth of possibility and the
promise of new beginnings.

Sign up for the Love Inspired newsletter
at **LoveInspired.com** to be the first
to find out about upcoming titles,
special promotions and exclusive content.

CONNECT WITH US AT:

LISOCIAL2021

She leaned back, watching him.

Curiosity about this man who could make the best of a difficult childhood—and who actually owned a garlic press—flashed through her, warm and intense. She didn't want to be nosy, shouldn't be. His childhood wasn't her business, and she ought to be polite and drop the subject.

But this man and his son tugged at her. The more she learned about them, the more she felt for them. And maybe part of it was to do with Landon, with his being the same age her son would have been, but that wasn't all of it. They were a fascinating pair. They'd come through some challenges, Dev with his childhood and both of them with a divorce, and yet they were still positive. She really wanted to know how, what their secret was. "Did you grow up in the Denver area or all over?"

"Denver and the farm country around it." He slid the bread into the oven. "How about you?"

"Just a few towns over on the other side of the mountain." Indeed, she'd spent most of her life, including her married life, in this part of the state.

He didn't volunteer any more information about himself and Landon, so she didn't press. Instead, she leaned down and showed Landon Lady's favorite spot to be scratched, right behind the ears. Now that they weren't working anymore, he was talkative and happy, asking her a million questions about the dog.

It was hard to leave the kitchen, cozy and warm, infused with the fragrances of garlic and tomato and bread. Her quiet home and the can of soup she'd likely heat up for dinner both seemed lonely after being here. But she had her own life and couldn't mooch off theirs. "I'd better let you men get on with your dinner," she said and started gathering up her books.

"You want to stay?" Dev asked.

The question, hanging in the air, ignited danger flares in her mind.

The answer was obvious: yes, she did want to stay. But an Unwise! Unwise! warning message seemed to flash in her head.

Spending even more time with Dev and Landon was no way to keep the distance she knew she had to keep. As appealing as this pair was, she couldn't risk getting closer. Her heart might not survive the wrenching away that would have to happen, sooner rather than later.

Don't miss
Her Easter Prayer *by Lee Tobin McClain,*
available April 2022 wherever
Love Inspired books and ebooks are sold.

LoveInspired.com